I WILL SEND RAIN

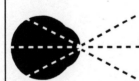

This Large Print Book carries the
Seal of Approval of N.A.V.H.

I WILL SEND RAIN

RAE MEADOWS

THORNDIKE PRESS

A part of Gale, Cengage Learning

GALE
CENGAGE Learning·

Farmington Hills, Mich • San Francisco • New York • Waterville, Maine
Meriden, Conn • Mason, Ohio • Chicago

GALE
CENGAGE Learning®

LIBRARY OF CONGRESS CATALOGING-IN-PUBLICATION DATA

Names: Meadows, Rae, author.
Title: I will send rain / Rae Meadows.
Description: Large print edition. | Waterville, Maine : Thorndike Press Large Print, 2016. | Series: Thorndike Press large print basic
Identifiers: LCCN 2016029903 | ISBN 9781410492173 (hardback) | ISBN 1410492176 (hardcover)
Subjects: LCSH: Rural families—Oklahoma—Fiction. | Dust Bowl Era, 1931–1939—Fiction. | Farm life—Oklahoma—Fiction. | Droughts—Fiction. | Domestic fiction. | BISAC: FICTION / Historical. | GSAFD: Historical fiction.
Classification: LCC PS3613.E15 I2 2016b | DDC 813/.6—dc23
LC record available at https://lccn.loc.gov/2016029903

Published in 2016 by arrangement with Henry Holt and Company, LLC

Printed in Mexico
1 2 3 4 5 6 7 20 19 18 17 16

For my mother,
Jane Elizabeth Ernster Meadows

CHAPTER 1

Annie Bell awoke in the blue darkness before dawn, her nightdress in a damp tangle at her knees. She'd dreamed about the baby, ten years gone, but all that stayed with her were stray details: the tang of sour milk, a bleating cry she couldn't soothe. Samuel slept beside her, his hand clenched, his face scrunched into the pillow. She inched away from him and sat up. There had been no rain for seventy-two days and counting. The mercury would climb past a hundred today and no doubt again tomorrow.

She rose quickly, quietly, and padded downstairs through the kitchen and out the back door. They would all be up soon, but in these last moments before the sun, cool air still hid in the shadows, and the hushed morning wind whispered against her arms. She stepped gingerly to avoid the grasshopper husks that littered the yard. As she rounded the barn and the darkness faded to gray, she noticed a mound of half-darned socks lumped on a hay bale.

Oh, Birdie. How often she'd thought this recently. About her daughter's lack of urgency, her inability to see what needed to get done. To her they were only socks with holes; but Annie knew, like any farmer's wife, that they were one of a thousand things that kept the place going.

Annie brushed the hair from her forehead; after nineteen years on the farm, it was now mapped with lines, making her look, she thought, older than thirty-seven. It was getting harder to stretch their means. Provide, provide, provide, she repeated in her head as she kneaded bread or wrung out the sheets or ground old wheat into porridge, while her daughter frittered away the afternoons. Thinking about a boy, she had little doubt.

Really it was Birdie's daydreaming that rankled Annie most of all. This wasn't fair, she knew. Part of being young was giving in to the feeling that your life was full of possibility. Annie knew she had done the same when she'd first met Samuel all those years ago, remembered what it was like to want things for herself. But now, here were the land, the farm, the house, her children, her husband.

She dropped the socks where she'd found them. Let Birdie be for now, she thought, try and give her a little space. She slid her toe in an arc across the hard-packed dirt.

A jackrabbit knifed in front of her and then was gone. The sun appeared, and, as it rose, would slowly take with it any respite from the heat. Birdie would soon drag her feet to the barn to milk, Fred would charge out to see the hens, Samuel would look around for a way he hadn't yet thought of to beckon life from the fields.

It was time to make the biscuits.

Birdie stepped outside the kitchen door into the arid wind. She rounded the house and made a visor with her hand. Nothing. Always nothing. Land as flat as a razor in every direction, a burned-out watery mirage. To the north was Kansas, and to the south, Texas; to the west were New Mexico and Colorado, and to the east, the rest of Oklahoma. The windmill was the tallest point on the farm, flanked by the barn. Her father had built the small shed off in front a few years ago, now mostly full of burlap sacks of grasshopper bait. The wind buzzed against her ears, blowing her hair in her face. Relentless.

She grabbed her hair into a ponytail with her fist, unwilling yet to tie it back with string or rubber band. Where had she left her green ribbon? She pulled down the bucket from the windmill and pumped the water up, brown at first before it ran clean. Now taller than the house, the grove of locust trees her father had planted in that first year on the farm offered better shade than the scraggly mesquites. She carried the bucket over and emptied it around the base of the trees. Last week her father had poured water on the roof of their house, which had made it sizzle and steam, but hadn't done much to cool anything down inside. At least she'd never had to live in the old sod dugout, which was little more than a roof on a mound of dirt beyond the barn. At least they now had running water and electricity in the house.

"Birdie," her father said from the open door of the shed.

Samuel Bell's ropy arms were reddish brown from the sun, and his hair had grown thin, as if the drought were eroding him, too. He used to laugh readily at Fred's clowning, even sing sometimes in the evening, stomping his foot to keep time, some lively tune he'd picked up in the barracks in his sharecropper days. But now any leftover energy went into worry, into thumbing through the tissue-thin pages of his Bible, its cover cracked like the veins of a long-dead leaf. You needed at least sixteen inches of rain to grow anything and they had had four. With only weeks until harvest, the plants should have been at grain filling, at milk stage, or even soft dough, but the kernels were still as small and hard as tacks.

Last week a man from Amarillo had come with charts and graphs, talking about rain.

"Haven't you waited long enough?" he'd asked a packed school gymnasium.

Here was a chance to do something, the farmers nodded. A way out of the drought. None of them had the money to spare but there was no choice, really.

"How do you go about that?" Samuel asked.

"Explosives. A heck of a lot of them," the man answered. "Give her a little shake up there," he said pointing at the sky. "We done it north of Las Cruces. And down there at Toad Creek, East Texas. Those boys in Washington could do it for y'all but they don't want to spend the money."

The farmers grumbled. Of course, of course. It would be up to them to help themselves.

"Let's bomb it to hell!" someone had

11

shouted.

The man had smiled and clapped, had kept on clapping until the farmers had joined in, even pounding their feet on the wooden floor.

The farm's small remaining patch of grass crunched under Samuel's feet, chewed to its roots by the cows and desiccated by the sun. The man from Amarillo would arrive midweek. Samuel was skeptical, of course, but they had all paid their share, come what may.

"Make yourself useful," Samuel said to Birdie. "Get some of that thistle off the fence." It was all that seemed to grow now and it tormented him to watch it cartwheel across the dry yard.

Birdie hated hauling tumbleweeds, which scratched her arms and face. Cy Mack had run his thumb along her chin and told her she was the softest thing in Oklahoma. He said he loved her freckled nose and the dimple in her cheek. He said she smelled like clover.

"That pile's too tall already," she said to her father.

"Start a new one."

She sighed and wiped the sweat off her lip with her arm.

"It's so hot," she said.

Samuel laughed a little. "You don't say."

Out on the western fence, at the edge of the largest field, she plied a tumbleweed thatch from the barbed wire and tossed it to the side. And then the wind paused. Birdie felt the quiet like a shiver, and in that still breath she could hear the meadowlarks chirping and beating their wings. In the distance, a black haze that looked like mountains. The heaviest clouds she'd ever seen were rolling toward them. Delight rose up in her as if she'd been handed a big, pink-bowed package. She ran back to her father.

"Look, Pop."

Her father looked up from the fence post he was rewiring. He took his hat off, ran his hand over his hair, and put his hat back on. Relief bloomed in his face.

"Well, hallelujah," he said. "Go get your mother. The rains have come."

Fred balanced a twig across two rocks as a bridge for the ants. He made a line of biscuit crumbs up the side to entice them to climb.

"Come on, little fellows," he thought. "Eat up."

Fred was knock-kneed and pallid, younger than his eight years. He had never spoken.

His parents had given up trying to get him to, and he'd settled into his own way of communicating, a proficiency of expressions and gestures that his family knew well. Now he wrote on a small chalkboard, which he carried to school, and he kept notebooks stashed around the house, pencils attached with yarn and tape.

The anthill was the size of a bread box. He was tempted to jump on it and watch the little black workers scurry, but he resisted. One of the ants skittered out, elbowed antennae quivering. Fred crouched down and pressed the marcher down softly into the dirt with his finger. He'd learned in school about how an ant colony operates as a unified whole, the ants working together for the good of the group. He wondered how many would need to die before the colony would notice.

It was getting hard to see, the dark specks of the ants indistinguishable from the ground. He blinked and rubbed his eyes with his fists. He stood, confused by the sudden darkness, and then he saw the clouds.

Rain would mean wheat would mean money would mean a bicycle.

"Mama!" Birdie cried, the door snapping

14

shut behind her. Inside the farmhouse it was hot and close, the windows covered against the sun.

"Now what is it, Barbara Ann?" Annie said. A lost button? A dress she'd seen in town? A splinter in her thumb that would keep her from milking? Her daughter found drama everywhere, her emotions so quick to bubble up to the surface. "I'm in the kitchen," Annie said. "No need to yell."

The ivy wallpaper Annie had put up five years before was curling away from the wall in the corners. The green leaves, the indulgence, felt mocking now, bumpy under her hand. She felt as if she had faded along with the ivy print, all the work and the wait had slowly leached her of color, too.

"Mama, come out. Come quick." Birdie was breathless.

Annie untied her apron in the doorway. She'd traded three dozen eggs for a last quart of mulberries from the Jensens, which she'd just finished baking into a pie. It was a rare extravagance. Her garden was still strong, at least. She watered it each night, bucket by bucket from the well.

"What's all your clatter about?" she asked.

She wondered if Birdie would finally tell her about Cy Mack. Annie already knew the girl was moony for him, that much was obvious. She had sensed for a while that Birdie had her eye on something beyond Mulehead. She would press for details about Kansas City, where Annie herself had only been once. Did the women have red-painted fingernails? Were the buildings taller than the grain elevator? When the radio had worked — the oiled-walnut box now on the floor shoved next to the sofa — Birdie would lose herself to the stories of *Ann of the Airlanes* or *The Romance of Helen Trent,* always eager for news of places far away. So the idea of Cy Mack courting her daughter needled at Annie, concerned her more than she wanted to admit. He was a farmer's son, already farming full-time. No matter what he might be telling Birdie now, Annie knew that Cy would never leave.

"Rain, Mama. It's rain," Birdie said.

Annie felt her face soften and rise. At last.

They ran outside together, mouths agape when they saw the wall of thick black clouds headed their way. Annie put her hand on Samuel's shoulder, a gesture of relief and solidarity both. Birdie noticed. It was more than she had seen pass between her parents in months.

"Where's your brother?" Samuel asked.

"Maybe over in that gulch near Woodrow's place," Birdie said. "I don't know."

"What if there's lightning?" Annie asked.

"He'll come when the rain starts," he said. "It seems it'll be hard to miss."

"We should celebrate," she said. "No need to wait for supper."

Birdie loved the musty, sweet fruit and larded crust of mulberry pie. Before she turned toward the house, though, she saw what her father now saw. The clouds were not gathering overhead as they should have been, they were instead moving at them like a wall, the sun lost in a hazy scrim, the winds picking up, dry and popping with electricity, biting and raw against her skin.

"What in God's name?" Her father squinted against the darkening sky, which turned brownish and then dark gray, even green in places where the sun was trying to burn through. It was midday but it looked like dusk, the sweep of an otherworldly hand.

Birdie started to cough.

"Fred," her mother said.

"I'll go," Samuel said. "Get inside."

He nodded his head to the old dugout, two rooms they'd gouged from the earth, where he and Annie had first lived when they'd arrived as newlyweds. Almost fully underground, it was the closest thing they had to a cellar.

He ran east toward Woodrow's place, hoping the boy had sense enough to head for home. If he even saw the clouds. Samuel knew his son could spend all day counting cow chips or following coyote tracks, oblivious, his face as open as a sunflower.

"Fred!" he yelled, though it was pointless given the wind. Dirt began to blow. The world had gone dark and haywire. Dear God, Samuel thought, what is this ugliness?

Fred ran in from the fence, scared. How close was he to home? Was that the barn up ahead? His spindly legs took him blindly forward, his flailing arms searching for anything solid around him. His name, faint and carried by the wind. Louder this time.

He barreled into Samuel, jolting them both with a zinger of a shock, a hundred times what he could get from rubbing his feet on the rug and then touching the doorknob. The dust generated electricity all around them. He held onto his father's hand as they ran, the wind whipping their clothes and burning their eyes, to the dugout door.

They closed themselves in and Fred scampered to his mother's feet. She smoothed her hand over his wiry hair. He is safe, she thought, be thankful for that. But she could not hold on to her relief. Surprise — she swallowed dryly — things can always get worse.

They sat atop sacks of surplus wheat from three years ago. Outside the wind groaned, grating against the roof. Birdie knew she should be ashamed for feeling excited, but her heart thumped, loud in her ears, like the time they'd waited out a twister in the Macks' cellar after a Sunday supper, she next to Cy, then sixteen to her thirteen. He'd leaned over and said, "You're safe down here," and her ears had burned.

"Samuel? What is this?" Annie asked. She pulled her dress over her knees and rocked her feet against the floor.

"I don't know, Ann. I don't hear any hail, though," Samuel said. "I suppose that's a good sign."

Annie stood and straightened the canned beets, parsnips, and beans, the dugout now their makeshift storehouse. When had he stopped calling her Annie? They had become more formal with each other, more careful. She could feel herself retreating. Today, though, standing next to him when she'd seen the clouds and, thinking they held rain, felt the tightness in her jaw ease, she had imagined again a carpet of wildflowers, trumpet vines, and pale green buffalo grass all around them, and she'd felt an old tenderness swelling. You and me and this family, she had wanted to say. She had offered her silent hand instead.

"Seems to have passed," Samuel said. "I don't hear much."

"How could there be no rain with clouds like that?" Fred thought. He was disappointed. There would be no bicycle.

Samuel dislodged the old door with his shoulder and climbed out into the light. The sun was out again, that much they could see. A moment later Birdie and her mother followed through the door, Fred trailing behind.

"Dust," Samuel said, as if they couldn't see for themselves.

The world was buried under it: the garden, the window ledges, the wheat. Birdie wiped her hand across her face, trailing a mix of sweat and grit. The wind blew the fine sand over her shoes. She could feel it in her eyes and in her throat. Her father looked dolefully out at his buried fields, but he seemed unable to move, unwilling yet to acknowledge what had befallen his land. Annie trudged straight to the garden.

"You ever hear of a dust storm before?" Birdie asked.

20

"I never did," Samuel said.

"Think it'll make the papers?"

"I think it will."

Birdie wanted to talk to Cy about it, to see how he looked at her. His eyes were the color of an April sky before you started to wish for clouds.

Fred coughed and hacked up blackened phlegm and spat it into the dirt.

"Learn some manners," Birdie said.

"Pill," Fred thought, squinting his eyes at her. Bossy pill. Wash your hands, Fred. Fill the trough, Fred, Leave me alone, Fred. The rest of the time she only cared about Cy. He'd seen her slip out of the house last night.

"Birdie, go check on the cows. Take a rag for their noses. Fred, see to the coop."

Fred tripped as he ran off and he narrowly missed the corner of the shed. He liked his sister, too. He could make her laugh. When they were smaller they would run into the fields and spin around to get lost and she would sing "Baa, Baa, Black Sheep" until he found her sitting, feet out in front of her, in the tall-as-him wheat.

Samuel watched Birdie walk away, her hair bleached like straw from the sun, and then started toward the fields to see how much had been destroyed.

■ ■ ■ ■

The pea shoots were lost, as if trampled by a horse. The pole beans hung limp, flopped over, pulled from the trellis and weighed down with dirt. Annie gently lifted a stalk and brushed the dust off its bruised leaves.

She refused to read the destruction of the garden as a larger sign. God doesn't use weather as a weapon, she thought. Even her father would agree on that. But she wasn't so sure about Samuel. With less to do on the farm, he had more time to pray, more time to listen for the still, small voice. "God is displeased," he had said when she'd found him staring off from the porch a few days before. There was a time when she would have tried to shake him out of it, but his new searching look, his eyes wild and cast up, kept her from saying anything.

As she set to work tending to her wounded plants, Annie saw how the years out here had ravaged her hands — her skin creased and dry, her nails thick and short. They were capable hands, though, and she did not begrudge them. On the night she'd first met Samuel, she knew she would choose the soil, the sun, the work, over a steady life as the wife of a minister like her mother.

■ ■ ■ ■

"One, two, three, four, five, six, seven, eight, nine," Fred said in his head, counting the leghorns, their white feathers now dirty brown, as they bobbed around. "Where are you, ten?" He counted again, but still came up one short. The birds screeched and pecked at his skinny legs, agitated from the storm, as he scattered the kafir corn.

He wanted it to be like it was before. When Miss Miller taught his class and he gave her a box of chocolates for Christmas before she left to get married. In the fall he would have sour Miss Peterson and they didn't have the money to give her anything and she would never leave because no one would ever want to marry her.

Where was that hen?

In back of the coop he found her on her side, dust clogging her eyes, panting through an open beak, her wattle limp against the floor. His lip quivered and he balled his fists to stop the tears. "Get up, get up, get up," he thought. He wiped the hen's eyes with the hem of his shirt. He loved these birds. He rubbed lard on their combs in the winter so they wouldn't get frostbite. He kept meticulous counts of their eggs — some 230 apiece last year — on a yellow ledger pad under his bed. Leghorns were a nervous breed, and he knew how to hold them in the crook of his arm to calm them.

He looked at the ravaged bird and knew there was only one thing for him to do. He put his foot on its body, grasped its small quivering head in his hands, and yanked as hard as he could. The neck gave way with a pop. Fred kneeled down and cradled the creature to his chest like a gift.

Birdie swept the kitchen floor. Dust had made its way through every crack and window seam, settled on every surface. The counters, the clock, the sink, the table, the telephone. But it felt good to clean up the mess, she was strangely invigorated by the excitement of the day. As she wiped a wet rag across the windowsill, she wondered what it would be like if she and Cy lived someplace like Oregon, where she heard everything was green and blackberries grew in wild thickets.

Later, when the storms kept coming, she would think back on this day and try to recall the expectation she had felt when the kitchen was clean and she'd sat down with a fork and the mulberry pie.

She scraped the dust off the crust, and dug in.

CHAPTER 2

The man from Amarillo wore a bone-white suit and a matching ten-gallon Stetson low on his forehead. He lifted the hat — his hair as slick and full as an otter's pelt underneath — to fan himself. Not that it wasn't windy already, and not that it would do any good, but he kept at it, every five minutes or so. Birdie moved closer through the crowd to get a better view, to see if the man was, in fact, handsome or if it was just the getup. Yes, handsome, she decided, if a little untrustworthy, particularly his ink-pool eyes, which he cast beyond the dell. He was lucky it was bright. It made it hard to see the dirt-edged cuffs of his jacket, the yellow smear on his lapel, the droplets of sweat that hung from one end of his long mustache.

"My friends," he said, replacing his hat. His voice was deep and slow, with a sharp Texas twang. Confident or cunning; Birdie couldn't be sure.

The crowd, most all of Mulehead and plenty from over in Texas County, quieted. In back of the gathering, Fred perched on his toes and peered into the man's straw-padded truck. Boxes marked "Dynamite" in big red letters.

"Are we ready?" the man asked.

The mayor, Jack Lily, glanced around and gave a small nod. He was skeptical of this man, the way he peddled hope, but the farmers were desperate.

The man from Amarillo had two other men with him today, burly fellows with rolled-up sleeves and work boots, and they had assembled a cannon aimed straight up at the sky. One of the men's hands ended in two bulbous knuckle stumps.

Some of the women had brought umbrellas, just in case the effect of the explosions was immediate. The Hollisters, faring better than most with family money from the sawmill, sat on a quilt and ate ham sandwiches and lemon cake and sipped iced tea. Samuel and Annie Bell stood close to each other in a piñon tree's meager shade, their hands heavy at their sides. Annie's soft curls lifted from her face in the hot breeze and the mayor had to look away.

Jonas Woodrow whipped his head around as if flies were darting at his face. Jack Lily wondered how Woodrow had possibly come up with his share of the man's fee. People used to say, Well, that's Woodrow, bad luck and all. Arriving too late for the boom years. Over-borrowing. The thresher taking his pinkie clear down to the palm. Now he was feeding his cows ground tumbleweed and salt, and his wife was feeding their six children fried dough and wild nettles. But these days everyone was hurting, and no one said anything about Woodrow's luck anymore.

Birdie glanced back at her parents, to see if they were watching her. They were almost the same height, their stances solemn — like two fence posts, she thought. She rolled her shoulders back and pushed her chest out, which made her look older than fifteen she was sure. As she set off to find Cy, she almost ran smack into the mayor.

"Miss Bell," Jack Lily said, as he inched out of Birdie's path.

"Lovely day for rain, isn't it?" she asked.

"From your lips to God's ears," he said.

She noticed with displeasure that dirt now covered her shoes and smudged her socks. There was a thread hanging from the hem of her skirt. Why wasn't Jack Lily married? He had a fine face and, in this town, a girl could do worse.

27

Fred ran by in pursuit of a zigzagging rabbit, and a moment after Fred came Cy's little sister, a flash of black hair and patched dress. Cy is here, then, Birdie thought. She straightened her blouse and strolled along the edge of the crowd near a murder of crows that had settled on the weedy bank along the dry creek bed. The birds cawed through green-black beaks, a hundred of them or so, more nervy as the villainous drought wore on.

Birdie and Cy had finally done it in the Macks' barn three days ago, and she felt different, better, as if she had blossomed, or as if they had.

"My sweet little bird," he had said.

"I'm not that sweet," she had said, even though she loved hearing him say it.

She knew they were supposed to be married first, but surely they would be married soon enough, so she didn't see it as any great sin. She was only fifteen but her mother had married at eighteen and what was the difference really? Cy didn't have to do much convincing. Love made it all okay, she told herself. She'd grown up around animals. She knew how they did it. It hurt, of course, but she didn't blame Cy. He kissed her. He whispered, "I love you," in her ear. He dipped a bandanna in cool water from the well and swept it across her forehead. She had skipped the three miles home, fueled by the glow of choosing and being chosen, each cheek a rosy nimbus.

"Birdie Bell."

She turned, the wind making it hard to tell where the voice had come from, and squinched her eyes against the glare.

"Over here."

Cy Mack sat sideways in the open front seat of his father's truck, his boots resting on the running board, his large sun-browned hands laced between his knees. He smiled, showing his slightly overlapping front teeth, which Birdie thought tempered his handsomeness with a hint of little-boy mischief. His hair was as black as boot polish. His eyes, blue and water clear.

"Hello there," she said. She felt an odd coolness settle on her skin, as if his presence alone could dissipate the afternoon heat.

"Looks like the show's about to start," he said.

"What's that?" she asked. She had forgotten, in the moment, why they were here.

He pointed up, but kept his eyes on hers. She laughed. Who cares about rain, she thought. I love you, I love you, I love you.

Cy hopped down.

"We could sit on the back of the truck if you want."

"I'd like that," she said.

He sat and reached his hand out to help her up. She held on even when he tried to pull it away.

Pastor Hardy, his thin tufts of pale hair afloat in the wind, took in the sight of the scraggy crowd, most of whom were members of his congregation at the Church of the Holy Redeemer. "Is it God or the devil withholding the rain?" they had asked him, each worried it was his own sins that had done them all in. "God's sending of the plagues upon Israel is not merely to punish," he had told them, "but to call his people to repentance." His answer had not satisfied anyone, including himself.

The pastor stepped up on a wooden crate.

"Such a momentous occasion requires deference to our maker," he drawled, his Arkansas accent more pronounced when he took to the pulpit. "Bow your heads and open your hearts."

As he did at the closing of Sunday meetings, the pastor closed his eyes and transformed, his voice booming, holy-rolling.

"I'm talking now about the Holy Ghost — hah — the third person of the Trinity —

hah — let the Holy Ghost come into your lives — hah — He will show you a new light on your experience — hah — the Holy Ghost will help you to see you have all those things in the Book — hah — you have faith, hope, and charity — you will see your experience by the light of the Holy Ghost."

He opened his eyes and looked up, blinking against the sun.

"Amen."

Birdie and Cy dutifully mumbled, "Amen," with the others, their sweaty hands intertwined.

"He thinks we're sinners," she said.

"We are." He squeezed her hand. She giggled, heat rising in her neck and cheeks.

"I mean all of us. Trying to make rain."

"He thinks chewing gum's a sin. You can't win."

They watched the pastor step down and trundle off toward town. The man from Amarillo stubbed out his cigarillo on the sole of his boot and flicked the butt away.

Birdie felt the metal of the truck bed like a spitting frying pan against her thighs, but she was content, waiting here next to Cy. Her brother slid his feet through the gravel and stopped at the truck.

"Freddie," Birdie said. "Your hair's sticking up."

The man in white straightened his tie and stepped up on the crate the pastor had vacated.

"We'll blast and reload, ten times," he said. "Ladies, you may want to cover your ears. Rain is in your future, my friends. Might not be today, mind you. But it'll come."

Fred couldn't get a good view, so he scampered up onto the truck bed and squeezed himself between Cy and Birdie.

After the first shot of the cannon there was a strange quiet, a collective held breath, as all eyes followed the bundles of dynamite through the air, their fuses flickering. Everyone stared into the sky until it erupted in thunderous bursts. The explosions panicked the crows, which took to the air in a mass of riotous wings, soon lost in sooty billows of smoke. The second wave of dynamite quickly followed the first, taking out the crows and sending down a shower of ash and oily black feathers.

Birdie gasped, sure her father would see the birds as some kind of sign, like in Exodus, when the frogs fell from the sky. Mary Stem, a girl from her class, screamed as she brushed black detritus from her hair. The Hollister women put up their umbrellas. Birdie wrapped her arm around Fred's shoulders as the booms continued to shake the ground and blacken the sky. Fred's upturned face was a canvas of awe, his mouth open, his eyes glassy. It was wondrous and scary, Fred thought, like the comics but real. The birds, all the birds.

"You okay, Freddie?" Birdie asked, but he could not hear her for the ruckus.

The man rocked on the heels of his boots and checked his watch. He looked up and caught Birdie staring. A slight tug of a smile pulled up one side of his mustache, and he touched the rim of his hat in her direction. He held her gaze and raised an eyebrow and she quickly looked away.

There was a lull in the noise.

"That it?" Cy asked.

Fred put up seven fingers.

"You sure?"

Fred nodded, just as the cannon went off again.

Cy took Birdie's hand again and she felt her shoulders soften. She could be anywhere as long as he was there next to her.

When Samuel and Annie had finally arrived in Oklahoma, the land didn't look anything like the brochure had promised. There was no river except for the Cimarron twenty miles to the north, no tree-lined streets —

not even much of a town to speak of. But a homestead was a little piece of something, even if it was in No Man's Land on the western edge of the Panhandle. As a young man Samuel had been a tenant farmer in Kansas, but here he got a quarter section, 160 acres of sandy ground under a thick turf of prairie sod. And it was free. For years he kept, tucked in his Bible, that torn piece of newspaper with the parcel number scratched on it, as a reminder, he told his children, of what they had.

And now here they were shooting bombs into the sky. How had it come to this? He knew it wouldn't work, this hocus-pocus. One couldn't make God do something. He had his own schedule, his own reasons for man's suffering.

Samuel remembered the pale green glow each year of the first shoots in the spongy, dark soil, how they grew into laden honey stalks. Their pungent sweetness. The dull plops of rain on thirsty dirt. The thwuck of tractor tires in wet mud. Rain had even seeped into his dreams now, thundering bountiful storms, an exhausting loop of want and wish.

Next year will be better, because it sure can't get worse.

"Ann," he said. "Let's go home."

But his wife did not seem to hear, her eyes cast upward at the chaos.

They'd met at a church dance. She had served him lemonade, and he was struck by the wide plains of her face, which made her look kind and solid, pretty but unaware of it. She had a delicate narrow waist, and as he watched her box-step with another man, Samuel knew he'd do whatever he could to win her.

In their second Oklahoma spring, before the house was up, they'd dragged the mattress from the dugout — Annie never liked the feeling of being underground — and had slept in the barn, amidst the crisp smell of pine, the sighing of the horses. They pulled open the door and in that milky celestial light they would sleep, her leg over his, her head on his chest, her hand held in his. They had nothing, but with her body fused with his, Samuel had felt they had the world.

Lately, though, Annie had grown remote, edged herself out of his reach. He feared that all these years later, a seed of regret had sprouted in the preacher's daughter. He watched her sometimes when she was in the garden, her arms whip thin, her back a graceful curve toward the plants she was tending. Gone was the softness in her hips she'd had when they married. She was carved now, sinews over bone. It startled him sometimes how much she had become part of the land, shaped and scarred and bound by it. But it scared him, too, how she didn't need him like she once did.

"Ann," he said again.

There was the slightest hesitation before she turned to him. The sun lit the ends of her hair like fire.

"This is an awful thing," she said. "Let's go home."

The explosions were finished and the smoke had begun to clear. A mosaic of charred feathers and remains now covered the ground. The man from Amarillo was already behind the wheel of his truck.

The chattering festive mood of earlier was gone. Samuel watched his neighbors pack up their picnics. Now it was time to wait, and waiting, it seemed, was all they ever did these days.

"There's Birdie," Annie said.

Samuel looked to where she was pointing and saw Birdie sitting with the Mack boy. His daughter was reedy still, though now nearly as tall as her mother. She was laughing, her head thrown back, at something the young man said, and Samuel saw, even from

36

here, the sparks charging the air between them.

"Well, now," he said.

"I had suspected something," Annie said.

"She's just a girl."

Annie laughed. "She's fifteen, Samuel."

He took her elbow and they walked toward the car, their old Ford Tudor gone rusty along the running board, its fender dented, bought off Warren Graves before any inkling of the drought. Fred, a crow feather behind his ear, bounced rocks off the back tire.

As they neared the car, Jack Lily eased himself away from a group of farmers, his hand raised in greeting.

"Afternoon, Mayor," Annie said. She tended to Fred, brushing dirt off his pants.

"Afternoon," he said. The light caught her hair as she pushed it back with her wrist. Jack pulled his eyes away, down to his oxfords, lace-up city shoes that alone differentiated him from the farmers.

"I see our friend is about to hightail it," Samuel said.

Jack glanced over his shoulder and shrugged. "I hope we're proved wrong."

"I didn't see your man Styron out here today." Styron was the deputy mayor, agreeable enough though often with more enthusiasm than sense. "This seems like something in his particular wheelhouse."

Jack snorted. "He does like a big idea, that's for sure. I sent him over to Herman. County meeting." He flicked his eyes to Annie, who sipped water from a jar. "Okay, then. I guess I'll see you all on Sunday."

"If Pastor Hardy lets us back in after this display," Samuel said.

The mayor nodded and waved as he ambled away, hands shoved deep into his pockets.

"Birdie's coming," Samuel said.

"Don't say anything about the boy," Annie said. "I'll ask her about it when the time is right."

He put up his hands in surrender. It hurt him, though, to think of his daughter now in a category somehow off limits to him.

"You'll just get ahead of yourself," she said.

"It always starts somewhere, doesn't it?" he asked, smiling a bit at his wife.

"Flirtation doesn't equal a wedding." She turned her head and let the wind blow the hair from her face.

Sometimes at first light Annie could hear the wind roll over the plain and she could imagine it was the soft rustle of a sea of wheat. She remembered dew sliding down blades of buffalo grass and collecting in honeysuckle flowers and slippery under bare feet before dawn. Mornings like a juicy pear.

The man from Amarillo checked his watch again and his men lifted the last of the paraphernalia into the back of the truck and hopped on. The crowd had thinned, had given up on rain today, the sky again bright. The truck rolled through the center of the clearing, dust and feathers coating its tires. The man waved, a thin smile barely visible under his mustache, and, before she could think better of it, Annie smiled and waved back, a small fan of her hand, which she hoped her husband hadn't seen.

She watched as the truck pulled out toward Route 287. She was a Kansas girl, and Texas had always seemed rough and large, dangerous even. Her heart rabbited as she thought of the man's hands on her. Hands that didn't hesitate. And that left her red in the face, blushing, disgusted. She shook her head to clear it. What she really wanted was something to wrest them from the heat and wind that bore down on them day after day. There seemed no end to the oppressive sameness.

She was certainly not her mother's daughter. A woman who shrank from loud laughter, got agitated by crumbs on the table, seemed incapable of breaking a sweat. Her

39

mother was a Presbyterian minister's wife, prim, unquestioning, content within the church's narrow hallways, those impermeable walls. Her placid bow mouth. "Are you doing good by God, Annie?" she would ask, if she caught her with an unpressed handkerchief or sneaking an extra cookie. Her mother believed she was doing good by God in serving her husband, no matter what he might have been up to.

Annie's life would have been quiet and restrained had she married William Thurgood as her parents had expected. He was in seminary. He kept his shoes buffed.

William had taken her to the dance, she in her yellow crepe dress with roses around the collar and he in a black wool suit — a suit! — as if it weren't July in Kansas. All she could think about was how hot his hand was on her back, a smoldering lump of coal, burning a hole through the fabric. He kept his hand there while they danced and even when the music stopped. Please move your hand, she thought, please move your hand or I will have to run away or scream. Sweat moistened his hairline and his lip. It was the approach of her father — he needed her help at the refreshment table — that finally made William drop his hand, leaving her lower back blessedly cool and damp.

She hadn't noticed Samuel. He blended in with the other young farmers with their awkward postures and mud-covered boots.

"Lemonade?"

"You squeeze these lemons all by yourself?" Samuel asked.

She laughed and handed him a small glass cup. "I had a little help from the church ladies."

He had mournful eyes, brown as molasses. His hands were tough-skinned working hands.

"Samuel Bell," he said. "Ready for lemon duty whenever you need my services."

"Ann Stokes."

"Nice to meet you, Annie."

It was bold of him to be so familiar, particularly in her father's church, but she liked it. Samuel had a quiet sureness about him, no matter his frayed collar. Standing next to him she felt as if she had time and space to breathe. She did not need the burning hands of William Thurgood, and this was a revelation, that she could choose something different.

Samuel was a more rough-hewn sort and, in those early days, his talk of homesteading made something rise up in her. She leapt for the wildness of the unknown, saw herself reborn as a farmer's wife. And Samuel's vision, his conviction, had been exciting, hadn't it? Even then she'd known she was tough; she just hadn't had a chance to prove it yet.

Birdie waltzed up and slid into the backseat with Fred. Her color was up, her eyes inward and dreamy. Do not marry that boy, Annie thought. Get yourself out of this place.

"Mama, Fred ripped his pants," Birdie said. "All the way down the seam."

Annie heard her, but didn't respond, afraid of what her voice might give away.

"Ann?" Samuel said.

She walked around the car and got in the front seat next to her husband. Annie looked at her family in the dirty old Ford and she was grateful, then, for what she had. But rain or no rain, she couldn't shake the sense that on this searing June afternoon, the man from Amarillo had changed her life, had left a little tear. Her faithlessness had been exposed, however briefly, and try as she might to forget it, it was there, held back by a few loops of thread.

Samuel reached for her hand but only got ahold of three fingers. She tried to readjust, but he thought she was pulling away, and then their hands returned to their laps as if they had not touched.

Samuel started the engine.

"Home," he said.

CHAPTER 3

The Woodrows, all eight of them, left sometime in the night, two weeks after the man
from Amarillo drove off leaving little more
than sunshine in his rearview. Jack Lily went
out to their place for some eggs and found
the front door flapping against its post, a
one-legged crow hopping from empty room
to empty room. The Woodrows were not the
first — the Morgantowns, the Nickelbaits
before them — but he was surprised that
Jonas Woodrow, beaten down so long by
that spit of land, had the gumption to
simply pack up and go.

Of course they hadn't told anyone they
were going. No one wanted to admit defeat,
Jack thought. Just yesterday he had seen one
of the boys digging out fence posts half-
buried by sand drifts. Desperation, he knew,
though, was not something you make a plan
for.

He tilted his chair back onto two legs and

looked out at the old farmers who were leaning against the post office, taking cover from the heat under the gutter's thin stripe of shade. The rain gutter. A cruel irony these days. He used to see Jonas Woodrow out there biting his fingernails, rubbing the scar where his pinkie had been.

The light in Jack's office held the dust like a snow globe, like the one he'd given Charlotte a lifetime ago — Chicago seemed impossibly distant now — a sleigh covered in buttercream snow, made in Germany, bought in that little shop on Michigan Avenue. The chime of her laugh when she shook it in her slender hands. That clarion sound, beautiful, mirthless. Her upturned nose and perfect marcelled waves.

So unlike Annie. She had one lock of hair that fell onto her forehead no matter how many times she pushed it back. Her laugh, always surprisingly gruff, as if she was letting you in on a secret. She called him Mayor — true, he was the mayor, but — with a shimmer in her eye that he couldn't quite read. Ever since he'd found himself momentarily alone with her at the church bazaar a year before, Annie had become something to him. He had only ever seen her with her family, an attractive woman, someone else's wife. But there, sitting alone behind a sun-sprayed table, neatening her stacks of preserves, he was at once struck by the angles of her face, her bewitching half-smile, as if he were seeing her for the first time. Would you look at her, he thought.

"Let me guess," she said. She closed her eyes and touched her temples. "Strawberry."

He stood there dumbly smiling.

"I'm right, aren't I?" she asked.

Was she flirting with him? He used to have an easy time of it back in Chicago. Before he had set his sights on Charlotte, there had been other city girls trying out their new-found independence. Flamboyant Helen with her trousers and dark curls who had, for a short time, set his heart ablaze. But out here was different. Early on he'd courted a sweet substitute schoolteacher named Laura for a few months, but his feelings had fallen flat. It had been so long since he had felt that uptick of his pulse, the charge of a small interaction, the warmth of a body close to his.

"Indeed you are, Mrs. Bell," he said.

"Lucky for you there's a two-for-one mayoral special," she'd said.

He'd bought six and lined them up along his windowsill.

"A giant ball of string," Styron said, slapping the desk and startling Jack. Styron, wiry and ruddy-cheeked, took to his duties with the energy and fervor of a missionary. They were trying to figure out a way to shore up the badly listing local economy, lure people to Mulehead, a place where apparently they couldn't even get people to stay. "Make it as big as a house."

"Who gives a mole's whisker about string?" Jack said.

"We make it a tourist destination. Tell people it's something to see. You know, like those faces they're carving in that mountain in South Dakota. Now *that's* inspired. I wish I had thought of that."

Styron was only a pretend frontiersman, his family trust a not-so-secret secret. At twenty-two, he'd come out here after Dartmouth College, on a whim, to start a newspaper although he didn't even know how to set type. After meeting Jack, who had been a real newspaperman back in Chicago, Styron saw that out here, he could think bigger. He could be mayor. He could be the one to single-handedly transform Mulehead into a thriving town. All before the age of thirty.

"The land of blowing dust," Jack said. "How about that?"

Styron ignored him.

"Get a sign up on the highway. Get someone to declare it official. The World's Largest Ball of String. I'd stop the car for that. Just to say I'd seen it, you know?"

"Good Lord." Jack laughed despite his weariness. It was a good thing he liked this kid. "I was thinking more along the lines of a manufacturing plant."

Styron winced a little, chafed by his boss's lack of vision. He would keep thinking. Great men had ambition, optimism, and opportunity. Styron believed big ideas were the way to redemption. He likened the strategy to football. A rushing game was tedious — he'd take the risk and rapture of the long pass any day.

"What about some kind of event? Like a yearly festival. Or a carnival?" Styron drew a circle in the air with his finger. "An enormous Ferris wheel lighting up the plains."

Jack stood and ruffled Styron's hair, a gesture both avuncular and condescending. Everyone had either come here looking for something, or, like him, was running from something else.

Styron scowled and dragged his finger through the dust on his desk.

"Come on," Jack said. "Coffee at Ruth's. Didn't you want to talk about the rabbits?"

■ ■ ■ ■

A few merciful clouds took the edge off the heat as Birdie walked along the edge of the east field, through the gulch and over the rise to the Woodrow place. She wanted to see if it was true. Birdie had ridden the school bus — a truck outfitted with crude plank seats — with Maggie Woodrow, thirteen, redheaded and shy, one leg slightly shorter than the other. Her father had fastened a piece of tire rubber to the bottom of her shoe to lessen the hitch of her gait. Maybe they would be happier somewhere west. Maybe Maggie Woodrow had finally gotten herself some luck.

The house appeared to slant, or maybe it was just that the dune of windblown dirt under the parlor window made it look off kilter. Up close, the paint was scratched away, and broken clapboards were roughly patched with aluminum scraps and tarpaper. The multiple sets of tire grooves in the dusty driveway would soon be smoothed away by the wind. Birdie knocked, just to be sure, before testing the door with her fingertips. It gave with little resistance, one of its hinges loose. Inside, it was surprisingly bright, as if, freed of its burden, the house was giving itself back to the elements. The kitchen window was broken out, a corona of glass on the floor below. Birdie leapt as a crow landed on the sharded sill, its black beak open and expectant, before it took off again with a papery swoosh. The Woodrows had left their kitchen table but they'd taken all the chairs.

She repositioned a bobby pin to hold back the wisps around her face. Cy had found her green ribbon, but he now kept it pressed in his Bible and that was even better. Birdie opened a cupboard. A patchwork towel. A rose-colored teacup missing its handle. An empty coffee tin. She felt as if she was snooping on ghosts. By now, maybe poor, short-legged Maggie had seen the sea.

A thump upstairs. Birdie was not alone. She stepped lightly through the empty sitting room toward the stairs.

"Hello?" she called. "Someone up there?"

Footsteps tumbled across the floor above her. She climbed slowly, her curiosity trumping her nerves.

Fred appeared at the top of the steps, with his scabbed knees and chipped-tooth grin.

"Dang it, Freddie," she said, stomping the rest of the way up. "I thought you were catching bugs or whatever you do." She pushed past him. "Find anything good?"

Fred ran ahead into a bedroom and came back beaming, a doll's head in one hand and a Coca-Cola bottle in the other.

"I mean like money or a diary or something," she said.

Fred was such a kid. He didn't understand a thing.

She had had a sister once. Eleanor was born when Birdie was five. She didn't remember much about her, but she did remember the hushed murmurs after the birth. She knew that something was wrong with the shriveled little body, her sister's breath wet and whistling. Three months later she was buried in the small cemetery behind the church, her grave marked with a little pink stone. Birdie's grandmother had come from Kansas — the first and last time Birdie had seen her — and had spoken in a low girlish whisper, as the heels of her shoes tapped against the wooden floorboards.

Birdie missed Eleanor in a teenaged way of wanting a sister to whom she could talk endlessly about everything. A mute little brother didn't quite suffice.

She followed Fred into a bedroom, where there were an iron bed frame, a crude broomcorn broom wedged into a corner, a cheap empty armoire, its doors agape.

"How'd they take everything?" she asked.

Fred shrugged and ran off to the other room. He sat and wiped the smudges from the doll's face. He did not want to think about the Woodrows. In two years, things had gone from good to broken for the Bells, too. They used to sit on the porch at the end of the day and he would dance like a chicken, his elbows out like wings, and Pop would laugh. Now at night all his father did was look at the sky and look at his Bible and not talk and not talk some more. Fred had written his name in the dust on the windows and the kitchen table and Mama had gotten short and then said she was sorry because she was really just angry about the dust. He was mad about the dust, too, mad about leghorn number ten, too sad to eat her stringy meat at dinner the other night — and so he ate biscuits instead, about twenty, he thought, or maybe four.

Fred heard an engine outside. The wheeze of creaking metal car doors.

Birdie stood in the doorway of the other bedroom, which must have been where the children slept, the cradle left behind along with a torn mattress on the floor. She imagined being here with Cy, how they could pretend they were in a house of their own. It would be better than the barn, romantic and dangerous at the same time.

Fred raced back in and pulled her arm. "What is it?"

From the window she saw two men she didn't recognize in dirty clothes and leather gloves, one carrying a crowbar, the other a hacksaw.

"Hey, McGuiness. What about the tin up here?"

"Can you get an edge? Yeah, let's pull it."

Birdie held Fred's shoulders, unsure whether to run or hide. Fred covered his ears against the terrible shriek of nails giving way as the men peeled a sheet of tin from the front of the house.

"Let's go," Birdie whispered.

McGuiness stepped inside just as they reached the bottom of the stairs. He laughed a little, and Birdie was close enough to smell his beery breath. He was missing half his front tooth.

"Well," he said. "Looks like we was beaten to the punch."

"We're going," Birdie said. She tried to walk around him, but he stood his ground, sucked his teeth at Birdie. She felt he could see through her pale pink dress and knew all that she and Cy had done together. Shame felt like thousands of tiny needles pressing on her skin.

With an exaggerated bow, McGuiness

53

moved to let them pass, and Birdie and Fred ran, leaving the scavengers to take what they would.

Birdie didn't want to go home — the run-in with that man too fresh — so she followed Fred, who tugged her hand. He seemed to have something he wanted her to see. They walked north on Gulliver Road into the land vacated by the suitcase farmers, men who used to show up once for planting, once for harvest. Rain follows the plow, everyone said so. Tractors ran all through the night, disk plows slicing through the prairie. But the rain had stopped, the fields left fallow, and now it was a wasteland of bitten topsoil and sand dunes, the road itself barely discernible. It was early in the day but the eroded earth was hot underfoot. Birdie ran to catch up with Fred, who had scampered down an embankment into an irrigation ditch.

"You're not taking me to see some silly animal bones or something, are you?"

Fred turned and pointed, and she could see something glinting in the sun, up high in the remains of a sun-bleached cotton-wood tree. They crossed the dead field and Birdie squinted up at a mass of tangled metal in the skeletal tree.

"What is it?" she asked.

Fred flapped his arms like wings and grinned.

She looked again.

"Crows?"

He nodded.

With nothing growing, no hay or twigs or leaves lying about, the crows had chosen the most plentiful resource: barbed wire, which littered the landscape, poking up through the drifts or hanging from buried posts. A giant barbed-wire nest.

"Isn't that something," she said. Why it made her feel better to see the nest she couldn't say, but she liked the stubborn way it looked. "Thanks, Freddie."

He raised his eyebrows together in quick succession until she laughed. He'd first noticed the nest months ago, and he sat out here every so often at the base of the dead tree, motionless, until a crow flew in. After the men had bombed the skies and killed the birds, he was relieved the nest was still occupied.

"I'm thirsty," Birdie said. "You coming?"

He wanted to hold her hand the way he used to, but he knew he was too old for that.

"The rabbits," Jack said. He smoothed his hand over his folded napkin, a faint brown stain on its corner.

"The rabbits," Styron said, taking a bite of a donut, the sugar coating the top of his lip. "The little critters are everywhere."

Styron had been fascinated by the overrun of rabbits, the plague-like nature of it. Only out here. But it was more than that. In those quiet dark moments before the sun came up, he knew the Panhandle had changed him and he couldn't imagine going back to East Coast life. What would he do, wear a suit and become a banker like everyone he used to know? He was different, wilder. The land was huge, the sky unpredictable, the elements punishing, and he had come to believe that it was good to feel small against all that. He could see opportunity even if no one else could.

"So they are."

Jack sipped his coffee and glanced around at the empty tables. Ruth's was the name of both the restaurant and the bar next door, where old Ruth herself, all four feet ten of her with her white bun and red lipstick, tended bar. Her daughter, Jeanette, ran the café, always ready with a caustic laugh and an easy sway of her hips. Jeanette's husband, Dwight, worked at the grain elevator; he was a charmed fiddle player who, when drunk, would often let his fists loose on

Jeanette. Jack had seen the black eyes from under her heavy face powder.

At the counter, Jeanette drawled mm-hmms to two farmers as she dried cups and saucers.

"What did they have to lose?" he heard her say. "I mean, good Lord. The whole sorry bunch of them."

Half the town had a crush on Jeanette. Jack wished Samuel Bell wasn't such a god-damn upright citizen. If you were going to covet your neighbor's wife, it sure would feel better if your neighbor was a son of a bitch like Dwight.

"Boss?"

Jack focused on Styron. "There are a lot of rabbits, yes."

"And people eat them, right?" Styron said.

"Yes, Styron, people eat them." Jack didn't have the patience for Styron's antics today. He felt sluggish, the coffee not yet kicking in. "You have sugar on your lip."

Styron wiped his face with his napkin, and still the sugar clung. "So I was thinking . . ."

Jack clunked his forehead down against the table. "Just get on with it."

"Come on, hear me out," Styron said.

Jeanette sauntered over with the pot of coffee. She was pretty, still, despite years with Dwight.

"More for you, Mayor? Or something to eat? You look a little pale."

"I feel a little pale," he said. "I'll have a bowl of chili. And more coffee."

"You ever serve rabbit here, Jeanette?" Styron asked. His voice came out too high, like a boy's, and he reached quickly for his coffee.

Jack shook his head. "Don't you mind him."

"Well, no, Mr. Styron, no, we don't. You don't see something you like?" She cocked her hip and Jack felt sad for her then, for the gesture of her younger hopeful self.

"Just thinking about our current abundance is all," Styron said stiffly.

"Plenty of people skinning and eating what they catch these days," Jeanette said, nodding hello to the fellows who walked in. "Just not sure they want to see it on the menu." She walked away calling back, "I'll get that chili to you, Mayor."

"Out with it," Jack said to Styron.

"Okay. People are angry about the drought, and here are these little animals multiplying, hopping around destroying gardens and what little crops are growing."

"Uh-huh."

"And people are struggling. Rabbits are meat."

58

"Styron —"

"An event. A roundup."

"A roundup?"

"We round up all the rabbits. Pen them in."

"We?"

"Divide up the meat at the end. Make it festive. It'll be a sporting event. A hunt."

"It's not a hunt if they're in a pen." Jack was already unsettled by the idea.

Jeanette returned with coffee and a small chipped bowl of chili.

"Don't worry, I'm not listening," she said.

As Jeanette walked away, Jack leaned in and lowered his voice. "You're talking about a bloodbath."

"Rodents," Styron said.

"Hares," Jack said.

"Pests. Whatever they are. Besides, it's not a big deal for these folks to kill animals."

"Jesus, Styron."

Styron lifted his hands in defense. "I bet people would come from all over the county for it. All's I'm saying."

Even though he usually drank it black, Jack dropped a sugar cube into his coffee. He pushed the chili away, the smell turning his stomach.

And then there she was. Annie Bell. Walking down First in a blue dress and matching hat, her eyes cast down but her pace brisk, a paper sack in her arm. As she neared Ruth's, she looked in and caught Jack staring. With a curious tilt of her head, she smiled back.

"I'll see you back at the office," he said to Styron, surprising himself as he sprang up from the table.

"Wait, what? What about the rabbits?"

Jack clumsily counted coins and spilled them onto the table.

"Do whatever you want."

Annie needed white thread, pins, lard, and cornmeal. Or so she'd told Samuel. She did need those things, but not today, not enough to make a separate trip into town. But standing in her hot kitchen, having swept the floorboards again, and put the bread to rise and chased grasshoppers from the windowsill, and snapped the beans, she thought about the Woodrows on a road to where it was green. Sure, there was no perfect life waiting for them in the West. She imagined them foraging for grubs and weeds in a highway ditch to fill their bellies on the way. But there had to be relief in leaving the drought behind. She wiped the hair from her face and felt a soft itchy flutter in her chest, like the beating wings of moths trapped in a lantern. I must get out, she thought. And once she had thought it, she couldn't shake it. She waited until Samuel had finished his lunch.

"Do you need anything while I'm out?" she asked, trying to slow her breath.

"I'm all right for now," he said. He licked peanut butter from his fingertips. "Oh, you know what? I need some stamps. If you could swing by the post office. You might ask after Edward's wife. Her joints are bad again." He pushed away from the table, rubbed his hands together and stretched his arms overhead. "I'll see you later."

Samuel felt himself pretending. All he could really think about were the dreams that visited him almost nightly now, the dreams of ferocious rain.

Annie had rushed to clear his plate and it clanged against the sink as the door swung shut behind him. He hadn't noticed anything. She ran upstairs, taking the steps two at a time. She splashed water on her face and washed under her arms and changed into a navy blue dress, one she hadn't worn since the Judson wedding two years ago, its sailor collar still flattering when she checked in the flecked mirror above her dresser. And she opted for a cloche hat, reddening some as she put it on. She was older than pretty, she knew, yet that didn't help temper the longing for something just outside of her periphery, something she could not yet name. Annie licked her lips. She had never in her life worn lipstick, but she wished she had some now, a little pink.

Samuel was out in the field tending to fragile shoots, which should have been heading but were barely jointing. There wasn't much to do, but he was still out from dawn to dusk every day. More and more, he saw the drought as a test of faith. More and more, she feared the drought would free this tight coil of restlessness in her, expose her as someone less than steadfast.

Annie had stuffed the hat into her handbag and skittered to the car. The tires spun and dust rose up around her until she jolted forward, onward, toward town.

Annie walked quickly along First, as if she had somewhere to be. She felt the McCleary brothers watch her as she passed, even though that was sort of the point. What was she doing, anyway? Trying to be different from the farm wife that she was? Her head was roasting in her dark hat and there was a pebble in her shoe cutting into her heel. The afternoon was hot and quiet. Her errands were done, all her purchases made in fifteen minutes, so she walked, the grain elevator looming at the end of the street. Ruth's was the last place on the block, and she considered stopping for an iced tea and an oatmeal cookie to resurrect her mood. But she couldn't stop, because of how it might look — dressed up and whiling away the afternoon alone — not to mention the fifteen cents they couldn't spare.

When she glanced in the cloudy front window, there, not for the first time, was the mayor looking right at her. Jack Lily. She smiled without showing her teeth, and kept walking.

"Afternoon, Mrs. Bell," he said.

She stopped and turned, shifting the paper sack to her hip as if it were a baby.

"Oh. Hello, Mayor," she said, registering how quickly he had managed to make it out to the sidewalk. She wished she'd had a chance to blot her face with a handkerchief.

"Solving all our problems?" she asked, nodding toward Ruth's.

He chuckled and crossed his arms. "Trying to rein in my deputy. He thinks everything deserves a plaque or a parade."

"Nothing wrong with a parade," she said. She should have kept going then, but there she stood, a tension between them both awful and delicious. "You can call me Annie."

"Can I carry that for you? Help you to your car?"

No one who saw them would have thought anything of it, and yet Annie knew different. What could people see anyway? They couldn't see the weight of a glance or the impurity of a thought. They were in plain view, but the town might just have easily fallen away. "No, no. I'm all right," she said. But she didn't move on.

"I don't mean to keep you." Jack glanced at the towering grain elevator at the end of the street. "Where are you headed?"

Annie could feel sweat above her lip as she looked both ways and then back to Jack Lily, his pale, smooth hands. Even after years out here, he hadn't lost the refined city way about him, an imprint of his old life in Chicago.

"I should have an answer," she said. "But I guess I'm just walking some."

"Walking is good," he said.

"The truth is I didn't want to go home just yet." She felt lighter having said it, a new hollow in her gut.

"Can I walk with you? I'm in no rush to get back to my desk."

She was pleased, but she knew it was not quite right for him to ask. Are you doing good by God, Annie? she heard her mother say before she could quiet the voice.

"Okay," she said.

"Okay, Annie," he said. "And you can call me Jack."

She nodded and switched her groceries back to her front. They walked a few feet apart down the block and beyond where the buildings gave way to dirt and scrub and the blackened, crumbled remains of the old feed store, which had burned down last year.

"It's not like Chicago, I bet," she said.

"No, it's not. But there are things I don't miss about the city," he said.

Glad to be moving, Annie felt the motion settling her down.

"I miss it and I've never even been there," she said, and laughed. "Not that I'd know what to do off the farm." The reference to the farm made her feel better; it held the mention of her family, of Samuel. They passed the loading platforms of the deserted silos and crossed the train tracks. And then at the same time they looked up to the sky. Where had the sun gone all of a sudden on a cloudless day?

"No," they said in unison to the darkness ahead. Another duster, this time, it seemed, thundering right toward the two of them.

Annie's hat lifted off her head and when

she reached up to grab it, the bag fell from her arms, spilling thread and lard and salt and baking soda and the cherry drops she'd gotten for Fred and the red ribbon she'd gotten for Birdie and the coffee and stamps she'd gotten for Samuel, across the road that led east out of town. She stooped to salvage her purchases as the wind whipped her dress and drove dust into her face, took her hat straight up into the air.

"Annie," Jack said, "leave it."

He took her hand and they ran.

CHAPTER 4

What hath God wrought. Ever since the first duster hit, that was what Samuel heard like a hammer on tin, over and over in his head. Shovel the sand. What hath God wrought. Spoon up the beans and gravy. What hath God wrought. Pump the well. What hath God wrought. Insistent like a heartbeat.

He watched Annie sleep, the rise and fall of the sheet. He wanted to wake her when the dreams came. But he didn't. She was exhausted, too. Each breath a heavy sigh. The dust was never gone. In their ears and eyes. In the sheets. On their toothbrushes and coffee spoons. In the butter. A layer of gray on the milk.

Pastor Hardy couldn't say whether withholding the rain and showering them with dust was a condemnation by God, but how can we not feel cursed? Samuel thought. Our land is on the wind.

Before Eleanor, before Fred, he and Annie used to sit together at the kitchen table when Birdie had gone to sleep and hold hands and bow their heads for just a minute or two before moving on to the tasks still needing tending. Those few minutes of intimacy were grounding, a reminder. But when the baby died, Annie stopped praying with him. She never said anything about it, just busied herself in another part of the house. Now Annie was distant. Annie was beautiful. She closed her eyes in church, but Samuel was pretty sure it was not to pray.

When they had first arrived, sleeping in the wagon lined with the mattress she'd slept on as a girl, he had never felt closer to her, to anyone. "Samuel," she'd say. "Samuel, tell me about the farm." And he would describe the place he imagined it would be when it was done. He had thought about it every day — working the soil for Ben Gramlin until his hands split — every day since he was seventeen. A sea of tilled fields flat and dark. A timber house with dormered windows and a grove of locust trees to remind her of Kansas. Together they carved out the barely-there hill for the dugout and planked two rooms that would shelter them until they could build the farmhouse. Centipedes clicked in the earthen walls, but it was theirs. At the end of each day their arms quivered and their palms were ground with dirt. He'd look over at her, his Annie who'd never done more than housework, sweat darkening her dress, and he would praise God for his good fortune.

Samuel had about a quarter of the wheat left. Scrawny plants that uprooted with the slightest tug. He could count the cows' ribs. The last duster had clogged the well.

And yet. I cannot leave this land that is ours, he thought, any more than I can crawl back to Dickinson County to work another man's acres, making a dollar from dawn until I can't see my hands. Or get on the relief. On relief you might as well be dead.

A farmer needs a farm. Didn't he know it.

The rains would come. The rains would come and God would show them the way back. Samuel had to believe that.

Cy rolled away from Birdie with a sigh. She poked his side, and he squawked and fell partly onto the floor, legs splayed.

"Hey now," he said, laughing a little and repositioning himself on the torn mattress.

The scavengers had picked the Woodrows' house clean, but they'd left the mattress, Birdie had been pleased to discover. She stared up at the mottled ceiling. Sepia water stains bloomed from the cracks, vestiges of rain. His sweat left her front slick so she waited to dress, thankful for the breeze that crisscrossed through the tumbledown house.

"You know it's my birthday coming up," she said.

"Oh yeah?" Cy propped himself up on his elbow. "When?"

"Two months. I'm giving you ample notice."

He laughed and lay back down. "Thanks for letting me know." He turned to the window and watched a gauzy cloud scud by.

Her birthday meant sixteen. And what she hoped for was that Cy would ask her to marry him. They had not talked about it yet, but they had confessed love, and to Birdie, this was as good as any promise. He made her feel like a new person, no longer just a daughter and sister, no longer a child. He was like a lantern held high, letting her see what might be possible just ahead. When he said, "I love you," she swallowed those words whole and they spread out through her limbs until she felt fortified, sated, as if she could live forever on love alone.

She sat up and pulled on her underthings. As she buttoned up her blouse, she saw one of the buttons had cracked and another was missing. She'd have to find some replacements. There were no new clothes now, only the mended and remended.

He laced his fingers with hers, and then lifted her hand to kiss it. His eyes went back to the window. Birdie recognized his searching look. She'd seen it in her father, in the other farmers. Worry had reeled him out of the room.

"What's wrong?" she asked.

"We lost two head of cattle, this last one. The others are sucking air. Wobbly on their legs." He let go of her hand and sat up. "Things aren't going so good."

How he could think of cows when they'd barely just caught their breath was beyond her. She scooched closer to him where the mattress was dry.

"It'll take them a while to clear it out. They'll be okay." She patted his arm, but he didn't look at her. What did it matter, she wondered, when they would go away, start somewhere else together soon. A porch swing and honeysuckle and big, leafy trees.

"And that patch we worked to save after the first one? Gone. Done." He rubbed the sides of his face with his hands. "I don't know, Birdie. It's a lot."

She was so sick of hardship. She just

wanted life to return to regular. The last storm had taken two more hens and her mother's pole beans and had buried most of the wheat shoots in the east field. She knew the government was paying a dollar a head to kill starving and sick cows, although it made her squirm to think of it. Can't sell them so they shoot them instead. Everyone was losing everything. It was awful. It was boring.

"You got me, right?" She pounced on his chest and knocked him back, wanting to shake him out of it, wanting to be enough to change his mood.

"Right-o," he said, planting a kiss on her forehead. He sat up again and pulled on his overalls. "We best be getting on. It's late."

She knew he was right, but it dug at her still. A wolf spider made its way across the floor. She stood and zipped her skirt, felt a rush of dampness in her underpants.

"We'll live somewhere else," she said, surprised by the resolve in her own voice. "Someday. Away from here." She wasn't too concerned with the details. She would work in a café in a town near the beach. Or she would see Cy off to work each morning and pick fresh flowers for the dinner table. Away, away, was all that mattered. Like Ann of the Airlanes in the radio show she used to love, "over valley and mountain, river and plain," buzzing about as the world spun.

Cy nodded, but busied himself with tying his boots. "Sure we will. It'll be good."

He smelled of dirt and hay and sweat and she leaned into his big warm chest. He held her hair in his fist, and a kiss to her neck sent a jolt to her toes.

"Maybe we should live on a boat," she said.

"Aye, aye, Captain."

"And listen to the water all day long."

"And sleep under the stars." Cy put his heavy hands on her shoulders and shook her gently. "I have to go."

"I know."

Hand in hand they walked out into the arid evening. To the west the sun cast its copper glow on the barren remains of the Woodrow farm.

"Glad school's out?" he asked.

"What do you think?"

"I saw Miss Francis in town yesterday. Looks like she's still a nervous Nellie."

"On the last day she teared up because Billy Trotter threw an eraser at Tom McGuane but it hit her by accident and left a white rectangle of chalk on her backside."

"I never thought I'd miss it. But I do sometimes."

Cy wagged his head and looked away. He was only a year out of school, but it might as well have been ten.

"It's a large backside. It's kind of hard to miss," she said.

He laughed and latched his thumbs on his pockets. "See you soon, Birdie girl."

In his mind Birdie was like sunshine, the early spring kind that got the chickens laying and the robins nesting and coaxed the grass green. Or used to. What do people do when there's nothing left to farm, nothing left to eat? Cy felt his stomach seize. Lately he'd been saving some of his dinner for his sister, who got last dibs. He took measured breaths and steps, his boots sliding in the dust. He couldn't stop for fear that Birdie was still watching. Birdie wasn't the kind of girl you could tell your troubles to. She was like a swift sparkling creek, flowing right over the sharp rocks to a place where the current ran smooth.

It calmed him to think of it, him and Birdie running off somewhere like she talked about, to think of her beside him. He pictured them on a train, an open boxcar, with rucksacks and apples in their hands. But he didn't have a rucksack and neither did she and she was fifteen, a schoolgirl still, and there was his father and mother and sister and the dying cows and the dying land. He was a son first.

Step, step, step, hop. Step, step, step, hop. "Look out, hoppers," Fred thought. "You better scatter while you can, because here I come, a giant boy with a sack of poison bait." He didn't really want to kill the grasshoppers, but he did what his father asked. Fred coughed and his breath felt grainy; the air was getting a little stuck on the way in and then again on the way out. When he ran, his lungs were heavy like sponges full of water. It annoyed him to have to walk all the time.

Even if he washed his hands twice, the stink of grasshopper bait still clung to them. Pop said the bait didn't do much, so Fred didn't know why they kept putting it out, but he couldn't ask him and it didn't seem worth it to write out all the words. So he did what he was told even if he got bored and took a break to follow tracks that could be bear tracks that led to a secret forest where the shade was cool and dark and smelled like moss and toadstools.

He heard his mother calling him in.

Birdie waited until Cy had disappeared over the drift of sand east of Woodrow's before running for home. By the time she rounded the fence she saw the sun going low and she knew she was late for dinner again. She stopped outside the front door, trying to settle herself, make sure her buttons were done up right, her skirt straight. She brushed her hair with her fingers, fishing out a twig.

"Where you been at?" Samuel said as she opened the door.

Her parents and Fred sat around the table, the stew and boiled potatoes untouched in the middle.

"Answer your father, Barbara Ann."

"Out walking," she said.

Fred made a kissing face across the table as she sat. She scowled at him and reached for a piece of cornbread as she sat.

"Birdie," Samuel said, his voice harsh. "We will say grace."

She looked down at her plate; a fine gray layer was already settling on the white porcelain. Even when the sky was clear, the dust never left them. There was no such thing as clean.

"Bless us, O Lord, and these, your gifts, which we are about to receive from your bounty. Through Christ, our Lord. Amen." Her father kept his eyes squeezed shut even after "Amen," and Fred kicked Birdie's foot under the table.

Annie folded her napkin in her lap and watched her husband's face, his eyes tight, his mouth twitching. It was irksome to her, how he held them captive after the prayer. And there her daughter was, running in from doing who knew what with Cy Mack and making them all wait.

Samuel cleared his throat and picked up the stew pot, exposing a white ring on the tablecloth. In the last storm, with Annie stuck in town, Samuel and the children had hung wet sheets over the windows to keep out the dust, but even in the house they still inhaled it with each breath, cobwebby in their noses.

"Looks wonderful," Samuel said.

"At least we'll always have potatoes," she said. "Elbows off the table, Fred."

He grunted, a yes of a kind, one of his few noises. Annie didn't pray anymore, but sometimes she would stare at Fred and try to will him to speak. Talk to me, she said to herself, you can talk to me. She already knew his voice, heard it in her head whenever he wrote.

Birdie pushed around a carrot with her fork before nibbling on a square of cornbread. Annie spied a mark on her daughter's neck, even obscured as it was by her hair.

For now, Annie held her tongue. Gathered there with her family, she couldn't help think of her own transgression. She bowed her head.

When the storm had hit, what followed her initial fear was the undeniable thrill of Jack Lily's confident hand leading her to the closest parked car. Inside they had huddled side by side in the backseat as the car was rocked by gusts, dust scratching against the windows. They breathed into the crooks of their elbows. When she realized they were still holding hands, she didn't pull away. The heat of the car, stifling, flushed her cheeks.

"Thank you," she said, when the wind subsided. Light filtered through the haze and she returned her hand to her lap.

"Annie."

Dust had coated his hair and shoulders like talcum powder, but there he was, smiling. She couldn't help smiling, too.

"I suppose I can make it to the car now," she said.

"Maybe best not to drive quite yet."

She knew it was probably fine — she was not some delicate rose, and the worst of the storm had passed — but she stayed, she wanted to stay, and she was glad to have the pretext. Who am I? she wondered as her heart drummed its erratic beat beneath her rib cage. Jack Lily had crisp brown eyes, steady and direct, and black hair that hung boyishly across his forehead. He was younger than she was by a few years, she guessed, but he was sophisticated, knew about a different kind of life. She was drawn to this man, liked the excitement she felt next to him. She had stayed sitting close.

"You hear that?" Samuel asked.

"What?" Flustered, Annie sipped her milk.

"Fred. When he breathes. There's a whistle."

Fred exhaled theatrically, and a wheeze constricted the tail end of his breath.

"Be serious," Birdie said.

He laughed silently and did it again. He had always had fragile lungs; his colds would settle in his chest and last for a month, with a tight barking cough that yanked Annie from sleep like the blast of a shotgun. Some things helped a little. Hot water and honey. Steam. That the dust was taking its toll she could hear now in his ragged-edged breathing.

"Feel okay, Freddie?" she asked.

The doctor over in Herman cost five dollars for the visit alone.

"The boy has asthma," the doctor had said last year when they took him. The liniment oil in his wavy dark hair made his collar greasy. "Pull down his trousers."

Annie didn't know what asthma was and didn't care just then. She did as she was told and whispered into Fred's ear, "It's okay. The doctor is going to help you." Fred had smiled even through his strangled breaths. Her good boy Fred.

The doctor jammed a syringe of epinephrine into Fred's thigh, and he shot up to sitting, shaking and sweating, but breathing.

"Doctor? What can we do for him?" Samuel asked.

"They say it's a psychosomatic illness."

"Psychosomatic?" Samuel asked.

"In his head. Psychological causes. Fear, stress, feelings of hopelessness perhaps. From the Greek verb *aazein,* meaning to pant."

Annie hated this man, his condescension. She ran her palm over her boy's clammy forehead.

"He couldn't breathe," Samuel said thinly.

"Oh, the symptoms are real. But most likely brought on by some strong emotion. Something upsetting you, son?"

Fred looked to his mother, confused.

"He can't speak," she said.

"Can't or won't?" the doctor said.

Annie felt Samuel squeeze her hand, and

80

she half hoped her husband would up and knock the doctor down.

"Well. Nothing much to be done, I'm afraid, except watch for symptoms. And don't let it get this bad before getting him help."

The doctor turned to Fred. "Tell your folks if it gets hard to breathe, okay?" He had leaned down close to Fred's face. "You can do that, can't you? I'm pretty sure you can."

And that had sent Annie spinning.

Birdie reached for her third piece of corn-bread. "I'm sure he'll be just fine with a plateful of sugar cookies and strawberry preserves," she said.

"Nothing your mother's cookies can't fix." Samuel grinned.

His compliment nettled her, so easy and bland. As she and Jack Lily had waited in the hot backseat, the light diffuse through the dirty windshield and cloudy air, she had felt outside of time, transported. Like someone else.

"I sure wouldn't have imagined myself here in No Man's Land," Jack said with a laugh.

She found she loved his voice, smooth and clear, laced with bits of his Chicago accent. They caught glances and turned away.

"Who would have?" she said. "I hoped Mr. Darcy would find his way to Kansas."

Jack Lily raised his eyebrows. "Austen?"

She reddened, caught showing off with the little she remembered from high school English.

"You are lovely," he said.

And there it was.

Annie stared straight ahead. She felt electric.

"I should go," she said, avoiding his eyes. She touched her fingertips to the scowl lines between his eyes before opening the door.

Her hat had been caught, wedged under the car's front tire, crushed. She had done nothing and she had done everything.

Fred had knocked his glass of milk to the floor with one of his unruly elbows.

"Get a towel, Fred," Samuel said.

"I'll get it," Annie said, leaping to her feet. He would never suspect. Never be jealous.

"No use crying over spilled milk," Birdie said. Fred stuck his tongue out at her.

"I'm going over to the Macks' place after supper," Samuel said. "He's got a bunch of sick cows. Needs to figure out what to do."

"Is there anything to do?" Annie asked as she sopped up the milk.

"I think he'll take the dollar a head. They

herd them over to Fairview gulch."

Annie looked up. "It's awful." All of it, she thought.

"Don't I know it."

Annie handed Birdie the last pot to dry, and took a rag to wipe down the table.

"You were with Cy. Earlier."

Birdie silently dried the already dry pot.

"Birdie." Annie turned to face her. "Barbara Ann."

"What?"

"Don't go sneaking around."

"I'm not sneaking." Birdie shoved the pot on the high shelf until it clanged against the wall.

Annie pushed the hair from her forehead, that stubborn curl that never stayed back. "It's becoming," Jack had said in the car, "how it always falls like that."

"You think you know everything there is to know, Birdie." She knew it was the wrong thing to say, but she couldn't help herself.

Birdie crossed her arms and clamped her lips together. "So you've said before," she muttered.

Annie took a breath, evened her voice, and tried to start again.

"Cy's a farmer like his father," Annie said.

"So what? You married a farmer."

I know I did, Annie thought. I know, I know. Jack in his rolled-up shirtsleeves. His clean cut-grass-and-mint smell.

"I'm not saying a farmer is a bad thing," Annie said, lowering her voice. "I chose this life."

"Besides, Cy doesn't want to stay here forever. You don't know anything about him."

"I know that you like him. And that's a wonderful thing. But you don't need to decide on someone yet. You're only fifteen."

"You don't know what it's like," Birdie said, her voice gone quiet. She bit her lip and shook her head, giving up trying to explain it.

I do know what it's like, Annie thought.

"Be a little careful with your heart. That's all I'm saying," she said.

"I'm not like you, Mama."

I'm not like me, either.

Fred watched his father set off toward the Mack farm, his steps quiet in the dust, and then the car chugging down the driveway, finally small against the horizon. The evening brought a light breeze, the clouds plum in the west. He would have liked to go along, but he had not been invited. He jumped off the porch and ran behind the

84

chicken coop to check his trap, which he'd fashioned from an old crate. If it worked, a rabbit would hop in through the door he'd cut, nibble at the piece of cabbage — stolen from his mother's garden — and the movement would knock loose a gate of chicken wire, which would fall and capture it. He didn't know what he'd do with it after he caught it, but maybe he could fashion a leash out of twine.

Fred panted, unable to get a breath in deep. He came around the henhouse to find the crate knocked over and the cabbage gone. This was his third failed contraption. He wandered toward what was left of the old grazing land around the dry pond to look for bones. There was a bone market out near the railroad, bone meal being the cheapest way to fertilize. They paid by the ton, he'd heard, and he was pretty sure he was getting there now that there were all kinds of bones to be found: coyotes, rabbits, birds, bats, raccoons, squirrels. He'd hauled a whole cow skeleton, piece by piece, from the middle of what was left of the pond. His pile of bones formed a white tower in the dying light.

He picked up a cow skull, heavy in his hand, still warm from the day's heat. He hurled it with both hands as hard as he could at the lone cottonwood on the pond's edge. The crack of breaking bone felt clean and good. He gulped in a not-quite-full breath and yawned.

Sugar cookies would make him feel better. Birdie was right. He scampered off, in the direction of home.

Samuel did not go to the Macks' farm. Instead he turned toward town and drove past the church to Pastor Hardy's small wooden house that the townspeople had built for him almost twenty years ago. The yuccas held the sand, but the elm they'd planted with the house was leafless and peeling. The pastor had lost his wife to diphtheria back in Arkansas soon after they'd lost their son in the trenches of the Great War. The pastor had answered an ad for a preacher needed on the High Plains, and had set off for Oklahoma alone.

Samuel turned off the car and waited while the engine knocked and settled. He would drop by to see Stew Mack on the way home, but he hadn't been able to bring himself to tell Annie that he was first going to talk to Pastor Hardy. Just as he hadn't been able to talk to her about the dreams, more disturbing and powerful as the summer wore on, afraid she might dismiss them as foolish. He could sense her impatience with the intensity of his prayers, his questions. She went to church, of course, but her Bible had been packed away for years.

Always now there was rain when he closed his eyes at night. Rain hurtling to the earth without letting up. But after the last roller he'd had a dream so lifelike he couldn't shake its haunting grip. It wasn't like the others, and it didn't dissolve the next morning when he woke, his throat gritty and parched. Instead, it seemed to gain weight and dimension as he went about his day on the farm, sticking with him like a physical presence. Torrents of rain pouring from a dark and savage sky, a deluge that wiped out animals, houses, the railroad, the post office. His neighbors bobbed along in the rising water as trees snapped like matchsticks.

Pastor Hardy stood in the open doorway and beckoned Samuel inside. They sat on wooden chairs at a small table in a circle of yellow lamplight.

"I brought some cookies," Samuel said, unfolding a butter-spotted napkin.

"Annie is sure a good cook," the pastor said. "I miss the kitchen smells. The small things can wrench you into misery when someone's gone." He took a cookie, not bothering with a plate, and his first bite dropped crumbs to the table in a constellation. "I'm grateful for the congregation," he said. "Keeps me busy."

Samuel nodded. "Hard to outrun it sometimes, isn't it?" He patted the pastor's sleeve, and quickly withdrew his hand.

"What's on your mind, Samuel? What brings you out?"

"I've been chewing on something. It's got me all tied up."

"Go on."

"We had abundance out here and now we have nothing. Worse than nothing." Samuel's words began to spill from him. "People leaving their land, not enough to eat. Questioning God. I know I have, I can't help it."

"Slow down, son. Let me get the whiskey."

The old man shuffled to the cupboard and pulled down a small jug and two cloudy glasses. Samuel took a sip and welcomed its calming effect.

"The jackrabbits, the grasshoppers. Even all the spiders. It just feels plain wrong," Samuel said. "If it's not retribution, this place we're in now, if God isn't punishing us for our sins, could it be a test, then?"

"When we return unto God, things will be changed for us," Pastor Hardy said.

Samuel rolled his glass between his palms

before the pastor filled it again.

"I'm afraid," Samuel said quietly.

"We're all afraid. These are frightening times. That's why some leave. That's why some stay. That's why we ration ourselves to cured pork and cornmeal porridge."

"No, it's something else. Why I came tonight. To talk to you."

"What is it, Samuel? Have you done something?"

Samuel shook his head and looked to the window, only to see the reflection of the lamp. It was ludicrous, this thought that wouldn't leave him.

"Then what's troubling you? Unburden yourself."

"I'm afraid of what I've seen in dreams."

"Dreams are difficult. They can feel like visitations, can't they?"

"Could they be?"

The pastor leaned back in his chair and shrugged.

"Sometimes God speaks in thunder. Other times in silence. Only you can know the voice that speaks to you."

"What if," Samuel said. "What if God has spoken to me?"

Annie sat on the edge of the bed and, in the moon's weak light, rubbed beeswax on her hands. In place of washing powder, she'd begun to use cheap lye, which left her hands rough and ugly.

Samuel had come home late, smelling of alcohol, but Annie couldn't bring herself to ask. Compared to what she'd done — her thoughts returned to Jack Lily in the car again and again — a night of drinking with Stew Mack was nothing. He'd mumbled something about cows and had then gone straight to bed, where he now slept, legs out, mouth open. This image of him — helpless, vulnerable — repelled her.

It is you, Annie, she thought. Don't blame this on Samuel. It is you and Jack Lily and what has taken root in you. Lust was new to her, a darker pull than she'd ever felt with Samuel, a barbed vine that snaked its way around every thought, gently squeezing everything else out.

Life was not good and fair. God had taught her this, hadn't he? She harbored this belief like a shard of iron lodged in her gut. Her baby, her baby. Beautiful and alive with her gurgling milky breaths and tiny pink hands and eyes dark like obsidian. Ten years and she could not forgive God for what he had taken. Jack Lily did not remind her of what she'd lost. What they were losing day after day.

Annie brushed the fine dust from her pillow and pulled back the sheet. She curled herself around her husband's slack body in apology.

CHAPTER 5

The next duster came quickly on the heels of the last, and the Bells scurried about trying to cover the beds, to wedge wet towels around the windows and under the doors. Wind burst two windows of the empty school. After the dust had followed the faintest black drizzle, which left only a smattering of drops on the dry ground before stopping. Fred and Birdie spent the storm's aftermath sweeping, wiping, cleaning, and tending to the farm's anxious animals. Annie tried to keep Fred inside as much as possible — his cough had turned deep and phlegmy — but he could not stand being trapped in a handful of hot rooms, so she gave up.

Samuel's boots crunched on grasshoppers as he toured the fields. There was so little to harvest. Enough of the feed crops had grown to see the animals through the winter, but the wheat was dismal — five bushels to an acre, maybe — a yield not worth the gas for the tractor to pull the combine. Last Sunday a farmer out near Beauville had come home from church and hanged himself from a beam in his barn. It's the waiting that will drive you mad, Samuel thought. Watching it all go, bit by bit.

The dream about the rain came to him every night now, and he'd awaken in ravaged sheets damp from sweat. The power and the horror of all that rain.

"What do you want me to do?" Samuel said into the wind. "I am listening."

It had been a few days since the storm, the sky again high and bright, but dust still hung in the air, a gossamer haze over everything. After his chores, Fred went to the gulch near the Woodrows', remembering the frogs he used to catch, but of course found it parched and empty save for what looked to be the thick webbing of a black widow's nest. He dragged a stick through the filaments and they made that telltale crackle, but he didn't see any spider. Webs were everywhere now, in every corner, crevice, and ditch, undisturbed by animals or rain. How long could spiders go without water? How long could anything? Where was God? The question nagged at him, though

93

it scared him a little to even think it. Maybe you weren't supposed to ask something like that. Round and round he went in his head. It just seemed like it would be pretty easy for God to make it better.

He didn't notice Birdie until she was right beside him.

"Don't tell Mama you saw me," she said. Fred covered his eyes with his hands. She stopped and squatted next to him.

"She doesn't understand," she said.

Fred was confused by the arguments lately between his sister and his mother. You don't understand no you don't understand no you don't understand.

"You like Cy, don't you?"

He nodded and handed her the stick.

"I do, too," she said. Birdie raked the stick across the silk. "It kind of sounds like paper being ripped, doesn't it?" She dropped the stick with a shudder. They stood, dust aswirl at their feet, and Birdie brushed the front of her dress, which the wind flattened against her legs.

"See you later, alligator," she said.

Fred squinted and tugged at his ear.

"What?"

He dug a smashed notebook and pencil nub from his pocket.

"Can't God make it rain?" he wrote.

94

Birdie shrugged. "I don't know. He doesn't seem to be doing much, does He. He makes it rain in California. I hear carrots are the size of baseball bats out there."

Fred blinked, not entirely sure if she was kidding.

"You're such a kid," she said, knuckling his head before he scooted away. She walked into the wind in the direction of the Mack farm, her hair whipping behind her.

Fred gathered a small stash of rabbit bones and hammocked them in his shirt, setting off for the pond.

The cottonwood at the edge of the dry pond swayed in the wind. He dropped the bones onto his growing pile. He stood in the tree's shade and ran his hand along the deep fissures of the bark. The seeds with their cottony tails had blown away a month ago, and Fred wondered if any of them had landed and taken hold. He saw his father top the small ridge.

"Your mother sent me to find you," Samuel said. "Figured you were going out to the bones again." He handed Fred a small tin of petroleum jelly. "Wipe it in your nose." Fred shook his head with distaste. "Go on. It'll keep the grit out some."

Fred smeared the goo inside his nostrils, disgusted by its cool sliminess. He wiped his hand on his shirt and then pouted, picking at the cottonwood bark.

"You okay?"

Fred pulled out his notepad and flipped to a page.

"Can't God make it rain?"

Samuel couldn't help but smile a little.

"I ask myself the same question. I mean, yes, I suppose God could make it rain. But why He doesn't, I don't know."

Fred found his pencil. "Noah?"

"Noah? You know that story. God was saddened by the wickedness of man who he created."

"God sent rain," Fred wrote.

Samuel nodded. "He did."

"He's sad again?" Fred wrote. He coughed and wiped at his nose. When He was done punishing them with drought, would He punish them with rain?

"It will come again," Samuel said. "The rain. I'm sure of it."

They sat together for a long while, the shade shifting, the sun hot on their necks.

Fred thought about rain, the rising water. He found a clean page in this notebook and began to draw. When he was finished, he held it up to his father.

It was a picture of a boat.

■ ■ ■ ■

Samuel, wrenched from sleep, found himself dry-mouthed and shaken, alone in the bed. He had the momentary, sleep-gauzed panic that Annie had deserted him. He careened into the kitchen. She was sitting at the table with a cup of tea gone cold.

"I was worried," he said, "when you weren't there."

"I couldn't sleep." Her hair was messy, her prominent collarbones visible above her nightgown. She looked away.

"I'm sorry if I kept you up. A bad dream," he said. "Another one."

He wanted her to ask him about it, but she was quiet and suddenly he felt shy about sitting down at his own table. He had not told her about his visit to Pastor Hardy the week before. In the light of day there never seemed a good time to bring it up. He pulled out a chair, the scrape loud against the floorboards in the night quiet. She recoiled, the slightest retraction of her shoulders. And Samuel had the awful urge to slap her.

Annie smiled at him as he sat, and he was grateful for that.

"Hungry?" she asked.

"Yes," he said, though he wasn't. "Or a little brandy maybe?"

She nodded. "I'll get the glasses."

Samuel reached behind the sack of cornmeal on top of the icebox and got down the bottle, pulling out the cork with a satisfying thwop. He poured a finger for her and two for him.

"Remember that first night?" he asked. "There was that tear in the canvas of the wagon and if we scooted to one side we could see the moon through it?"

She nodded and smiled, hands around her jelly jar of brandy.

"I was scared we'd get eaten by coyotes. Or the horses would run away and we would be stuck in the middle of nothing," she said.

They had arrived at their parcel, marked by a small stake with a number painted on it, barely visible in Indian grass two feet high. Their horse-drawn wagon was lined with a mattress, and around it were packed tools and jugs of water and boxes of canned food. Roped to the back was a trunk filled with dresses, linens, and dishes her mother had insisted they take. It was 1916. The wind carried the cow stink from the ranches over miles of grassland. They had been jittery from the bumpy trek south over the plains. The next day they would start digging out their house. But they could do little in the dark. So they lay together in the wagon, and as he held his wife in the cool spring evening Samuel had felt blessedness swell deep in his chest. Annie Bell, he had said. Annie Bell.

Samuel finished his drink with a large gulp. "I had everything I wanted."

"Except a roof."

"Ah well."

"We were so young," she said. "I thought we could dig out the house in a day."

"You were beautiful. Are still." The alcohol was loosening him.

"Samuel." She reached across the table and covered his hands with hers.

"We need to talk about something," he said.

Her eyes widened.

"I believe it's going to rain," he said.

She felt a leaden relief pour through her. Here Annie had thought, in that terrible moment, that Samuel had found out about Jack Lily. She would not meet him again, would bury the giddy spark.

"I hope so." She felt herself return to Samuel, allowed herself to believe in what they had built together.

"No. I mean rain the likes of which we've never seen. Rain to end all rain. Rivers of it.

A deluge."

"Deluge?" She let go of his hands and pulled hers to her lap. "What are you talking about? Out here?"

"To wipe out the ruined land. So we can start again."

He held her gaze trying to bring her with him, to carry her.

"The liquor's got you going."

"No."

"Let's go back to bed."

"God has shown me. In dreams."

"Dreams, Samuel?"

"It feels like more than dreams."

Annie finished her drink and rubbed her face. Samuel waited for her to speak but she didn't.

"Fred and I were talking," he said.

"Fred?"

"He has an idea. About the rain. About how to protect us when it comes."

"Fred is an imaginative little boy."

"I think he's right," Samuel said.

She shook her head, trying to regain the clarity she had felt a moment before.

"We're going to build a boat," he said, feeling the idea solidify for the first time.

Annie hid her eyes with her palms and dug her fingertips into her forehead.

"I know how it sounds," he said.

"Do you?"

"It's not crazy, though."

"Please, Samuel. You are a farmer in a drought."

Her bitterness stung him.

"Psalms 46, verse 10. Be still, and know that I am God," he said.

"Please don't quote Scripture to me." She dropped her glass in the sink with an angry clang.

Samuel sank into himself.

"Fred is right," he said. "I know it. And I will do what I have to do to keep us safe." His once tentative question about the rain, over the past weeks, had with Fred's help crystallized into belief. With time, Annie would have to see the truth of it.

"Stop!" she shouted, covering her mouth quickly with her hands.

"There's no harm in it. To be prepared."

Annie left him there at the table. Samuel seemed more lost to her than ever.

Annie hadn't been to the Woodrow house since the family had disappeared, and to see it now with its sagging roof and gaping door — how fast nature reclaimed itself when people weren't looking — she stopped, her feet half buried in the sand. What separated the Woodrows' ruin from their own was the finest of threads. Through how many bad harvests could they continue to piece together an existence? She realized in her haste and nerves that she was still wearing her oil-stained apron. The house had been her idea — meeting at the mayor's apartment in town was not a possibility — but the physical emptiness of it now scared her, so she sat outside in the mesquite's stingy shade to wait.

As a girl she'd loved her father's church. Bentonville had been a frontier town where Presbyterians held meetings in homes or shops before her own parents had arrived, fresh from seminary in Topeka. Her father had overseen the church's design and construction, and its cool walls of Kansas limestone, its Gothic tower, and its turrets felt castlelike. He wanted a beacon, he had said, to attract worshippers from all over the Plains. In the stained-glass sanctuary, awash in sun and color, she would close her eyes and feel the warmth of the spirit, as the staccato of her father's stern voice lulled her.

Once when she was eleven, she went to call her father home for lunch. The day was bursting with the earliest hints of spring, the snow melting in rivulets down the sidewalk. Her unbuttoned coat flapped as she bounded up the church steps. She was early. Inside the dark vestibule, which always smelled of books and must and candle wax, she heard the murmur of voices, a woman's laugh. Annie rested her ear against the office door.

"Let me help with that," she heard her father say.

"Thank you, Reverend," the woman said, followed by a childish giggle. "It's hard to zip it up myself."

"You best get on your way now," he said.

Confused and hot, Annie had rushed out of the hall, down the stairs, back outside. Mrs. Simpson, a wealthy widow who headed up the church's women's committee, emerged, blinking hastily against the day's brightness, lifting her skirt away from the meltage underfoot. Her dark hair, piled high on her head, leaned to the side, and a hairpin dangled from it like a fishhook.

"Oh," she said, seeing Annie, who pretended she had just arrived. "Hello there, Annie. I had to deliver what we collected for the poor Jameson family. Everyone was very generous."

Mrs. Simpson's cheeks were pink, and she swung a big empty basket as she descended the steps, the smell of rosewater in her wake.

The first flash of anger Annie felt was

toward her mother. For the grooves on her face, her little puckered mouth and insipid voice, for somehow being responsible. Are you doing good by God, Mother, by pretending that you don't see? Annie thought. She couldn't then, not for a long while, accept that her father was not only just a man, but a fake.

Here she was, no better. A hawk circled above her. I am not weak, she thought, and stood, brushing off her dress, and turned to go home. But she heard an engine on the wind, and soon she saw that green Model A any of the neighbors would recognize coming toward her.

Jack Lily emerged into the fierce glare, his hair still damp from bathing, a nick on his chin. He stood in front of her with his hat in his hands. Dressed in a white shirt and a black tie as he often was, out here it made him seem like a visitor from another time.

"Annie."

She tried to smile, but the heat bore down and her mouth felt heavy — for a moment she thought she might faint. He offered the crook of his arm and she took it, leaning into him, aware of how he felt different from Samuel, less muscled but more substantial. He smelled of soap and toothpaste. His hands were clean.

"I was afraid you wouldn't come," he said.

"No one was home," she said.

They walked up to the door, open and off one hinge, leaning against the house.

"We could drive somewhere. To Beauville. No one would recognize us there."

"Samuel will be back before long."

They stepped over the dried rabbit pellets and drifts of dust in the entryway. He took her hand and she was grateful to be led. At the sight of the old mattress on the floor, Annie knew there had been others here. She looked at Jack Lily, then surprised herself by laughing.

"The maid took the day off," she said.

He laughed and folded her into his arms, and a hunger bubbled up in her, pushing away the guilt so that all she felt was the weight of a man who was not her husband pressed against her. Here was a man who knew about the world, who saw something in her, wanted her. Her body felt borrowed. She was not wife or mother or mender or cook or scrubber or canner or weeder. She did not have a husband who believed he had to build a boat in the desert. She did not have a baby who lived inside her for nine months and died outside after three. They had no history. It was almost too much, her breaths small and quick, and she felt she might pop.

"I have a blanket in the car," he said. "So we can sit down."

He jogged out and she stood motionless, closed her eyes against the dirty floor and broken doll's head and the field mouse nest in the corner, and tried to leave herself behind.

When he returned, he pulled her to him and she was for a moment afraid of the need and gratefulness in his eyes, so she kissed him. How strange it was, she thought, this unfamiliar insistent mouth, the taste of another's lips, tongue, and teeth. She kissed Jack Lily again and again with an abandon she never dared show Samuel.

He untied her bonnet and lifted it from her head.

"Annie," he said. "Is this really you?" He pushed her hair back from her face and cupped her shoulders as if she might float away. He grinned and let out a small whoop, which made her laugh. She touched the small blood spot on his chin.

"I was nervous," he said. "Not the best time to shave."

She felt self-conscious then, for she knew she must look wilted after a morning pulling carrots and boiling bones.

"I'm sorry I didn't freshen," she said. "I

106

would have liked to."

He shook his head, kept shaking it, and smiled. "No need."

He took her hands in his — soft hands, not working hands — and they stood in the middle of the near empty room. Annie glanced out the cracked window and in the distance were the locust trees Samuel had planted and the house he had built. That is there and this is here, she thought. Jack followed her gaze.

"Let's sit," he said.

He unfurled the quilt over the mattress and they sat side by side, their knees up awkwardly high. She wanted to loosen his tie, but didn't want to suggest it.

"I heard about the rabbit hunt," she said.

"Styron's idea. I'm hoping no one shows."

"I don't know. I hear Win Johnson and his band are playing. Bessie Strom's sewing up sacks."

"Sacks?"

"So folks can carry home the meat."

"Ah."

"Fred is angry with me because I won't let him go."

Jack nodded. He had straightened at the mention of her boy and hoped she hadn't noticed. He tried not to think past the afternoon, this moment of sitting close. Annie, here with him. It was astounding. He hoped his skin could contain his body's exuberance — blood rushing, breath racing, heart boomeranging in his chest — so as not to frighten her. Slow, he told himself. Slow.

He had never felt this way with Charlotte. Her cool beauty had been intriguing, her father's stature enticing, and Jack had been seduced by the trappings of what his life could look like. A beat reporter at the *Daily News* from the South Side when he met her, Charlotte Burkette, the only daughter of a publishing magnate who dabbled in whiskey running. He would be made an editor at the *Herald Examiner,* have a house on the shore. When she broke off the engagement, her hair newly cut into a severe flapper bob that didn't suit her long face — "I'm sorry, Jack. You understand how my father is" — it was as if she were passing on a book he'd offered to lend her. No tears, no hint of sadness in those blue eyes beneath her thin arched brows. Only later could he admit he hadn't loved her.

"Hello, Mayor," Annie said.

She leaned in and kissed him again, and in a sudden rush he wanted all of her. He took her hand and kissed her fingertips, her nails edged in dirt. He gently pushed her back and she did not resist. He lay down beside her, unsure, all of a sudden, of what came next.

"You can take off your tie if you'd like," she said.

But then came a voice from outside.

"Isn't that the mayor's car?"

It was Birdie. Annie shot up. Through the window she could see her daughter and Cy, the top of Birdie's head not even reaching his big shoulders, and, mixed with her distress of being discovered was the sickening realization that Birdie and Cy had lain on the same mattress, her daughter who was not yet sixteen.

"I'll go talk to them," Jack Lily said.

"No!" Annie whispered.

"It'll be okay." His voice was gentle and firm and she believed him. He jumped up and jogged out, his feet quick on the steps.

"Let's go," she heard Cy say.

"Come on," Birdie said. "What's he going to do?"

"I thought I heard voices out here," Jack said.

"Hi, Mr. Lily," Birdie said.

"Sir." Cy nodded.

"You know you're not supposed to be out here, right?"

"Just out walking," Birdie said.

Annie stood with her back to the wall beside the window. A mouse skittered by her feet. This was the toll then, this hiding and worry. Shame should have been enough to end it for good, but she was discovering she was not the woman she thought she was. The moment was over — she would go home as soon as it was safe to — but she would go to Jack Lily again because she knew now what he felt like, how her body hummed, and she would think of little else until then. She would avoid looking Samuel in the eye but she would hug him out of nowhere, leaving him slightly embarrassed but secretly pleased. While putting up the green beans she would imagine Jack coming up behind her and get too close to the hot water as it bubbled and she would blush when Samuel asked her how she got the burn on her arm. And later, when she realized she'd forgotten her apron in the bedroom of the crumbling house, she would vow to sneak back while her family slept.

"See you kids in church," Jack Lily said.

Birdie dug at a rock with her toe. Cy tugged on Birdie's hand.

"Tell your father I said hello," Jack said to Cy. "I owe him a call."

"Yes, sir." Cy lifted his free hand in a wave.

"Bye, bye," Birdie called over her shoulder. The mayor stood with his hands on hips watching them go.

"Come on now," Cy said, pulling Birdie along down the path toward her house.

"What do you think he's doing in there?"

"I don't know. He's the mayor. He can do whatever he wants."

She looked over her shoulder.

"Think he knows what we were going to do?" she asked, elbowing him in his side.

Cy smiled and draped his long arm over her small shoulders. Her hip knocked into his leg as they walked. The sky was dark to the west, veined with dry lightning, and the air crackled around them.

"Dust or rain?" she asked.

"Hell if I know," he said. "Don't make a lot of difference."

"What do you mean? 'Course it makes a difference."

"Not for us. We mowed the big field. We said it couldn't get any worse and then it goes and does."

They kept walking and Cy didn't say anything more for a half mile. Birdie wanted to make him feel better, pull him down right there and give herself to him. But there ahead was her father's truck returning from town. She led Cy behind their barn and he pushed his body into hers, kissing her hard, rough, her backbone scraping against the timber wall.

"I love you, Birdie Bell. You know that, right?"

"I know that," she said.

She heard the truck door slam shut.

"Come say hello to Pop. He wonders why you never come around."

"I best be getting along."

"See you at the rabbits, then?"

He nodded, turning away. He cut quickly back through the locust grove and out to the county road.

"Help me here, will you, Birdie?" Samuel called. His arms strained to hold up a bundle of wooden planks of different sizes. "Get the ends there."

Birdie lifted the longer pieces and moved with him to the side of the barn. She yawned. She had been so tired lately she'd fallen asleep midday twice this week. She'd just sat down on a bale of hay out of eyeshot of her mother and nodded off. The dark clouds scuttled west without so much as a drop.

"Here's fine," he said, dropping the pile with a cascade of clacks. "That Cy I saw slinking off?"

"He just had to get back to work, is all. They mowed one of the fields. The big one."

"That right?" Samuel whistled. "That doesn't leave them much. Down half a herd, too." He nodded to the cows foraging for fodder. "At least the disease hasn't gotten them."

"Are you building something?" she asked, pointing to the old lumber she was helping him unload.

"A steam box. You get wood all steamed up and it gets nice and pliable. Makes it so you can bend it."

Birdie nodded, not really listening. She scanned the horizon but couldn't make out Cy.

"Fred and me got ourselves a project," he said.

"Okay, Pop."

"Your mother home?"

"Haven't seen her. I'm going to go wash up. I'll call you in for supper."

Inside the house, Birdie yawned and poured herself a glass of water from the kitchen sink. She listened for her mother or Fred but heard only the ticking of the spinning windmill and the groans of the settling house. She ducked into the bathroom and pulled down her underpants. Still nothing. The menstrual pad was lily white, as it had been for three weeks.

Yellow starbursts of coreopsis, pink poppy mallow, lavender verbena, and white bell-flowered beardtongue. Blue morning glories and the fiery tendrils of mountain sage. Patches of green-leafed cowpeas with their waxy lavender blooms, and millet with its floppy bunched stalks, and the russet of broomcorn. Earth as rich as chocolate.

Golden ripe wheat. The kernels full and heavy on the stalks. The buzz of tractors day and night, the vibrations in his bones from the work, and the trucks back and forth to the granary, as fast as they could be loaded and unloaded. Feet burning through his boots on the hot metal of the combine platform.

That's what Samuel remembered.

When the day had been done, and the last scatterings of grain had been swept up for chicken feed and the machines sat quiet and the prickly chaff was rinsed from his sweaty and spent body and the mourning doves cooed from their hollows, he would lay his proud self down on clean sheets and sleep like the dead.

Now the drifts of silt blotted out all the colors of the prairie. We swallow hard, he thought. We give away another load of wheat for twenty-one cents a bushel, less than the cost of production. We huddle from the furious skies. We wince when we trade a whole bushel for an oil-stove wick, twelve dozen eggs for a pair of overalls, five gallons of milk for a pair of work gloves. Jenkins breathes in the stink as he gathers cow chips from the pasture for fuel. The men in suits come and take away everything Astor has, down to the false teeth he hasn't paid out on.

Samuel had heard the men down at Ruth's, who'd been able to scrape a few pennies together for a splash of whatever Ruth might have to offer, their desperation shoved to the side for the slimmest of moments. They laughed and coughed and nursed the last in their glasses until Ruth shooed their jaw-flapping selves out to flounder home to angry wives and broken-down fields and all the hours of wait. The choice was California or WPA, and $22 a month couldn't hardly hold a family.

We stay, Samuel thought, because we remember how it was.

Fred filled a bucket with rodent bones and added them to his collection. He dug out a cow femur half-buried in a drift of sand and the exertion brought on a spasm of coughing he couldn't shake. His chest felt constricted, a belt cinched around his lungs. It was all the time now, this hard work of breathing, and he tried to tell himself it was getting better, that maybe it wasn't as bad as yesterday. If he didn't run and stayed away from the cattle and went inside when the dust was up, he could manage. He had to rest up for the rabbit hunt. He was set on going. All those bones! And all the boys were going with their slingshots and bows and arrows and he didn't want to be left out, even if he'd never been that kind of boy.

After a spell the coughing subsided, and he decided to take a detour to the Woodrows' place on the way home. He hadn't been back since the run-in with the scavengers, and he wanted another look. The sole of his right shoe was coming loose and it flapped like a mouth as he walked. He wondered if glue would hold it, or maybe a rubber band. The soapweeds' spearlike leaves scratched his bare legs. He stopped and pulled apart the petals of one of the few flowers, loosing the yucca moth vibrating inside. At night the flowers would open and moths would fly out into the darkness in search of other soapweed flowers in which to lay eggs and pollinate. Fred had a sudden urge to pop open each flower and pluck out the moths, but he let them be. "So whoever knows the right thing to do and fails to do it, for him it is a sin," his father was fond of reciting. Fred walked on.

The roof of the Woodrow place sagged in the middle like the body of an old mule. Critters had moved in, taking up shelter in various nooks and corners, and spiders had taken over the bathtub where water no longer ran through the pipes. He crunched over dust-buried glass in the kitchen and found a box of matches under the sink, which he slipped into his pocket. His shoe slapped against the stairs, which set off a click click click of little clawed feet somewhere above him. In the old children's bedroom, the mattress had been dragged nearer to the window and the room had been swept with the broom now leaning against the doorframe. He suspected Birdie and Cy came here, though he didn't really understand what they might be doing. And then he saw on the floor, half underneath the mattress, familiar faded red gingham. He held up the apron. The red square patch and the embroidered yellow "A" in the corner. It was his mother's. How it had gotten there, he had no inkling.

But he was sure she would be happy he had found it.

CHAPTER 6

I am not pregnant, Birdie thought. I am fifteen and eleven months old and I am going to marry Cy and we will leave the wind and dust and go west to where it's green or to a big city like St. Louis where we'll ride streetcars and go to clubs where people play jazz music and smoke cigarettes and I'll wear lipstick in a color like poppy red.

She hadn't told Cy because each day she thought maybe the blood would start tomorrow and there was no reason to worry him. She thought it was her fault somehow. Really she hadn't thought about getting pregnant at all. Cy never said anything about it either. He had slid her green ribbon between the pages of his Bible, and that was enough for her. How weird, Birdie thought, that lying with a boy and having a baby were connected. They didn't feel like they should be the same thing at all.

She cleaned out the troughs and shoveled

the shit and spread the hay — already dipping into winter stores — and then she drew a bath, not bothering to heat the kettle to warm it. She lowered herself into the cold, dust-rimmed water.

God makes no sense, she thought. He took baby Eleanor, whom her mother wanted, and gave other people babies that they didn't. She stared at her abdomen and willed the blood to appear. Please, God, make the blood come.

Maybe she would tell Cy and he would lift her up into the sky and say, "Birdie Bell, be my wife," and she would be happy. Maybe she would have a baby girl and dress her in a pinafore dress and push her around in a carriage on the shady sidewalks of some town far from Mulehead. Birdie and Cy and a baby girl would make a little family. It didn't sound so bad.

I don't want a baby, she thought.

The water in the tub started to shake and soon it was too dark to see anything. She cursed, knocking her shin on the edge of the tub, and grabbed her dress from the floor, yanking it over her head. She stumbled out of the bathroom to join her mother in trying to get wet sheets over the windows in time. She called outside to Fred though she knew he wouldn't be able to hear above the din. They were all getting used to these, and she figured he would be fine out there in the henhouse with the birds. She didn't get it about the chickens — they smelled bad and pecked her feet — but Fred would put leashes on them if he could.

Samuel came in bringing with him a rush of dirty air and helped get towels under the door, without a word to Annie. Birdie thought it strange how this had been going on, something between her parents that was quiet, heavy.

The storm was a smaller one this time, brief, the dust reddish so Samuel said it must have come from New Mexico. He got a candle lit and they sat at the table and waited until the sun came back outside. Annie stood at the window and looked through the crack the sheet didn't cover.

Birdie thought of Cy's slightly crossed front teeth, the rough skin of his hands, a cowlick at the whorl of his hair that he ran his hand over when he had something to say. When she saw him she felt it in her fingers and toes, a tingle in her scalp, like she couldn't feel anything before and now she could feel everything. Her mother thought she was too young, frivolous. She doesn't remember what it's like, Birdie thought. Birdie did not want to spend her days weeding a garden and washing clothes, a Sunday trip to church the only thing breaking up the drudgery. She eyed her mother's frayed, ill-fitting dress and wondered when she'd started looking so weary. Her mother had bought the dress — a cotton floral more ornate than she usually wore — years back when the crop was good, on a whim one afternoon trip to Beauville. When did Mama ever do anything on a whim? Must have been the only time ever.

Cy said he didn't want to be a farmer, but he didn't know what he wanted to be or how to be anything else. Birdie didn't know what she wanted to be, either, but she knew she didn't want to be her mother, nice and regular and bound up by the farm and this cruddy town. Where was the fun in that? That felt like giving up. Birdie wanted to be with Cy and she wanted something bigger, and knowing that was something.

I am not pregnant, she thought.

The site of the roundup was northwest of town, out toward Black Mesa, at the base of the small hills above Mulehead. Styron busied himself with the chicken-wire fences, which he'd fashioned into a large three-sided pen. People could take what they wanted, and the rest of the animals would be carted away and buried in a pit he'd had dug two miles farther west.

He'd fashioned a banner, clothespinned to a barbed-wire fence, which he'd painted in red, white, and blue: First Annual Mulehead Rabbit Hunt. The mayor was still not on board, he knew, even though a fellow over in Texas County had told them that each jackrabbit could account for $10 worth of farm damage, and hundreds of them had come down from the hills looking for food. Styron saw the roundup as a community unifier, a way to give folks agency who felt they had none. He'd gladly take credit for it. He was a leader, he knew he was, and each day he felt that self grow inside him, like the luna moths he remembered from his youth wiggling around in their silk cocoons, and when they did finally emerge from their drab pouches, there they were with their ethereal wings sweeping around at night, flashes of pale green and haunting eyespots in the lamplight. So he was not humble, but great men rarely were. He wished he'd planned to have more water. The ladies of the church were bringing lemonade, but they weren't arriving until noon. Styron sat on the open front seat of his car and wiped off his hands with a towel.

He'd been seeing Hattie Daniels for six

months. She was a genial woman with an attractive enough face helped by wide-set gray-blue eyes, but she was a little more ample than he preferred — her body the shape of a bell — and a little too chatty. She lived nearby in Herman, where she was a schoolteacher, and sometimes he found himself saying nothing more than "uh-huh" for minutes at a time as she told him about her students' antics. But a lack of eligible women was one of the major drawbacks to life on the Plains.

Why had he invited her today? It was the excitement of the pending event that had gotten him, and last night as his hand had reached under her skirt as far as her girdle, he'd blurted out, "Come with me tomorrow." She had looked so pleased, her eyes shiny with tears even, that he'd felt terrible and had vowed to be kinder to her. But here he was today, the morning of the roundup, wishing she weren't coming at all. He would have to leave soon to drive all the way to Herman to pick her up and be back before the townsfolk arrived. There was no way he would miss his chance to fire the opening pistol.

Annie had found her apron hanging with the potholders next to the stove. She was reluctant even to touch it at first — how in the world? — before looking around the empty kitchen. Last night she had considered slipping out of bed and over to the Woodrow place, but she feared Samuel might wake up. Now here was the apron, as if she'd sleepwalked to retrieve it. She couldn't ask. She wiped the dust from the counter again, floured its surface, and turned out her biscuit dough.

She had told Fred he could not go today — too young, too sensitive, and too curious about what would happen to all the rabbits once they were trapped — but after Pastor Hardy preached last Sunday about supporting your neighbors, how the only way to survive this mess was to pull together, she and Samuel had decided they would all go. Jack Lily would be there, of course. It had been three days. For three days she had felt like her body was filled with tar, a hot and heavy ooze. Yet somehow she carried on, outwardly unaffected, working to exhaustion. Outside the window, white sheets baked in the sun, snapping in the wind like flags of surrender.

"We really need to go to this fool thing?" Samuel smiled, since he was the one who had insisted. He had changed from his work clothes into a clean shirt and navy trousers, which were held up with a belt and hung loosely from his whittled frame.

"You dressed up for the rabbits," Annie said, putting biscuits in the oven. "I'm sure they'll be pleased."

"You don't look so bad yourself, Mrs. Bell." Samuel was trying for lightness. He sat at the table and retied his shoes, unsure of what to do while he waited. His dreams were getting more frightful — rising black swirls of water, cars floating by like river bugs — but he didn't know much about how to build a boat. The steam box was a start, even if he couldn't tell Annie, even though the line between faith and becoming unhinged seemed perilously narrow.

"I redid the ribbon around the hem," she said, hand brushing against the fabric of her dress. "Changed out the faded blue for a red I found in the bottom of my sewing basket."

He nodded. "It's pretty. I've always liked that dress on you."

Annie turned back to wipe the flour from the counter, her head in a bashful tilt, a gesture that charmed him.

"Saw Cy ducking away the other day. Strange he doesn't even come by to say hello. Don't you think it's strange?" Samuel asked. "He's always seemed a polite young man. You'd think he'd want to keep up the good impression."

"Birdie doesn't say peep about him to me. I worry about it, though," she said, thinking of the mattress at the Woodrow place. "About what they're doing. What do you think they do together?"

"Do?"

Annie glanced through the kitchen window before turning back and lowering her voice. "Do." She widened her eyes.

Fred came bounding in from outside and began coughing wildly, his hands on his knees. He was pale, despite the heat, and noticeably thin, his knees knobby — his feet looked too big for his body. When the last storm had rolled through, Samuel had found him huddled on the floor of the coop with a hen in his lap, the others bobbing and squawking fearfully around him. He was covered in the reddish dirt, his hair matted, his eyes white against his stained face, and he was gulping for shallow tugs of air. Annie had mixed kerosene with lard and rubbed it on his throat. It had taken a full day for his airways to ease.

"Sit, son," Samuel said, guiding him to a chair. Annie placed a glass of milk in front of him. Fred drank and then coughed some more. She patted his back until he could get some breaths in.

"We're taking you to the doctor," Annie said. "Day after tomorrow."

Fred shook his head.

"No fussing," Samuel said. "It's decided."

Fred slumped. "I will try harder," he thought, "walk not run, breathe slowly, stay in when the dust comes, say prayers, be better." He felt the familiar tickle in his chest and tried to stifle a cough.

"You best go get cleaned up," Samuel said. "We're all going today to see the rabbits. That means you, too."

Fred perked up and slapped his palms against the table.

"Go on," Annie said. "Oh, and let Birdie know we're leaving at noon."

"Your apron's untied," Samuel said, reaching for the strings behind Annie's back. She had sewn it their first year in Oklahoma by lamplight in the dark dugout house. When he'd first seen the swoop of the embroidered canary yellow "A," it was a flourish that had made him feel flush with buoyancy, a sign of her optimism and eagerness for their life.

Samuel finished the bow with a tug.

"Thank you," she said, without turning from the sink.

They had been married only a week, had

yet to spend a night alone together, when Samuel said let's just go, and Annie said yes. Her parents had given up trying to persuade them to stay. Samuel had settled up with Gramlin, the landowner of the farm he worked, and procured a wagon and a team, which they packed in the quiet early morning. The horses snorted, their exhalations visible in the chilly dawn.

Her mother came out from the house, a shawl around her shoulders, and held a small wooden crate.

"A tea set," she said.

"I won't need that, Mother," Annie said.

"What will you drink out of? Your hands?" It was a rare moment of levity from her mother.

Annie took the crate and shoved it into a small crevice she found along the side of the overstuffed wagon.

"I'll write," she said, knowing she wouldn't, knowing she would relish the distance.

"You are married now. Before God," her mother said. "You know —"

Annie hoped she might divulge something to her, some motherly advice.

"You can't come running back here when it gets hard," she said. She stood with her feet perfectly together, her hands pulling her shawl tightly around herself as if she were trying to take up as little room as possible.

I never would, Annie thought.

" 'Wives, submit to your husbands as to the Lord.' " Her mother's mouth twitched, and Annie couldn't say if she'd seen a smile or a grimace. "You make it work."

Samuel came from the house with the last suitcase and Annie felt herself swell with relief at the sight of him in his old work clothes, his felted hat.

"I do wish you well, Annie," her mother said.

There were no kisses or hugs — her father never even came out to say goodbye — no waves as they set off, the two of them close on the buckboard seat, so ready for everything.

After they'd arrived in Cimarron County, at the end of a long rough ride, Annie looked in the crate to find the teapot in pieces, the saucers chipped, the sugar bowl's handle broken. Only two teacups made it. Months later, when the well had finally been dug, she and Samuel had toasted each other with teacups full of the coldest, sweetest water she had ever tasted.

Why Styron had decided to hold this thing

at midday in July was lost on him now. The brutal sun beat down on the crowd, which had swelled to upward of three hundred. The wind shook the tent he'd put up over the refreshment table, and underneath it, the churchwomen handed out cups of lemonade and water as fast as they could.

"We sent Betsy back with the truck," Mable Helmsly said. "Block ice from Thurston's and water from the nearest well."

Styron nodded, intensely aware of Hattie on his arm, but trying not to look like it. He took the glass of lemonade Mable held out to him and gave it to Hattie, who drank a greedy sip and then another, emptying the glass before they'd even moved beyond the table.

When he'd picked her up that morning, he'd felt great relief that she looked pretty good. She filled out her pink dress, but the fabric didn't strain. They drove to Mulehead with the windows down, which made it too loud to hear much of what she was saying. If today went well, he wondered if tonight he would get beyond the girdle.

"Good Lord," she said, blotting her face with a handkerchief. "Seems like there're more people than there could possibly be rabbits."

She took the handkerchief and rubbed his face.

"There," she said. "You don't want your picture in the paper with a smudge on your face, now, do you?"

Sweat from his armpits soaked his undershirt. Styron parked her in the shade of a straggly juniper.

"Wait for me here?"

He walked away before she responded, eager to get the hunt going. Win Johnson's band launched into "Deep Elem Blues." Dwight's sure hand with the fiddle was one of his few redeeming qualities.

"Hello, Mr. Styron," Birdie said. She held Fred's hand, and he held up his other in greeting.

"Birdie," Styron said. "Fred."

"Say, you haven't seen the Macks yet, have you?"

"One of them in particular you looking for?" Styron smiled, and wished, as he had before, that Birdie Bell were a few years older.

"I suppose I am. Yes," she said.

"I haven't seen Cy," Styron said, "but I'll keep my eye out for him."

Styron climbed up onto the flimsy stage. His hand trembled as he lifted the megaphone. The mayor stood off to the side, his arms crossed, bemused.

"Hello," Styron said. No one could hear him. Someone motioned to the band to stop playing.

Styron shouted, "Hello, hello, hello," until people quieted some.

"Welcome to Mulehead's first annual rabbit drive!"

The crowd clapped lethargically, ready to get on with it.

Birdie and Cy hadn't set a meeting place — no one had any idea people from all over three counties would be here — and now in the glare and the crowd, it seemed they might not find each other.

She and Fred moved closer to the stage as Styron went on. Bodies pressed in around them, everyone charged up and eager for action.

"But they don't call these the Great Plains for nothing. This is God's land," Styron bellowed, so lifted was he by his own speech. "And we're tough enough to make the Plains great again. So I pledge to you today, I will stay on. And darn if we're going to let some rabbits make it harder for us. Am I right?"

The whoops and hollers rose.

Fred tugged Birdie's hand as the crowd

surged forward.

"You want to go up?" she asked. Their mother had instructed them that they were only there to watch, but when she looked over, she saw the mayor talking to her parents. They wouldn't notice.

Fred nodded and jumped twice in excitement.

Styron pointed the gun in the air like he had practiced, and he fired three shots, sending the throng of people running toward the hill.

"Let's do it," she said.

They joined a group moving up the far side of the line. Jackrabbits scooted this way and that, jumping into the shrubs. Birdie swept the faces but didn't see Cy among them. She had washed her hair and left it down long, just as he liked. She had used the last of her powder on her neck. Afterward they would walk together and she would tell him. Or she hoped she could.

Fred ran off with a boy from school. Birdie stood next to Gladys Abernathy, the librarian, and took her small hand with a smile. On her right, an older man touched his cap in her direction. He shyly held out his hand and she took the knotty fingers in her own.

■ ■ ■ ■

After Styron's speech, Jack Lily had come right up to Annie and Samuel, clearing his throat, she supposed, to steady himself. When their eyes had met it was too much, so she'd focused on the space above his shoulder. He and Samuel talked, but she couldn't concentrate enough to get the details. His hand, only a foot from hers. She had kissed that mouth. She felt like hot wax was spilling down her limbs.

"I'm going to get water," she said, sensing both men watch her as she walked away.

Jack forced his gaze away from Annie, though he could barely look at Samuel. He had designs on the man's wife, for Christ's sake.

"Maybe you can help me with something," Samuel said.

"Sure, whatever I can do." Jack checked himself for sounding overly solicitous. "What's it you need?"

"Lumber. But I can't afford to get it green."

"How much are we talking?"

"Enough to build a boat."

"A boat?" Jack leaned closer. "To go on water?"

Samuel smiled. "I think there will be rain enough, when the time comes. I've had these visions."

Visions? Jack thought. Bell thinks there's going to be a flood in the middle of this drought?

"It was Fred's idea, really. The boat. He's going to help me with it. Need to get him a little stronger first."

"Good to work on something together," Jack said, unsure about how to proceed. He'd never been comfortable with the spiritual fervor that sometimes took hold out here, and he hadn't seen it before in Samuel Bell. "Know anything about boats?"

"Not a lick," Samuel answered, laughing a little.

It was a crackpot idea. Jack Lily was amazed that Samuel had no qualms about telling him. So sure he was in his faith.

The shots from Styron's gun rang out. The two men watched most of the town head up.

"If I think of any leads on wood I'll pass them along," Jack said, eager to extract himself.

"Obliged," Samuel said.

Jack had walked away with a wave. What must Annie think of this boat business? Before he could stop himself, he thought:

This might not be such a bad thing for me, for us.

It was beautiful. All of them linked like a chain of paper dolls against the blazing sky, hand in hand stretched out along the rise. As he watched his neighbors banded together, Samuel was sorry he'd been such a stickler about not wanting to be a part of the hunt. He took Annie's hand.

"I saw Birdie and Fred go up," she said.

"Ah well," he said. "Good for them."

She nodded. "Styron will shoot again, I imagine. To bring them down. He looked in rapture firing that gun."

Samuel snorted. "So he did."

"The mayor seemed a little distracted, didn't he?" he asked.

"I don't know," Annie said. "I guess I didn't notice."

They heard the crack, crack, crack of the gun — Styron somewhere at the top — and the wave of people started to move.

"Here they come," Samuel said.

Annie watched them all walk together, like sleepwalkers, she thought, jackrabbits trying to outrun them. The two ends of the line pulled in to form a semicircle, a giant net of humanity.

■ ■ ■ ■

Fred and Jeb Claren broke off and tried to
catch rabbits by their ears. The animals were
everywhere all of a sudden, herded downhill,
scared out from shrubs and holes, a hopping blur. Fred forgot his breathing and
delighted in the chase, got hold of a tail only
to lose it, and laughed silently as his shoes
slid on the packed dirt. "Get them, get
them!"

Cy was not here, that much was clear.
Birdie had gone down the entire row. She
sighed, disappointed, but also relieved to
keep her secret another day. Rabbits kicked
up dust before her as the crowd closed in.
She felt bad for the critters, even though
she knew they dug out crops and ruined
gardens and gnawed anything, even tree
trunks. They were still soft and cute, still
alive. As the group approached the pen, rabbits ran in, flinging themselves against the
fences, piling on top of each other in a bawl-
ing crush. No one held hands anymore. The
circle drew tighter, sending a multitude of
rabbits into the squared-off fence.

"Birdie, Birdie, over here." It was Mary
Stem from school. Birdie waved but no

longer felt so festive.

"We got you now!" a man jeered, while others laughed in response.

Birdie looked around for Fred, ready to get away from all of it. Styron and Garland Mitchell tried to close off the fence with a fourth side, but something had shifted, and they could not make their way through the crowd to pen them in. Anger rippled through the desperate men. They had no intention of backing away.

It was, she saw, the man McGuiness, the scavenger from the Woodrow house, who lunged first, a piece of wood suddenly in his hand as he whacked the frightened animals, crushing skulls and spines. He held up an armful of carcasses like the spoils of war. Birdie backed away as the mob cheered. She called for Fred, but it was useless.

The rabbits sounded like babies crying, a horrible wailing. Men took up whatever stones or sticks they could find and slaughtered the rabbits, charging into the cage with glee and fury. It took only minutes. By the time it was over, heaps of limp furry bodies were piled in the blood-spattered dust, spoiling quickly in the wretched heat.

Samuel shook his head at the brutality. The devil, he knew, could only take what you give him.

Two men began shoveling dead rabbits into a trailer. Samuel closed his eyes. He would begin in earnest on the boat tonight. He and Fred together.

"Where are the children?" Annie asked, her eyes darting about.

"They'll find us. They know where to find us," he said.

Birdie came up to them then, her face ashen, and Annie took her in her arms and kissed her forehead.

"I don't feel well," Birdie said. She leaned over and threw up, splattering her shoes. "I couldn't find Fred," she said, wiping her mouth on her sleeve. "I lost him up there." She could not take care of a baby. She couldn't even keep her eye on Freddie, and now it was her fault he was lost in this vile mess. Her stomach rolled, a burning in her throat.

Annie spun away, in a panic. Two steps one way, two steps another, trying to find Fred in the chaos of bodies and heat and death, her arms slack at her sides, limp and useless.

When the group had cooled, the bloodlust passed, there in the corner of the pen, hunched over the last rabbit quivering in

140

his lap, was Fred, blood on his clothes and caked in his hair. Annie heard his warbling, a feeble high-pitched moan, before she saw him.

She fought her way through the men and scooped him up, the rabbit jumping from his arms, dashing away toward the mesa. When she tried to walk she buckled under his weight until Samuel lifted him from her arms. The dreadful sound that was still coming from his son pierced him with awful precision.

"I'm here, Fred," he said. "We're here."

Fred's whispered breath barely lifted his chest. His lips were blue.

CHAPTER 7

The first contraction had brought Annie to her knees and the labor barreled along fast and unwavering. Three weeks too soon. The midwife had barely arrived from Herman in time, ushering Samuel out of the room, away from the groans of his wife. Annie pushed just three times and, without a sound, out came the baby girl. She slipped from the midwife's grasp and slid out onto the floor like a greased melon, tethered by the cord. Only then had the baby made a sound, more like an animal mew than a cry, until the woman got ahold of her and she went silent. She was bluish, too much so, Annie knew, and they rubbed that little body with hands and towels until the pink came in. Give her to me, Annie said. She was so much smaller than Birdie had been. Almost weightless. That little warm head in the palm of her hand.

They didn't have electricity then, only

those dirty kerosene lamps that gave off dim yellow light. Shadows like ghosts on the walls.

Birdie was five. The commotion woke her. She rose from bed and stood in the dark corner pie-eyed as the placenta came out, the sheets soaked in blood. Annie looked over and smiled to reassure her. Everything is all right, she said. Come see your new sister. It's a girl, Mama? Birdie asked, peering over. Eleanor, Annie said. She's beautiful, isn't she? But even then she knew, from the baby's weak suck and floppy arms and legs, that something was not right. The warm spring breeze raised the curtains. The sun was coming up. They had all the grass then, and it had rained through the night and the smell of green took away the smell of blood and she had willed away the worry by counting Eleanor's perfect fingers over and over.

Annie still felt carved out when she remembered, when she woke at night or cleaned the turnips or set the table or shoveled out the dust. She felt replaced by some other version of herself, roughly stitched together. Time will heal, everyone said, but time had merely deepened the feeling that something was missing. She and Samuel never talked about the baby. A few years ago, on Eleanor's birthday, Annie had said, "She would have been seven years old today," and he had said, "Who?" and she knew that it was different for him. People lost babies all the time out here. Mourning was a luxury. There was work to be done.

But when she touched Jack Lily, when she thought of him, the sadness receded for the sweetest of moments. For an instant, half of one, believing she could have what could never be hers.

Fred had a fever of 104 and sipped air like a sparrow. Small, quick breaths. She packed flour sacks of ice chips — a large block of ice sent over from Ruth's — around his body and told him everything would be all right even though she knew it meant nothing, even though everything was not all right. The doctor from Herman had met them at the house with another shot, but its effects hadn't lasted. Get him to the clinic, he had said. She'd wanted to kick him and say, "You said it was all in his head. What about now?"

It was two o'clock in the morning and the only sounds from outside were the shake and hiss of the katydids. The wind was mercifully quiet. Fred's eyelids fluttered and he smiled at her and it squeezed her heart. The sound of his strangled wail as he had closed his eyes against the rabbits. A child should never make a noise like that. They would drive to Beauville at the first light and wait until they unlocked the clinic door.

In Genesis, God asked Abraham to sacrifice his son on the mountaintop in Moriah. Abraham did as God asked. He bound Isaac on the altar and took a knife in his hand to slay him when God called to Abraham.

Here I am, Abraham answered.

Do not kill him, God said. Now I know you fear God.

Annie had known this story her whole life, understood its message of faith and abidance. When she became a mother, though, she no longer accepted it. What kind of God would ask this?

I am not here, she thought. It is a vengeful God to come after my boy.

Dust pneumonia. The doctor at the clinic said he'd seen three cases in the last week.

"They're calling it the brown plague," he said. "I'm afraid there's little we can do." He was a stooped older man, his white hair ruffled, and he looked at them through thick lenses with gentle, watery eyes. Fred's eyes were closed, his mouth open. "Keep up the fluids and rest. Make him wear one of these outside." The doctor opened a drawer and handed Samuel a mask. "The Red Cross just gave us these. Call me if things get worse."

"You're sending him home, then?" Samuel asked.

"I'm sending him home," the doctor said.

Samuel laid Fred down in the backseat with his head on Birdie's lap. Annie was silent, her face to the window. She twisted a handkerchief in her lap.

"It's nobody's fault," Samuel said, reaching to calm her hands. She held them still and rigid. "We will pray for him. Ask the congregation to pray for him." He had to say it, couldn't help himself, but she felt a barb of contempt lodge in her throat.

"You do that," she said.

Birdie needed to talk to Cy. She wasn't mad he hadn't come to the rabbit hunt — she assumed it was some kind of farm trouble that rose up — but she felt let down. There was so much to say, she didn't know how she'd keep ahold of all of it. She'd woken up feeling queasy again, but kept everything down on the drive to the Beauville clinic, passing on the boiled eggs her mother had brought.

Back at home, her mother sat as a sentry with Fred, so Birdie set about tending to the cow, her udder engorged. They now had three Holstein females — two were spring calves — and one bull, bony under their black-and-white hides. The lactating female needed to be milked twice a day and she had missed the morning because Birdie had refused to stay back. She had never really worried about Fred before, but after the rabbits there was no way not to. She'd been afraid that if she didn't go with him to see the doctor, he might not come back home.

With little grass to chew, the cattle didn't roam, but instead sought out the shade of the locust grove near the house. Birdie drew a bucket from the well, then pulled Greta — named by Birdie for Greta Garbo after she'd seen the movie poster for *Romance* in Beauville — by the collar into the dark hot barn and led her to the hay in the manger. When the cow was occupied, Birdie tied her to the post and patted her side.

"Sorry for the delay," she said. "You big nuisance."

She soused soap in the bucket and washed the udder, red and scaly from the heat and dust, and patted it dry. Greta swished her tail in Birdie's face.

"Hey," she said. "I'm trying to be gentle."

The cow snuffed and went back to munching, her milk letting down from the washing.

Cy would have heard about Fred. Surely he would come by.

Birdie leaned on her stool, a clean tin pail between her knees and lanolin on her hands, and she took hold of two diagonal teats, squeezing through her fingers, bringing the milk in strong streams that pinged against the sides of the pail. Fred could only do one teat at a time, which meant he cared for the chickens and Birdie had the cows. As much as Birdie usually complained about milking, she didn't mind it all that much. It was satisfying to come away with a gallon of milk, the richest cream coming at the end. These days, though, there was less milk, Greta struggling like the rest of them.

I know he can't call, she thought. The Macks' telephone service had been cut off last month. But couldn't Cy use the truck? Her feelings smarted. Okay, she was angry.

She pumped until the milk slowed to a dribble, flexing her fingers before starting again on the remaining two teats. She imagined her own breasts filling with milk, bestial and revolting. The menstrual pad was still hopefully pinned in her underpants.

A day after the dead rabbits had been

cleared away, Jack Lily nabbed Styron as he came into the office. Ruth's was empty, and they took up their usual table near the window.

"That was a disaster," Jack said. He hung his head over his coffee.

"The end got a little frenzied," Styron said. "I admit that."

"Frenzied? More like rabid."

"It was pest control. With a helping of community bonding."

Styron stabbed at his ham, unwilling to concede that it had been anything less than a success. Luckily Hattie had been far enough away from the mayhem so she hadn't heard Fred Bell's eerie cry.

"Jesus, Styron. I didn't know you were such a cynic."

"Gentlemen, you okay over there?" Jeanette wiped down the counter, tucking some stray pennies into her apron.

"We're fine," Styron said.

Jack sighed and downed what was left of his coffee.

"They're doing it in counties all over western Kansas. Using rifles even."

He held up his hand. "Doesn't make it right."

Styron leaned back with a thud against his chair. "Dead is dead. The vermin were going out either way."

"It was, at the very least, undignified."

Jeanette swayed over to the table. Her stockings made a slight swish as she walked.

"I heard it was quite a thing on Saturday." She poured the mayor more coffee.

"You could call it that," Jack Lily said.

"Dwight sure can make that fiddle sing," Styron said, looking Jeanette's way. "You'd never guess just meeting him."

"No, I suppose not," she said. "How about you, Deputy? Have any hidden talents?"

"Grandstanding?" Jack said.

Styron pointed to himself and laughed, and the other two joined in, glad to have the moment lightened.

"Well, I'll say this for you. You got people talking," she said. "That was a nice picture in the paper."

Pride blossomed in Styron's chest. It was a success, then.

"I'll leave you to your business," Jeanette said, scribbling out a check.

Jack Lily looked out the window, hoping Annie might come strolling by. It was selfish, he knew, with Fred infirm, to even think about her, but he couldn't help himself. The mere sight of her zinged his body awake, galloped his breath. Who did he think he was? Annie was not free to be his. But he wanted her nonetheless, and maybe, he admitted, even more because of it. Sure, he had felt attraction before, but here was a woman who felt right, who, when he thought of her, clicked into place like a suitcase clasp. And what of her husband, building a boat in the dustiest place on earth? Jack imagined going somewhere else with Annie, back to Chicago even. It was foolish, juvenile. But there it was, and he didn't push the idea away.

"Town meeting is set for two weeks out," Styron said.

Jack Lily squelched his musings and sipped his coffee.

"Governor's supposed to allocate FERA funds to the county but hell if any of us out here has seen anything," he said. "They think people'll become dependent."

"People go hungry before they go on relief," Styron said.

"Tell that to the statehouse. Not to mention rumor has it Oklahoma City's got a surplus."

"Who's coming?"

"Someone supposed to tell people how to apply for funds. Only three men showed up in Beaver. Afraid, I guess. Our job is to talk it up, get notices in," Jack Lily said. It would be such a relief to leave his responsibilities,

Mulehead, behind, the whole dry mess of it.

"How's the boy doing, anyway? Any word?" Styron asked.

Jack tensed his shoulders up toward his ears.

"I don't know any more than you. I'll pay a call this evening." How Annie would react to seeing him, he couldn't say, but it would be more noticeable if he didn't visit.

Styron shook his head. "A nice kid." He wiped toast through the grease left on his plate.

"Say, you've been holding out on me," Jack said, changing the subject.

"Pardon?"

"Your lady friend."

She seemed a slightly odd choice for Styron. A little matronly, a little frothy even, going on about the lemonade. And Styron had seemed sheepish in his introduction and then relieved when she'd finally stopped talking.

"Hattie. Hattie Daniels. Lives over in Herman. Yeah, well. I don't know. I didn't know if things were going to work out."

"Have they?"

"I suppose yes. Yes," Styron said. "I like her."

His tone had the practical conviction of

someone appraising a tractor, but Jack didn't pursue it. Styron was still young, and Jack knew he had no advice to give about women.

Jack stood. "I have a meeting with the dinosaur people. You can sit in if you want."

"That one's a little far-fetched, even for me," Styron said.

Fred's temperature had come down some, but when the coughing came on, spasms overtook him until he spat phlegm like mud into the bucket next to the bed. The curtains were pulled against the sun and a fan was aimed directly at the bed. As ice and sweat wet the bedclothes, Annie changed them, rolling Fred from side to side. After he had slept, she propped him up and fed him some beef broth, which he sipped eagerly. On his tablet he wrote, "Look out for birds," and then pointed to the ceiling.

"Birds?"

"Flying low," he wrote, and pointed again.

He was still delirious from the fever, his eyes like embers. There was a small part of her that liked taking care of him like this, as if he were still her baby boy. She ducked her head and he nodded.

"What color are they?" she asked.

"Blue orange," he wrote.

153

"They're quite lovely," she said. "Pretty little wings."

Fred laid his head back on the pillow and closed his eyes.

"Freddie?"

He opened his eyes and lifted his eyebrows in response.

"Do I have you to thank for finding my apron?"

He smiled and nodded. He pointed in the direction of the Woodrow house.

"Yes," she said. "I must have left it there when I went to have a look at the place."

If her answer had been vague, it seemed to work for Fred, who wasn't suspicious to begin with. She patted his hand, feeling unclean about the lie, but relieved nonetheless.

From the direction of the barn came the sounds of a hammer on nail and wood. She had not asked Samuel about the boat since their argument; she thought — hoped — he might come to his senses and forget the whole thing.

She tried to pinpoint why Samuel's obsession riled her so. Because they lived in a veritable desert and even when it did rain again it could never rain enough to raise a boat from the ground? Or was it that they used to decide things together, but now he

154

was going ahead with the boat without her? They'd built a life side by side: Should we buy the tractor? I'll hold the team while you work on it. Do you like this dress? What do you think? Let's call her Birdie. I think you're right about more wheat. What do you think is best? We will be fine. Hold my hand.

But now he would not listen to reason; her voice did not matter.

She was, she realized, frightened by this turn in Samuel. And there was the mayor, like balm.

At the window she pulled back the curtains and saw a light on in the barn, the glow of sundown behind it. There was a knock at the door.

"How is he?" Birdie popped her head in and then came and sat next to Fred on the bed.

"Fever's down some. Got a little broth in."

"I took care of the chickens." Birdie yawned. "You can tell him when he wakes up."

Birdie's face had begun to thin out as she neared sixteen. She was — Annie had the sudden melancholy realization — no longer her girl. She had hoped her daughter might go to college, might go further than she herself had gone. Annie was afraid Birdie had already cast her lot with Cy, waiting to be asked to be a wife.

"I set an egg pie to bake if you're hungry," Annie said. "Your father will come in to eat sometime soon."

"I'll check on it." Birdie scanned her fingernails.

"Are you feeling better?" In the commotion of the last two days, Annie had forgotten that Birdie had gotten sick at the rabbit hunt. "You look a little peaked."

"I'm fine," she answered hastily. She stood and dug at one thumbnail with another, fidgeting on her feet. "Just the heat was all."

Fred stirred and he was at once racked with coughs. Birdie patted his back and wiped his mouth when the spell subsided. He fell back to sleep.

"Birdie?"

"Yes, Mama."

"How is Cy?"

"He's okay, far as I know."

"Are you —"

"What?"

"In love?" Annie could barely get the words out, her voice gone small and husky, flustered as she was by such frank talk.

Birdie sat back down with a heavy plop onto the bed beside Fred.

"I love him. And he loves me."

Annie couldn't ask further, afraid of the

asking and of the answer.

Last fall Birdie had walked all the way to town, six miles, and back, because she'd wanted to make oatmeal raisin cookies and she needed the raisins. She wanted what she wanted, not one for temperance. Part of Annie couldn't help admiring her for it, but she feared her daughter's impulsiveness. Birdie had always been headstrong, and Annie guessed there was little she could say about Cy to make much difference. New bodies together were not easily cooled.

Annie glanced at Fred, panting in sleep.

"You know I was supposed to marry someone else," she said.

A hint of a smile pulled at Birdie's mouth. "Instead of Pop?"

Annie nodded. "His name was William Thurgood. I was barely older than you are when we began courting."

"What did he look like?" Birdie leaned eagerly forward.

"Dark hair. Serious Scots-Irish eyes. He was to be a minister like my father. He always had these little peppermints in his pocket. His father owned a mill outside of Bentonville. They had the nicest house in town. They had a maid who wore a black dress and a white apron." Annie laughed. "Can you imagine?"

157

"I wish we had a maid," Birdie said. "What happened?"

"He seemed right, I liked him, but he didn't make me excited for the future. And then I met your father." Annie gathered the fabric of her skirt like an accordion and then smoothed it out over her knees. "The first one is not always the right one."

"Mama, Cy is the right one. For me," Birdie said, resolute.

"Barbara Ann, you don't know enough about life yet to know!"

They were both startled by the rise in her voice. Birdie stood. Her eyes twitched and sparkled in the lamp's glow.

"I know Cy. And when I see him I feel like I could burst. I don't need to know any more than that."

And with that she spun around and flounced out of the room.

Annie's heart felt like a handful of sand as she stared at the space her daughter had left. Oh, Birdie, she thought. Even with all that teenage bravado, there was a sliver of vulnerability she couldn't hide. I was you once, Annie thought. I know, I know.

It had been the cusp of spring, the late afternoon light pale through the bare tree branches, the wrens in a dither. Annie had come upon her mother nibbling a biscuit with her tea, a copy of *The Lady's Realm* on the table in front of her. She had worked up her nerve, finally, to face her mother, but she had also wanted to shock, wanted to proclaim herself.

"I'm going to marry him," she said.

Her mother placed her teacup carefully back on its saucer.

"You cannot marry a sharecropper."

"He's going to have his own farm. We will."

"What do you know of farming, Annie?"

"I can learn."

"Life is hard without you trying to make it harder. William Thurgood —"

"I love Samuel."

"Love." Her mother sniffed and her gaze grew vague. "There's more to it than that."

Annie felt her anger crackle behind her eyelids. For you, maybe, she wanted to scream. Do you know what love is? That hot and tangled knot at her throat. Her life had felt like a dim hallway until Samuel had come along and the walls teetered over and there was space and light.

Everything about her mother was small: her feet, her hands; even her teeth looked to Annie like baby teeth.

"Your father won't give his approval."

"I'm eighteen, Mother."

"You are the reverend's daughter. You are not some country girl." Her mother rose from her chair.

"What does that matter when he makes me happy?"

There was an adjustment her mother made then, a slight giving in, a relaxing of her shoulders, as if she wondered for just a moment what that kind of freedom might feel like. She sat down, though, and turned away to wipe a trace of fingerprint from the window, her face impassive as a doll's.

"Where will you live?" she asked, not looking at Annie.

"Oklahoma. They're giving away homesteads." Annie couldn't stop herself from smiling a little as she said it. The adventure of it.

"They only give away what's worthless to begin with," her mother had said. And that had been the end of it.

Why couldn't she tell Birdie she understood what it was like? Annie wondered. Because the words would come out flat and wooden, as they always did now when she tried to talk to her daughter, their meaning, intention, lost in the space between them. As hard as it was for Annie to accept, maybe Birdie was right about what she knew, what she felt for Cy. Could it be, she thought, that what Birdie needs is different from what I think she needs? Samuel had once made her burn for all the next days. It didn't matter how difficult she knew they would be. She went to the window again, the light in the barn a beacon in the twilight.

Could she feel that way again with Samuel? She could swallow her sin deep and return to the man she had vowed to love.

Go to him, she told herself. Go to your husband.

Samuel knew nothing about boats, had never even been on one. The closest he'd come was a beached rowboat he'd helped pull in from the Cimarron. The ark Noah had constructed was an enormous boxy cargo vessel built to withstand storms on the open seas. Samuel just needed a boat for the four of them, and maybe a couple of animals. Would he need sails? A motor? Fred had given him more books from the library, and Samuel studied them, sitting in the tractor. What angle of transom? How long a body? He got down on his knees and closed his eyes, prayed for guidance.

Day by day, he told himself. God will provide. With Fred, with the boat, with the farm. He focused on finishing the steam box first. The temperature inside needed to reach 212 degrees. He attached an aluminum gasoline can to one end of the box to force the steam in. Once a piece of wood is steam-bent into shape, he read, it'll be less likely to crack as it bends. Steam the wood until it's wobbly.

It was time to check on Fred. And his hunger yowled. Samuel rubbed his eyes in the too-warm alcove. He'd put up the modest post-and-beam barn with the help of Stew Mack and a few of the other farmers when they still lived in the dugout, when all that existed of the house was a foundation. Wheat first. They plowed with horses in those days, and the gambrel roof gave him plenty of room for the mow. The old tack room was where he now kept his tools, and it still smelled vaguely of horses. He tidied up his work area, hanging up his hammer and saw, sweeping out the sawdust.

Outside the stars made a fierce spray of light.

"Samuel?" The mayor closed his car door. "Hope I didn't startle you. It's later than I intended."

"Jack, is that you?" He walked closer to the car, and the two men shook hands.

"I'm awfully sorry about Fred. I feel terrible about what went on."

"I don't have any blame for you. It's the

162

dust that done it. Why don't you come on in? Have you eaten?"

"That's mighty kind, but I can't stay. How's he doing?"

"He's sleeping in between fits of coughing. But Ann said the fever's down a little. The doc said keep him away from dust." Samuel shook his head at the idea. "Thought about sending him and Ann to Kansas, to stay with her folks for a while."

Jack Lily swallowed hard and kept his gaze steady. "They going to go?"

"She wouldn't hear of it. Can't stand her mother. Besides, Kansas is near as dusty as Oklahoma now."

Jack hung his head. "It's a hell of a thing." He wasn't sure whether he meant that he loved the wife of a good man, the interminable drought, the bedridden boy, or all of it.

Annie walked straight downstairs and out the door into the darkness. She heard her husband's voice before she could see him, and then her eyes adjusted and there he was and there was Jack Lily standing with him, hat in hand. The sight of these two men standing together in the milky light was enough to make her woozy. She reached for the banister on the front steps and gripped it tight.

"I can't get the mayor to stay for supper," Samuel said. "I tried."

"Just here to see how you all were doing," Jack said.

She found his eyes before she found Samuel's and her resolve faltered.

"You should stay," she said. She'd spoken so quietly she wasn't sure he'd heard her. If only Samuel would take her hand, she thought. That might be enough to lead her back. But he didn't reach for her, and she couldn't reach for him.

Birdie sat in the dark in the broken-backed chair behind the house, the one her mother used for peeling potatoes or shucking corn or standing on to get the sheets on the clothesline, and looked out at the vast expanse of nothingness. Her breasts ached. Dear God, she whispered. Dear God. She heard her father talking but couldn't make out the other low voice. Cy has come, finally, she thought. Cy would make it better. She rose quickly and walked around the edge of the house, stumbling on a clot of dirt. But as she neared, the voices grew sharper. She heard the mayor speak and then her mother. It was not Cy. She stopped and leaned against a wall of the house. The clapboard siding, abraded from the dust

164

storms, stuck and snagged her dress, but she didn't care enough to move.

"I'm okay," Jack said. "But thank you."

Birdie remembered how he'd been at the Woodrow house, chatty and evasive and eager to move them along. Could he have been hiding a woman up there? The mayor? It seemed unlikely but one never knew. So many secrets.

"I'm going back in to Fred," her mother said. "Evening, Mayor."

"Oh, before you go. I wanted to tell you both. I'm afraid I have some bad news."

"What's happened?" Samuel asked.

"The Macks. They left."

"Left?" Samuel asked.

"For California, I guess. The whole family."

Birdie pressed her lips together and dragged her palms across the rough wood behind her. There was nowhere for her shock to settle, a slow-motion spinning as the realization rose up and throbbed behind her eyes. She sat down in the weeds and tried to feel the splinters burrowing into the pads of her hands, but the pain was not enough.

She felt like the crushed petals of a violet, dark and limp. No, no, no. She bit her knuckle until she tasted blood.

Cy was gone.

CHAPTER 8

"A preacher and a soap maker go a-walking. After a ways the soap maker turns to the preacher and says, 'Look at the world. All the trouble and misery. Such sin and sadness, even after so many years of teaching about goodness. If religion is good and right, why should this be?' "

Pastor Hardy paced in front of the congregation. There was a pulpit, but he never lasted long behind it. It was a plain church without stained glass, unadorned but for a large oak crucifix above the sanctuary.

Mrs. Turner turned to listen, sitting at the church's small fold-up organ, a gift from a pair of Swedish missionaries who had passed through town. Pastor Hardy's wife had been the organist back in Arkansas, and he missed her acutely whenever Mrs. Turner — her small spidery hands — would play the opening chords of "Love Divine, All Loves Excelling" or "Abide with Me." A warmth would travel up his spine and then fly off, leaving him more lonesome than ever. In front of his flock, he sometimes could feel the abyss of despair open beneath him. He feared these moments and felt the hand of the devil in them.

"The preacher says nothing. They keep walking," Pastor Hardy said. He stopped and looked from face to hungry face. As the drought wore on, his people had thinned and aged, desperate for succor.

"They walk until the preacher sees a child playing in the dirt. The preacher says to the soap maker, 'Look at that child. You say that soap makes people clean, but see the dirt on that boy. What good is soap? With all the soap in the world, the child is still filthy. I wonder how effective soap is after all.'

"The soap maker stops. 'But preacher,' he says, 'soap cannot do anything unless it is used.' "

Pastor Hardy nodded and touched his temple. "And you know what that preacher says? He says, 'Exactly.' "

Samuel Bell smiled. The Bells sat, as they did every Sunday, in the third pew. Pastor Hardy was glad to see Fred in attendance even though, behind his mask, he looked sickly. The pastor had not attended the rabbit slaughter, thankfully, but he was saddened to hear about the violence. Killing animals for food was one thing. A bloody frenzy was quite another.

"Faith requires action. Let me say that again. Faith requires action. It doesn't take much to listen. Listening to the Word is not enough."

There were a few murmured assents in the audience. Samuel nodded.

"Listen to what Jesus says in the Sermon on the Mount: 'Not everyone who says to me, "Lord, Lord," will enter the kingdom of heaven, but only the one who does the will of my Father.' Not all who profess themselves Christians shall be saved." He stopped pacing. "Who among us is ready to heed the call?"

The congregation sat silent.

"I said, Who is ready to heed the call of our Blessed Savior?"

"I am," came the weary reply.

"I can't hear you. And if I can't hear you, then certainly God can't hear you. Now say it louder now."

"I am." People sat up tall and looked straight at the preacher.

"Proclaim it. Louder."

"I am!" A baby started crying, startled by the fervent response.

Pastor Hardy pressed two fingers to his

lips for a moment and then began again.

"James says, 'Obey God's message. Don't fool yourselves by just listening.' So I say to you today, don't fool yourself that the devil isn't pleased when you hear God and don't act."

His congregation always pricked up their ears at invocations of the devil. He moved to the pulpit and lowered his voice.

"Let the Gospel be your guide in everything you do. Pray. Do good works. Follow the teachings of Jesus Christ our Lord and Savior. You do not exist without Him."

Mrs. Turner struck the familiar opening bars and the congregation stood, needing no hymnals as they sang out words they had known since they were children.

> Sowing in the morning, sowing seeds of
>   kindness,
> Sowing in the noontide and the dewy eve;
> Waiting for the harvest, and the time of
>   reaping,
> We shall come rejoicing, bringing in the
>   sheaves.

This was not her father's church. At times Annie missed the order, the rhythm of the same structure each week. The lighting of the candles on the communion table. The

Lord's Prayer. The doxology. She missed the beauty and airiness of the building itself. The quiet bustle in the narthex before people funneled down the aisle to their seats. But out here there was the Church of the Holy Redeemer or nothing. The church itself was boxy and raw, stuffy in any weather. After a few years in the Panhandle, though, even the Lutherans relaxed a little and cast their lot with Pastor Hardy.

It had taken a week of bed rest and requests for the latest Krazy Kat comic strip for Fred to emerge, weakened but returned. He wore his mask out of the house with little reluctance. He wrote, "I am a bandit," and then pointed his fingers like a gun, his eyes crinkled. Annie was brittle, Fred's illness a demon that would not cede its grip. He was better, but he was by no means well. He was still Fred with his fragile lungs. And now that Cy had abandoned Birdie without even a goodbye, she was a sad sack of potatoes, as silent as Fred.

"I'm sorry," Annie had said to her.

"Are you?" she had shot back.

Annie had wanted to pull her on her lap then and stroke her hair, but Birdie was right, she wasn't really sorry. She was sorry for her daughter's pain. But glad that Birdie hadn't settled on her life at fifteen, hadn't tied herself to Mulehead before she had a chance to see anything else.

Samuel sang as if there were no one else in the church. He had a beautiful voice, that strong baritone, and Annie loved it still. She reached for his hand and held tight. He glanced at her and smiled as he sang. Each afternoon now, he went to the barn with clear-eyed purpose. She was glad, at least, that building the boat distracted him from his anxiety about the farm. He no longer stared out at his dying fields or ground his teeth at night or pored over what they owed, what they'd lost. Last night he had pulled her to him and she had not resisted. His hands tentative and gentle, his eyes seeking hers in the darkness. She felt comforted by his weight pressing her down and she closed her eyes and imagined his body a ballast — until he murmured, "Blessed be," and rolled off onto his side of the bed. This is my family, she had told herself. This is good and right. She had tried to hold on to the tenderness she felt for her husband then, the warmth of his body inches from hers, but she kept seeing Jack Lily in the slanted sun of the Woodrows' bedroom, his eyes the color of coffee, his elated grin when they had finally taken a breath after that first kiss.

In the pew in front of her, she could see

that a seam of Helen Mason's dress was coming loose, the fabric worn so thin she could see through it to the woman's freckles.

Pastor Hardy closed his eyes as the spirit moved him, hands outstretched.

"The Kingdom of Heaven awaits all who do God's work," he said. "Now hear it. Feel it. The Lord is my light and my salvation — hah — the Lord is my strength and my song — hah — I will praise him — hah — I will exalt him — hah — the Lord is God and He has made his light shine upon us — hah — be our strength O Lord in these times of great distress — hah — our everlasting light. Praise our heavenly father. Can I hear an Amen?"

"Amen," Annie said.

At Ruth's, Samuel sat at the bar, the midday sun leaking in through the small window. He'd come in a few times over the last weeks to talk harvest with some of the others, to unburden his mind of churning thoughts about the flood. The steam box was ready, and he was eager to have Fred well again, back working beside him. But Samuel had moments of wishing he had not been called. He wasn't proud of those thoughts, but sometimes he wanted to just be a regular farmer again. Here at the bar it was a relief to be, for an hour or so, just like everybody else.

"Olafson seen them up near Kenton. Kid on a mattress on top of a truckload. Had a goat in a pen jerry-rigged to the running board. The boy was retying the back," his neighbor Ford said.

"I'd gone to see Stew days ago," Samuel said. "Didn't let on."

"What'd he say to Olafson?" Jensen asked.

"Nothing much. Said they were out of luck here. Heard there were farms needing help in California. Going through Colorado for some reason, then down to 66."

"They had all their cattle shot, I know that. Took the thirteen dollars a head on six good ones, a dollar on the rest," Samuel said.

"Anyone know they was heading out?"

"A surprise to me," Samuel said. "Even to Birdie. Cy never said anything to her."

The men wagged their heads.

"Had a cousin took off from Dalhart. Haven't heard from him since."

Families had begun leaving in year two of the drought but it took a while before anyone realized it would be an exodus. Where did they go? What did they find? It was all rumor, conjecture, California as exotic and unknowable as Calcutta.

"Word is they end up picking peaches for pennies."

"It's been a long time since I had a peach. Remember those cobblers Mrs. Turner used to make for church social?"

"Me and Garland Mitchell once saw Mrs. Turner in all her glory," Ford said.

"Good Lord. She must be up near seventy," Samuel said.

"Thirty-some-odd years ago. We rode out that way on two of Mitchell's horses, back when there was bluegill in the Cimarron. Came up on her coming out of the river. Buck naked. Water running off her, shining in the sun. Man, oh man." Ford laughed a little and sipped the dregs of his beer.

"She see you?" Jensen asked.

"We were downwind. Hid by yuccas. But I'm not convinced she didn't know we were there. She took her sweet time and shook out her hair. Long and reddish back in those days. Skin like new milk."

"No wonder you remember the cobbler," Jensen said.

"A finer woman I never did see."

"I won't tell your missus."

"All she needs is something else to harp at me for. 'Stop all the drinking.' 'Go to church.' 'Apply for the relief.' "

"I'll never think of Mrs. Turner the same

175

again," Samuel said, the alcohol fuzzing his tongue.

"You're welcome."

"How'd it get up on noon so fast? Eight more hours before I can turn in," Jensen said.

"Say, what was Olafson doing out there, anyway? Pretty far from Beaver Flats," Samuel said.

"Driving the dinosaur diggers around."

"The what?"

"They think there's bones out there. Want to dig them up."

"They want to dig, come out to my place," Jensen said. "I've got some posts need digging out."

"Listen up," Ruth called over the chatter, hitting a fork against a glass. "A roller's been spotted about thirty miles southeast out near Texoma."

"Cover your beer, boys, here comes another one."

It was harvest time — had been for weeks. No one in the county felt rushed to pull in the sorry yield. What kernels had emerged were a little soft, but there seemed no reason to believe they would mature further without rain. So Samuel prayed on it, then oiled the combine and hitched it to the tractor and told Annie to keep the coffee brewing and the lemonade cold. There was no money to hire out a reliever, so Samuel told Birdie to get on her dungarees and rest up, because she would be driving shifts. Fred sulked because he wouldn't get a chance.

In those first years they'd had the draft horses, pulling the riding plow to make the furrows, the harrow to break up clumps, and the cutter for harvest. When the wheat was ripe, it was cut, run through the binder, and tied up into bundles, which were kicked off into the mowed windrows. Then in the evenings, they would go out and put the bundles up in piles so they could dry out. That sweet grassy smell on the field, quiet except for birds, the mix of pride for what was done and nerves for what wasn't. In the good years, those evenings were enough to bring tears to Samuel's eyes.

He loved the charge of the first bundle in the thresher maw, the loud buzz as the wheat was separated from the straw, the chaff against a hot sky, and how by the end of the day, the prickly remnants stuck everywhere, even, somehow, between his toes. Farmers came together and worked in crews, feasting from meals the wives laid out, platters of fried chicken, potatoes and gravy, beans and squash, bread and butter, peach pie and strawberry shortcake.

In 1924 he had bought a John Deere D tractor. Starting the tractor was always a joy to him, a reminder of what God and the farm had provided. Open the petcock over the valve and turn the fly-wheel, which would suck the gas in, and it would fire. Shut the little petcock off. And when it warmed up a little, turn it from gasoline over to kerosene and it was good to run on and on. In the boom years, he'd traded up for a Case tractor with a front crank. And now he had the combine, which he still owed on.

There was no stopping technology. What used to take five hours now took one. But Samuel missed the simplicity of the horses. With horses, and the deeper furrows made by the plow, he thought now, the topsoil might have had more chance at holding.

The tractor engine roared and groaned as it towed the combine over the rutted land to the fields. Samuel was sweating already and it was not yet eight. With Birdie covering while he ate and emptied the grain tank, he hoped to do thirty acres today.

Praise the Lord for this harvest, he said. Bless us with wheat.

Annie came out and waved. The sight of her as he set out lifted his spirits. Since

Fred's collapse, she had been different toward him, placing her hand on his arm at the dinner table, leaving a sandwich for him when he came back from the barn. They didn't speak of the boat, but in the week leading up to harvest, he felt her opening up to it, to him. The feel of her at night was new and familiar at the same time. She was thinner, more angular than she'd been as a younger woman, but her skin was softer, her touch gentler, and he was grateful. She kept her nightgown on, as she always did, but she moved with him instead of lying still. He had looked at other women, his head turned by beauty like any other man's, but he'd never really coveted another. With Annie there always seemed more to figure out, and it kept him wanting.

He drove out to the western field, the dry rustle of the wheat lost to the din of the machinery. The stalks were patchy, but the Lord would provide. He set the combine wheel along the edge of the dirt and fired it up.

What have I gone and done? Birdie gulped fast and shallow through her mouth, unable to fully catch her breath. She set the glass churn onto the ground and kept her head down between her knees for a moment so she wouldn't faint. She could hear her mother clanking bowls and pans in the kitchen, preparing the mid-day harvest meal, preoccupied enough not to notice Birdie doubled over in a chair out back. For the first few days, Birdie had not truly believed Cy was gone, sure he was coming back for her. She listened for a pebble against her window and looked for him where they used to meet up at the trio of piñon trees behind the school; she checked the mailbox for a note.

"Did you know?" Mary Stem had asked, cornering her after church, the mix of glee and horror in her whisper barely contained.

"Of course I knew," Birdie shot back. "You think he would just leave without telling me?"

"I heard they left on Saturday."

"So?"

"You just seemed so cheery at the rabbit thing. For someone whose boyfriend had just flown the coop."

Birdie didn't have the energy to pretend. She had just walked away, leaving Mary standing there lucky in her dowdy smocked dress, no baby growing inside her.

She took hold of the worn red handle of the old butter churn and started to crank it again, the butter, three quarts of it, finally starting to firm. She turned and turned the handle, a blister forming on her thumb. He loved her, but family came first. Everyone knew that.

Annie was invigorated. Despite its probable dismal returns, harvest was harvest, and she delved into her preparations for the late afternoon meal. She had steeled herself not to see Jack Lily, had stuck close to home since he had come out to the house. Through work she would redeem herself, she thought, as she plucked the stray quills — Birdie had done a lackluster job, not doing the wings right out of the boil — cleaned the chicken and cut it up into parts. She had splurged on a young chicken from the McClearys, bartering with milk, carrots, and peppers instead of going with one of the old laying hens that went for less. She arranged the pieces in a deep skillet, added a chopped onion, parsley, salt, and pepper, simmering it all in just enough water to cover. The ham had been in for two hours and was close to done. The bread dough had begun to rise.

Chicken and corn pudding had always been one of Samuel's favorites, something he remembered his mother used to make. Annie took the knife and shaved the tender kernels from six cobs, the juice sweet and milky. It was a small gesture of atonement. She would be a better wife.

"Birdie?"

Annie found the churn outside the door and her daughter gone. She sat and worked the handle until it was done. Birdie would not talk about Cy now. She would not talk about anything. Time would chip away at the heartsickness, Annie was sure. For her upcoming birthday, Annie had been working on a dress from navy-and-white-striped fabric she'd saved for three years, with a tailored front and puffed half sleeves, a straight skirt and a red tie around the waist. A dress for a city girl.

She scooped a cupful of butter from the churn into another pan, and when it bubbled, added the corn and some salt. She whipped four eggs with a fork and stirred them in with some of the broth from the chicken, beating until it was a thick batter. She smeared butter in a baking dish, poured in the corn pudding, arranged the chicken pieces inside, and set it in the oven.

As she pulled the blue-and-white serving platters from the cupboard, peeling back the stiff brown paper she'd wrapped them in last year, Annie felt a sudden rush of baby longing, skin to her skin, the warm clean

182

smell, the perfect heft, wrinkled tiny feet. These spells came on once every few months, making her, when they passed, feel like an empty bowl. She wondered, as she leaned against the counter to steady herself, if it weren't a kind of haunting, from the baby that was and then wasn't.

Her mother had come a week after the baby died, the only time Annie had seen her since she'd left Kansas. Her hair gone white, her dress starched stiff, her small hands as dry as paper. Annie had wanted her mother to make it better. What she got was "God decides what's right for us" and a butter cake she'd packed from home, made by someone in the congregation. Maybe something truthful, some real emotion from her mother, might have been a small bridge Annie could have crossed. But hers had been a family of hidden feelings, held tongues. "Life is so hard out here," her mother had said, unable to wipe the sigh from her voice, the disapproval, as if the Panhandle — Annie's choice — was somehow to blame for the baby's death. Annie had been too grief-tired to get angry, but she had had the thought, when she looked at her mother's stolid face, that she would probably never see her again.

Fred had arrived two years after Eleanor,

and Annie had felt so full, restored for a time. With a baby, she knew who she was supposed to be. The needs immediate, her importance absolute. As the years went by, though, it became clear that there wasn't going to be another child, as much as she had hoped for one.

Annie went to the garden to dig out potatoes. They were small still but would mash up well with butter and salt. As she worked the pitchfork to loosen the soil, and the sweat ran down her sides, she remembered Jack Lily's hands on her waist, his lips on her ear, his breath that tasted faintly of peppermint. She pushed the thought away. She sank to her knees and dug her hands in the dirt.

Jack read the letter again. His father was sick, his brother wrote; it was time to come home. He hadn't seen his father in eleven years. He wrote birthday cards and Christmas letters and called on the telephone once a year, but Chicago was far away and he was afraid of getting pulled back into a life he didn't want. And now there was Annie.

His father was a quiet man with tobacco-stained fingers and a raspy laugh. He made a decent living with the creamery, supplying the city with milk and butter. His mother had been a tall and handsome woman who was quick with a smack of the wooden spoon. She'd spent her days talking to the neighbors over sugary, cream-filled coffee, where she died one summer morning from a heart attack. Jack had been his father's favorite, but when he had refused to work at the creamery, his father wore his disappointment every day, his shoulders humped, his mouth downcast. They never spoke of it. And now it had been so many years since they had seen each other. He knew he must go home.

Jack had not seen Annie in over a week and it scared him. She had looked away from him that night with Samuel there, had not given him the slightest sign. As the days passed, he feared he might have made their relationship into something it wasn't. Before Annie, it had been so long since he had held a woman. Longing sent a kick of energy through him. Had he been too eager?

Yesterday he'd seen Samuel in the old McCracken lot, kicking through the remains of rotted wood, looking for scrap. Jack had forced himself to go talk to him, as he would have otherwise.

"Sorry I haven't come up with anything for you yet," Jack said.

"Got some to start with from that fallen-in

shed out on 287." Samuel picked up a length of wood, gauging its softness with his thumbnail.

"Still at it, then?"

"Can't do much else," Samuel said.

"It will be something to see."

Jack had felt a little shriveled inside, encouraging Samuel as if the boat were the most normal thing. He'd quickly taken his leave and ducked into the welcome shadows of Ruth's.

Styron backed into the office balancing a stack of books and dropped them with a thwack on the desk.

"Municipal projects," he said.

"Did we get a windfall I don't know about?"

"Something to pitch the WPA folks. Get some of our guys working. I wouldn't mind a public swimming pool with wages paid by the feds."

For someone who didn't get more than a stipend, Styron was sure industrious. Jack Lily would give him that.

"Say, I have a question for you. If you needed a fair amount of old lumber, where might you go looking for it?"

"Building a tree house, boss?"

"Not quite."

"The rail yard out at Herman. Where all

the old boxcars die. I saw it the other day. Heaps of wood. Some painted and such."

"I think you're going to like this one," Jack said.

"What's that?"

"Bell. He's building a boat."

Fred would get to steer. That was what his father had told him. The rains would come fast and hard, the likes of which they had never seen, and the water would rise up and up and spill into the house and carry off the coop and knock down the barn. Fred had decided he would bring the chickens and the cows even if the boat was only for the family. Noah had brought two of every animal on the earth — even cheetahs even hippos even boa constrictors — so Fred thought they could make room for their own. They couldn't just leave them. They didn't know how to swim. Two winters ago, one of the cows had gotten stuck in the pond when the water was too cold and they couldn't get her out even pulling her with a rope and the tractor. The water had frozen around her and she died. A frozen cow in the pond all winter long. Now that the pond was dry he'd found her bones right where he'd seen her last and added them to his stack for the bone crusher. His father said

187

he didn't know if they were paying anymore since there weren't many takers for the meal. Maybe next year. Everything was maybe next year.

"When the rain stops?" Fred wrote, and Samuel said he didn't know what would happen but that God would show the way just like he had always shown the way. They would plant again, and there would be no more dusters. "Other people?" Fred wrote. "You ask good questions, son," his father said. "I wish I had good answers but I don't." Fred thought he would be sad if the flood washed Caroline Hawlings away because she smelled like honeysuckle and took the chalkboard he wrote on at school and drew flowers on it before giving it back. He wrote, "Thanks," and she took it back again and wrote, "You're welcome."

Fred wore his mask out of the house, but then he took it off. Who wanted to wear a mask when other kids weren't wearing them, especially when you were already the one who didn't talk? He was tired all the time, like he'd been running through the night when he woke up in the morning. The mask just made it harder to get the air in.

He wondered if his father was going to tell everyone about the flood. Fred thought he should warn them. It seemed like some-thing people would want to know. It was probably good the Macks left, Fred thought, even though Birdie was sad all the time and even he was a little sad because he liked Cy and his little sister. He wrote to Birdie, "What are you going to take with you?" And she just rolled her eyes like he had said they were going to fly to the moon. "You think all of a sudden it's going to rain from the heavens?" she said. "Have you been outside lately? A boat can't float on dust. Pop isn't thinking straight with the heat and the crops and people leaving. He'll come to his senses."

But Fred thought his father had come to his senses. He would build the boat, and Fred was going to help him. He read:

The lumber should be largely free of knots. Wood won't bend properly if there are knots of any size, although knots smaller than a pencil eraser should be fine. Sec-ondly, the grain should be as straight as possible. Watch for areas where the grain runs off the board, which will affect the strength and bending properties of the wood. Third, the material should take and hold fasteners strongly. Wood that is too hard to drive a nail in, or too soft to accept a screw without splitting, is not right. Last, avoid warped boards. Softer woods like spruce, pine, fir, cedar, cypress, and juniper are good options.

The only thing that grew out here was juniper and sometimes ponderosa pine, but felling those wouldn't yield enough. Fred hoped his father had already figured that part out.

They couldn't get to work on the boat until harvest was done, so he just kept reading and thinking about it. Today it felt like he was breathing through a straw. Tomorrow would be better.

Birdie didn't believe it about the rain, but Fred did. He knew the flood was coming because he'd heard the rabbits scream.

The barbed-wire nest the crows had built was still there, but the tree trunk now leaned, its roots jutting out of the sand. A crow took flight with a whoosh of wings as Birdie approached. She sat in the shade of the nest and watched the skimpy puffs of clouds drift overhead. The breeze carried the sounds of tractors, harvest time. There would be a baby and she would be a mother without a husband and she would live in her parents' house milking the cows and scraping grit from her fingernails. Stop thinking, she told herself, stop thinking about any of it. But the loop continued: Cy gone; baby; life, or any real life, over. The baby was the weight that would keep her here forever. A crying, flailing baby that was hers alone. She wondered if she could hurt herself enough to lose the baby and not die. She'd heard of a pregnant girl in Herman who'd drunk kerosene. Birdie imagined the fire in her throat, the fumes tearing her eyes, the terrible pain in her belly. There had to be another way. She stood on the roots of the tree and reached for a knot, finding a depression for her foot and hoisting herself up. The tree was smooth, its bark long gone, and her other foot couldn't find a wedge. She groped for another handhold until she found a nub of a branch, her free foot searching blindly until it caught a small ledge. She was four feet off the ground but as she looked to check her progress, her hand slipped and she fell back off the tree, landing without enough force, she knew, to do anything other than give her a sore back-side.

A car moved along Gulliver Road from town, its tires leaving a trail of dust behind it. Birdie stood and tracked the car as it approached, knowing it wasn't her father, who was out in the field. A green Ford, the mayor's car. Birdie waved, hoping he'd stop, eager now for the distraction and a ride home. But if he saw her he didn't slow until up at the crossroads, where he turned on the county road in the direction of the house.

The crust of the bread was golden and crisp as Annie pulled it from the oven, setting it on a rack to cool. She stood back and looked at the bounty she'd been able to pull together, satisfied and proud. Ham, chicken-and-corn pudding, mashed potatoes, green bean salad, baked squash, strawberry pie. A good wife, she thought.

A knock on the door was such a rare occurrence, she assumed it was Samuel hammering at a sticky part of the combine. The second knock startled her. She untied her apron and pushed the hair off her face as she walked to the door. There was Jack Lily behind the screen.

"Afternoon, Annie," he said.

It was what she had tried not to want. He stood with his hands in his pockets, his hat low. He smiled and her mouth trembled into a smile in return. She looked quickly around, even as she knew Samuel was in the field, Fred was out near the old pond, and Birdie had run off.

"You weren't in church," she said. It was not what she had wanted to say. She held her arms to keep from opening the door.

He squinted off in the direction of the field where Samuel's tractor droned.

"Thought it best," he said.

She nodded, naked to her want. If only someone else had been home.

"I don't know what to do," she said.

"Samuel had asked me about wood. I have an idea I wanted to discuss with him."

"Wood?"

"For the boat."

Annie closed her eyes and exhaled. "The boat."

"Annie," he spoke softly now. "Are you alone?"

She dipped her head in a half nod. She could hear Samuel's tractor finish a row and then it turned, slipping out of sight.

"Meet me again. At the old house. Tomorrow late afternoon."

"I will try to get away," she said, knowing that there, inches from him, she would find a way.

He leaned toward her, his forehead against the screen. She did the same.

It was the mayor all right, Fred recognized

the car. He ran his finger through the dirt across the car's rear window. But when he came around the back and saw him up at the house, he didn't bound up to wave hello. Why didn't his mother open the door? He pulled down his mask, hoping it might help him think, but he didn't want to go up to the house, even though he'd come back for a pail to help with the smaller bones. He hoped they weren't talking about the boat, trying to get his father to give it up. He would have to ask Birdie about it later. She understood grown-up things better than he did. He retreated and set off for the pond.

CHAPTER 9

Her faded forget-me-not-print dress lay in a crumpled heap, and her stockings — the toe of which she'd crookedly mended with ugly black thread — snaked across one of her shoes, which had fallen on its side. Where was her other shoe? Jack Lily was asleep beside her. She was tired, but her body thrummed. A bristly wolf spider skittered into the debris-filled corner of the room. It was a female as big as her palm, a white egg sac on its back.

By the door was a basket of eggs Annie had brought to deliver to the Jensens. She had been gone an hour or so. She ran through the list again. Samuel had gone in with a load of grain. Birdie was driving the combine in the far glade. Fred was cleaning out the coop. It would take fifteen minutes to walk from here to the Jensen place. She might make it back even before Samuel returned. But she couldn't make herself get up just yet. Just one more minute. The musky smell of him. The warm wind on her bare skin. She was only ever naked to bathe, but she had no urge to cover herself now. He had brought a quilt again for the mattress, but it was on the floor where he'd dropped it, gathering her to him as soon as they had crossed the threshold.

She hadn't thought that much about sex after she and Samuel had settled into their marriage. There had been moments of passion, certainly in those early days — finally they could be together in that way — but she relegated her needs to a shelf just out of reach, as she thought she should, as women did. And it wasn't as if she could talk about it with Samuel, couldn't even imagine talking about it. Eventually she saw sex as part of being a wife. It was enjoyable enough sometimes, made her feel closer to him, but she didn't feel she was missing out. After the children, she did not long for affection, and she often wished she could go to sleep when she felt his body hug hers, his needy hands seeking her out. The only other man she'd kissed had been William Thurgood, and when he'd pushed his wriggling tongue into her mouth she'd thought she might gag.

Now she was afraid she would think of nothing but sex for the rest of her life. What a crazy thing to have a new body with hers. Jack was taller, fuller, sure of himself as he unbuttoned her dress and slid it off her arms to the floor. But it was his undisguised hunger that fed her own, his confident hands and eager mouth that had made her feel warm and slithery. Wanting was dangerous.

Get up, Annie, she said to herself. She raised herself up on her elbow and put her hand on his chest, feeling it rise and fall in a quiet rhythm. He did not wake. She shook out her undergarments and got dressed, shoving the stockings in her pocket. The other shoe she found under his pants, which she folded into a neat square.

It was only outside in the sun and heat that she began to feel the weight of what she had done. Her feet were terribly hot and slipping in her shoes, and the sand worked its way in. With each step she fell more into herself, and her stomach roiled with the curdled truth of her betrayal. I can see you, she imagined God saying. The basket of eggs hit her hip and one shell cracked, freeing yolk and white into a slippery mess, which dripped through the wicker and landed in thick shiny drops on her skirt.

After Jack had told Styron about the boat,

word was all over town in a matter of days. Did you hear? Samuel Bell is building an ark. It made people laugh, but it also made them uneasy and then angry. How dare Bell think he'd been chosen?

Styron loved it. He was positively gleeful. An ark! In Mulehead, no less. He couldn't have dreamed up a better idea on his own. When Jack returned to the office, he found Styron sketching billboards on the back of an envelope.

"I probably shouldn't have told you," Jack said.

"Everyone knows anyway. I overheard the fogies yammering about it last night at Ruth's. It's going to put us on the map."

"We're already on the map." Jack pointed to the Cimarron County map tacked to the wall.

"What do you think?" Styron slid one of his sketches in front of him.

"Easy there, Styron."

"You think we should wait until it's finished before advertising it?"

"I think you're getting ahead of yourself."

Jack stood at the window and watched the gaunt McCleary brothers crouched on their haunches, chewing tobacco and spitting into a can shared between them. He fidgeted with the piles of papers at his desk. With his thumbnail he scraped at a smudge of dried glue on the filing cabinet.

"You okay, boss? You look a little flushed."

"I'm fine. Feel pretty good, actually."

Styron glanced up, wondering, not for the first time, if Jack had a woman. He ran through the short list of available ladies in town, but couldn't settle on any likely candidates. There was a rumored woman for hire over in Beauville who worked in the hat shop or a candy store — he'd heard different accounts — but the mayor seemed a little too straight for a working girl.

"I have to go to Chicago," Jack said. "Probably leave in a couple weeks."

"Chicago?"

"My father's not doing so well."

"I'm sorry to hear that," Styron said, already clicking ahead to when he would be left in charge. He could bring Hattie to town to see his office. She always told Styron that he should be the mayor, that he would be mayor, that he was meant for great things. They had lain on his couch together and he had pressed himself against her stockinged thigh and she had run her fingers through his hair, before he excused himself to the bathroom, quickly turning away to shield from view his tented trousers, while Hattie took out her latest issue of *Ladies'*

World and returned to a dog-eared recipe for hush puppies, which she thought sounded quaintly Southern and gosh-darn delicious, and wouldn't he like her to make them for him next Saturday night?

"I don't know for how long," Jack said.

Without Annie, as short a time as possible, he thought. He felt buttressed by their afternoon together. The smell of her neck, the curve of her hip. She had been waiting at the door for him and fell into his arms without even a hello. Afterward they had not talked much — he felt a little sheepish at having fallen asleep so quickly — and then she had left. But it didn't worry him, not with the wildness of their bodies coming together like that. He'd planned to tell her about Chicago, but, as soon as he saw her, he forgot everything. They'd barely gotten upstairs before he had slipped her dress off her shoulders.

"Maybe the ark'll be finished by the time you come back."

Jack peered over at Styron's drawings.

"Something tells me you'll be keeping pretty close tabs on Bell's progress."

Jack felt a small ding of guilt about not going home immediately. He could barely admit to himself that he hoped his father would die before he arrived so he could

200

remember him as he was, not as an old, sad man caged in a wasted body.

"Hey, you never told me if anything came of the dinosaur meeting," Styron said.

"They think there might be bones out there near the mesa. A hundred and fifty million years old."

"A hundred and fifty million years?"

Jack shrugged. "I don't begin to get the science of it."

"That's million, with an 'm'?"

"That's what I said, Styron. I'm not sure how well it'll sit with folks trying to keep their fields from blowing away to know some eggheads from Oklahoma City are after prehistoric bones."

"They really think they're going to dig up a dinosaur in Cimarron County?"

"They really do."

"Things are looking up around here," Styron said.

It was supper, day three of harvest, and Samuel could barely lift his fork, having worked through the day and most of the night before. He would go back out to finish the last load before nightfall. In the flush years, they'd hired men and the neighbors helped and afterward they all feasted together, but this year it was just the four of them. Fred was already through a drumstick of fried chicken, his mask hanging loose around his neck. Birdie picked at a wing. They had moved the table outside into the shade of the locust trees, as was tradition. The fans of leaflets sent polka-dotted shadows across the bounty.

"It's wonderful," Samuel said.

"You haven't even taken a bite," Annie said.

"It's still wonderful," he said. "We're blessed."

"Can you tell how much is coming in? What do you guess on yield?"

"Five. Five and a half." It was meager, but it was something.

Despite his weary body, Samuel was feeling recharged. For hours he'd swung the tractor through the rutted dry rows, the combine devouring the wheat; the rumble of the machine and the rush of grain spitting into the tank blocked out all sounds of the natural world. In his head he saw in vivid relief how the boat should be. A three-chined hull. Humble but elegant. He had prayed on it, and returned again and again to an image of the four of them on the boat.

"People are talking," Birdie said, pushing her peas into a little pile. "Isn't that right, Freddie?"

Samuel looked up from his plate and Fred nodded, his pale face dappled in shade. Annie wiped the blue-checked napkin across her mouth, about to chastise Birdie, but then stopped herself.

"And what are they talking about?" he asked.

Birdie cocked her head, her eyes insouciant. "What do you think they're talking about?"

"Birdie," Annie said sharply.

"No, it's okay. Let's get it out there. The boat, right? What are they saying?"

"I've been stuck here, remember? Ask Fred," Birdie said.

His daughter's edge was flinty, unnerving. His sweet girl! Samuel swallowed a bite of mashed potatoes but it moved down his throat too slowly, a warm and pasty lump. He turned to Fred, who scribbled something on his notepad and slid it across the table: "Where you going to get 2 elephants?"

"Do you laugh when they say things like that? It's okay to laugh," Samuel said. "It's good to laugh."

Fred smiled a little, but shook his head.

"They're making fun of him," Birdie said.

Annie wasn't jumping in, Samuel noticed. She was letting him fend for himself. He set down his fork and sipped more water. A fly landed on his buttered bread.

"Forget it, Freddie," Birdie said, softening her tone. "They're just being dumb kids."

"More chicken, Samuel?" Annie asked.

He looked down at his full plate. "I'm okay, thanks."

"Pull your mask up as soon as you're finished," she said to Fred. "The doctor said." She rearranged the serving platters, her hands jumping around the table like crickets.

Samuel wanted to place his hands on hers to still them. She seemed restless and bothered. Earlier in the day she'd dropped a serving platter, porcelain shards all over the floor. Her eyes darted away from his when he tried to meet her gaze. He could see that the boat was weighing on her, but he was doing this thing. The boat was under way and he could not turn back. He just wished he knew how to make her see, make her believe in what he saw.

"What did the mayor want?" Birdie asked.

"The mayor?" Samuel asked.

"Saw his car coming this way yesterday."

Annie quieted her hands, palms flat on the tablecloth.

Fred looked at his supper. He should have kept it to himself. He would keep everything to himself from now on. No trouble, no trouble, no trouble.

"I forgot to mention it. You collapsed so soundly when you came in," Annie said.

"What'd he want?"

She breathed through her mouth, concentrated on the crooked lines of kernels on her corncob. He doesn't know anything, she thought, he doesn't know anything at all.

"He has an idea. For wood. Or Styron does. Something about boxcars."

"Boxcars?"

"A mess of them at the old yard."

"That's good news. That's real good news." He smiled, and she braced herself for the three words that she knew would follow. "The Lord provides," he said.

She felt like upending the whole table, running until her lungs burned and her insides retched. With little wind, flies landed on the relish, the chicken, the rhubarb cobbler.

"Funny he came all the way out here. Could have called. Not that I don't appreciate it."

Fred studied his father's face. Yes, it was strange, Pop, he thought.

Birdie rubbed her shoes against the dirt, the small stones pressing into her feet through the thin soles. Her arms ached from helping her father with the grain bins, but she was secretly glad for the hard, silent work. When did you tell your parents you were pregnant? When did you come clean about lying with a boy before marriage, a boy who ran off, leaving you with a baby, which left you no choice but to stay here forever?

Samuel sighed and rested his chin on his hand as he chewed. He eyed the level of the sun and sipped his milk.

"I best get back out there," he said, sinking some even as he said it. "If I'm going to do thirty today."

"You barely ate," Annie said. "Won't do you much good to collapse while threshing."

"Get through it every year. I'll do it again."

He winked at Annie whose mouth lifted only ever so slightly in return. Birdie knew her mother was angry about the boat, but she would never admit it. Fred flung a pea at her with his spoon. It landed in her hair. She slid it out with two fingers and whipped it back at him.

"Children," Annie scolded.

"He started it," Birdie said.

"Birdie, please," Samuel said.

"Barbara Ann, I do believe you will be sixteen next week. Let's try to act our age."

"Okay," she said, sighing, tired of being so

mad, suddenly seeing her parents' disappointed faces when they found out she was pregnant. She would be due in the spring. Baggy clothes and a big coat through the winter — maybe she would be one of those girls who didn't show much — and a trip to the hospital in Beauville where she would give the baby away? Surely there were families wanting babies. She'd have to ask Mary Stem to drive her, think of a lie to tell her parents. By the time Mary told someone else, despite promising on her life not to tell anyone, Birdie would have given birth, the baby whisked away by some happy family, and she would be herself again, free to say goodbye to Mulehead, go all the way to the ocean. It was a child's fantasy. She couldn't even play it out in her head without feeling sunk.

"Don't wait up," Samuel said.

"Good luck," Fred wrote. He smiled, his mask on his chin.

"Grain tank's near full," he said.

"I'll be ready," Birdie said.

"Ann?" Annie shifted her gaze from the horizon to Samuel. "Thank you."

"I'll wrap some chicken for you," she said, knocking over her chair as she stood. "And a bottle of milk." She rushed off to the house without righting the chair.

The three remaining Bells looked at the chair for a spell until Fred hopped up and set it straight. A wet cough racked his body.

"Get your mask on, son."

Fred pushed the mask over his mouth and nose, slumping back in his chair.

"When the grain's in you'll help me with the boat?"

Fred nodded, placated. Birdie retreated to the kitchen, her shoulders rounded under the weight of the dishes. The thin wispy clouds had bulked up.

"I don't have timber enough for the frame, but we can start cutting the ribs soon. Need forty or so."

Fred flipped to a blank page of his pad and wrote, "I will measure."

Samuel was about to protest. Fred's skin was sallow, and ashy half-moons shadowed his eyes above his mask, a reminder that he was still not well.

"As long as the animals are tended to. And your mama doesn't need help with anything."

Fred clapped once and scurried inside, leaving Samuel alone at the table. He picked up a green bean with his fingers and dipped it in the pool of butter at the bottom of the serving bowl before folding the whole thing into his mouth. A large cloud had darkened, and he watched it inch its way across the sun. It sat high overhead. Instead of the black or brown of a duster it had a deep blue cast.

Annie came out with a metal lunch pail in one hand and a thermos in the other. In the flat light she was an apparition. A beautiful ghost. He stood to meet her.

"We should talk," he said.

She stood still, and the breeze picked up and blew her hair across her face. She made no move to brush it away. He took the pail and thermos.

"Tonight, maybe," he said.

She didn't answer, just looked at him with those honey eyes.

"Ann? Annie?"

She blinked and looked up at the sky and then he felt it too. On his hand. Then again on his head.

Rain.

CHAPTER 10

The tears came with the rain. They mixed on Samuel's face in warm rivulets and it was as if God had brushed him with his fingertips and all he could do was stand there with his face to the sky. Droplets ran into his ears and he didn't care. Annie was laughing and he didn't know which was more startling, the rain or the sound of her jangling laugh that had always gotten him in the gut, that laugh he had missed without knowing it. He took her hands and twirled her around and his heart felt light. And now Fred and Birdie were here, too, whooping and spinning until they fell down, limbs out like stars, eyes closed to the patter of rain.

Samuel breathed in the smell of wet dirt and didn't even care that the tractor and combine were out to get rusted because he felt like a boy, joy expanding so full under his ribs he needed to run. So he did. He ran a large circle around his children and his wife and said thank you to the Lord. He still had seventy acres left in the ground to drink it up. Water dripped from the ends of their noses. The insistent rush of rain the most beautiful hymn. He peeled off his overalls and shirt, even his shorts. Birdie screamed and laughed when she saw him, and then Fred followed suit and tore off his mask and his clothes until he was naked, too, all spindly limbs. He too was a boy again, returned to himself, without fear of choking on air.

The sky was dark but not menacing. Maybe now the water wouldn't rise up and they would not need the boat. Samuel didn't know what his visions had meant, but he would not dwell on it in this moment of wonder.

Birdie, her hair already soaked, took off her shoes and socks and rolled up her pants, and Annie, Annie! She unbuttoned her wet dress and stepped out of it, her slip soon stuck to her frame, and it was all Samuel could do not to take her in his arms and bury his face in her neck and lie with her in full view of the world.

"Rejoice," he said. "Rejoice."

The ground was softening in the hard rain. Fred hucked a wet glob of dirt at Birdie, hitting her shoulder, and she went after him and ground a handful into his hair. Annie, like a toddler, sat down and rubbed mud onto her bare legs. The rain washed her clean. A pair of crows sat high in a locust tree and cawed as the leaves dipped and swayed in the rain. Below, the bowl for the beans caught drips.

But Birdie noticed first. She held out her hands. The drops were lightening, beginning to taper, and Samuel looked at Annie. No. It was not enough. It was worse than not enough. It was a punishing reminder of what once was and he had to steady his thoughts. Samuel squeezed his eyes shut and said the Lord's Prayer again and again, trying to push away the darkness tugging at him.

He would be tested. He would abide.

The rain stopped. The Lord giveth and the Lord taketh away. He was naked and wet and filthy. Fred was wheezing. Birdie angrily tied her hair in a knot. Annie shook out their wet clothes and piled them on her shoulder like a limp body.

Under that bright, withholding sky, no one said a thing.

Samuel pulled in the rest of the wheat. There was no more rain, but no dust either, and for that he gave thanks. The lines at the granary were short. Many of the farmers simply plowed under what was left of their crops. At not quite six bushels an acre, Samuel would not break even. It took three years to go broke, they said, maybe another year to hang on hungry, scraping by on handouts and on eggs from their chickens. The talk at Ruth's was whose luck would finally peter out. A farmer in Beaver County had taken the government's offer and watched as his threadbare cattle were herded into a ditch and shot, all for not even enough to save his tractor from the bank. Then he kissed his eight children and his wife and went out into a field and shot himself in the mouth.

It was the end of July. The late harvest left little time for Samuel to get the next crop planted. After he bundled the hay, he had to turn right around and plow. The grasshoppers were worse than ever. With no plants to gnaw on, they had set themselves on the trees and even the fence posts. Annie had mummified her garden in chicken wire and grease-stained cotton muslin she had salvaged from behind the mercantile in Herman. Fred had helped her spray a mixture of strychnine and molasses over the top, so when Annie came out to weed and water, she had to shake off a layer of dead grasshoppers, hundreds of them hitting the ground with a brittle crackle.

In daylight, Samuel plowed and furrowed and spread seed and talked to God, and by lamplight he went back to the boat.

He finalized his crude design with the help of books. With a pencil and ruler and a roll of butcher paper, he drew and redrew, recalculating the dimensions until the engineering felt sound, the lengths and widths, how each piece contributed to the vessel, how much lumber he would need, how much oakum to pack the joints.

"Lard?" Fred wrote. He had kept reading, too, now that he was a boat builder.

"Might seal the wood a bit," Samuel said. "Good thinking. Worth a try, anyway."

Fred tapped his temple. He took a two-by-two from the box-car lot the mayor had brokered on their behalf. The board towered over him when he stood it on its end. He imagined sailing expertly across deep water, a red flag snapping above. He measured the wood as his father had showed him, scowling with seriousness at his task.

Boards lined the walls, and they began treating the wood in the steam box, testing the bend they could get, holding the curves in C-clamps as the planks dried.

"It's going to darn near take over the

whole barn," Samuel said. "Once we get her framed out."

Fred nodded, unable to quite fathom how the boat would look, how massive it would seem.

"Guess we'll roll it outside once the thaw comes."

"Who gets on?" Fred wrote.

"Us."

"Hens," Fred wrote.

"We can probably bring some birds," Samuel said.

Fred set the board between the grips of a vise.

"You can saw it," Samuel said. "You know what to do. Seen me do it enough times now. Watch your fingers."

It was a moment like Samuel could almost remember with his own father, working in the smoky light of an oil lamp in the rough-cut tongue-and-groove barn back in Kansas. His father sharpening the steel share of the walking plow, his arms moving in a rhythmic row above the spinning whetstone. He'd been only ten when his father died, and sometimes he groped for a memory other than the few well-worn ones he'd already turned over in his mind so many times. He couldn't recall his father's voice, but he still knew the halting cadence, the long silences.

215

Samuel's father had passed on to him the belief that you must be grateful for the land, no matter what it gives you back.

In Fred's small hand, the saw looked cartoonishly large, but he worked it slow and steady, gnawing through the old wood with concentration and purpose.

"You're doing good," Samuel said.

They worked in quiet tandem until his mother called Fred in for bed.

On Sunday, the Bells headed to church, not speaking during the car ride over. Since the tease of the rain, it seemed there was little to say. Annie refused to talk about the boat, and Samuel could think of little else. Birdie brooded in the backseat, hoping the car would run into the ditch. Fred poked her arm and showed her a long splinter wedged into his middle finger. She squeezed it between her fingernails until its head popped up from the skin and he yanked his hand away.

"Let me get it," she said.

He held his hand in his armpit until she shrugged and turned back to the window. He worked on his finger with the dirty nails of his other hand.

"Your mask, Fred," Annie said, glancing behind.

He glared at the back of her head and went back to the splinter, without putting on the dingy mask jammed in his pocket.

"I'd like to have Jack Lily over for supper," Samuel said. "In appreciation for all his help with the wood."

Annie did not look at him. "All right," she said.

The looks were impossible to deny when they took their seats in their usual pew. Glances over the shoulder, narrowed eyes. Gladys Abernathy, who had helped Fred with boat books at the library, got up and moved to a different pew. Somehow the small rain, the indignity of the hope it inspired, was the Bells' fault. The Bells and their stupid boat. If Samuel seemed oblivious, Annie understood too well, familiar as she was with reading the meaning of what went unspoken. When Annie was a girl, her mother had stood beside her father to greet the parishioners for Sunday service. When Mrs. Simpson, her father's mistress, had arrived, laughing loudly, Annie had watched her mother's frozen, tight-lipped smile, as she turned slightly away without offering her hand. The anger in a squint. The snub of a lifted chin. Annie exhaled her agitation.

Samuel's obsession was no longer just his own.

She hadn't seen the mayor come in, though she knew he was behind her somewhere. She could sense the heat of his gaze, her hair prickly, her neck warm. How thrilling it was to feel this way, rattled by his mere presence, wanting only to give in to his pull. But desire was awful, too, full of trapdoors and sharp hooks.

"I'm going to get some air," she said to Samuel.

"You okay?" he asked.

"I'm fine. I'll be back before the opening hymn."

"Birdie, go with your mother."

"No," Annie said abruptly.

Annie squeezed past Samuel's knees to the end of the pew, a sharp tang in her throat. Darkness pushed in on her vision and she rushed for the door without looking up.

After a few minutes, when she had not returned, Samuel nudged Birdie. "Go see to your mother anyway."

Birdie rose and moved to the door, pushing through to outside and all that brightness. She didn't see her mother, but she was happy to be out of the hot church. At least out here the wind made it seem cooler. She sank down to the shaded bottom step and dropped her head against the heels of her hands.

Dear God, she thought, please take this baby home. Take it like you took Eleanor. Take it and I'll do anything else you want. I'll even help Pop with the boat. Or make Cy come back, you could do that too. Or instead. Whichever one you think is best. Amen.

Around the side of the church, Annie leaned over, guzzling air, until the faint passed.

She saw the tips of his shoes first, black and freshly shined, before she raised her head.

"I was worried," Jack said. "You looked so pale."

She looked around. "I'm torn up inside," she said quietly. "This is a mess we've got going."

He nodded and dropped his chin to his chest.

"You can talk to me."

But Annie had spent her life not talking. Her mother could have found a gold bangle bracelet on her pillow — Mrs. Simpson used to wear three of them, which jingled together on her wrist — and still she wouldn't have said anything to her husband.

She took her lumps with steely Protestant resolve. And despite Annie's contempt for her mother, she was really no different, unable to tell Samuel how she really felt about anything. You wanted what your husband wanted. You didn't complain. You worked until your back ached and your hands split and your hair fell out from worry. Talk was selfish. She wouldn't know where to begin.

Organ chords rang from the other side of the wall, and Jack's hand found hers and then her lips found his and there they were, out in the open for anyone to catch them.

And then she thought of Samuel, felt the unbearable weight of his constancy. She pulled away and shook her hair — the wind had picked up — not meeting Jack's eyes. A tumbleweed barreled close and snagged her stockings.

"Best to go on in," she said. She turned away and left him standing on the side of the church.

"Annie?"

But she kept walking.

As Birdie stood, she saw her mother nearly running from the side of the church, her head down, hair askew.

"Mama."

"I'm fine," she said quickly. "We should

go in." Annie tried to comb her hair into place with her fingers. She reached for the door just as Fred opened it from the inside, smiling.

"The wind's getting kind of crazy," Birdie said, but neither heard her for the singing of the hymn. As she turned for another look, she saw the mayor come around the corner, following the path of her mother. He walked quickly, his brow furrowed, hands in his pockets. She scooted inside behind her mother, pretending she had not seen him. Why had she done that? Something in his face, a trouble there.

They made their way back to their seats as the hymn concluded and the congregation sat. Samuel raised his eyebrows and Annie answered with a slight nod and an even slighter forced smile.

Why had they both been back there? Birdie thought. Her mother and the mayor. She didn't like the feeling it gave her to put the two of them together.

Pastor Hardy's hair hung flat and greasy, and his tie was loose around his neck. The Bells sat close enough to the front that Birdie caught a whiff of something stale, like yeast, when his pacing pulled him near. Even him, she thought. Everyone was coming apart.

"How do you cope in a world gone astray?" the pastor asked to the space above their heads, his eyes cloudy and beseeching.

How indeed, Birdie thought. Cy had to be in California by now. She imagined trees full of oranges. Juice on her chin, sticky on her hands. Even the sun had to be different there, golden, soft. She checked each day for any bulge in her belly, but was relieved to find none, not yet.

Her father nodded along to the pastor's sermon, Ezekiel, again. Her mother stared. Fred, in the light from the window above, looked for a moment like a newly hatched chick, with his twitchy little head and blinking dark eyes and face open to the world. Birdie felt something like fear then, something ragged and dark lurking just out of sight. Fred could die just like Eleanor did, just like the Wallace boy who'd gone to bed with a headache and died in the night when a blood vessel exploded in his brain. The slimmest margin separated life from not-life. Pastor Hardy boomed on and on.

"We must be overcomers or we will be overcome," he said.

When it was finally time for a hymn, the pastor fell into his seat in a spent lump, and the congregation, the whole bedraggled bunch of them, rose to their feet.

Next to Birdie, Luke Carlton's mother sang like an ailing warbler. His father had gone on relief and hadn't been seen in church since. Luke, who would be a senior, a head and shoulders taller than his mother, ran a finger between his buttoned-up shirt and his neck, halfheartedly singing every third word.

When the hymn was over, Luke folded his mantis legs in on themselves in order to fit in the pew. He looked over and smiled at her — his elastic grin a little goofy, his hair a slept-on mess — and she felt a fading sadness at having been left.

In the shuffling quiet, before Pastor Hardy began again, the high windows rattled as the wind whipped against the church in jabs and gusts. People looked up, unable, for a moment, to bring themselves to move, each hoping it would go away.

"The Book of Ezekiel calls us to join in a renewed encounter with the God of Abraham. It asks to recognize the depth of evil that can lodge in each human heart."

Samuel stood. "Pastor," he said. "I'm afraid we've got something brewing."

"Let it come," he said. "We're talking about the Lord."

"All due respect. I've got to get to the

223

animals," Joe Brevers said, rising with his hat in hand. When he opened the door, the wind blew it back with a crack. The rest of the congregation jumped up and scuttled to the door.

"Stay calm," the mayor said, though it was unnecessary. They were calm, resigned to the storms that had, over these months, worn them thin. How fast a new normal took hold. He watched Annie as she shepherded her children down the aisle, tying a mask on Fred even as he resisted, Samuel's hand on her back. That hand was crushing to him.

Outside crows and nighthawks and kill-deers filled the sky with swooping, squawking chaos as they flew pell-mell, as if they'd been hurled by slingshots. Blue sparks zinged off barbed wire from the static electricity. The dark clouds were a few miles off, thousands of feet into the sky and rolling east, sweeping up the dirt in their path, straight toward them. Even though the sun was still bright, the air had the acrid taste of what was to come. Jack Lily helped the old Hollisters to their car.

"You going to ride it out at the office?" Styron asked.

"Go on. I'll seal it up best I can."

"It looks like the end of the world, doesn't it?"

Jack nodded, just as the Bells drove by.

"Even in defeat and despair God's people need to affirm God's sovereignty," the pastor said to his empty church. His face blotched pink under a waxy sheen. "Even in despair."

He sat in the first row, his hands lifeless in his lap. He didn't want to go around to his house behind the church, couldn't even muster the energy. He guessed he had some time before the worst of it. He closed his eyes and slipped into a jagged bout of sleep.

The first dirt hit soft like light snow, and then the gusts picked up, rocking the wooden church as sand hurled itself against the windows.

The pastor woke up to the cross above him, its burnished wood as smooth as alabaster.

"I just don't know," he said.

He fingered what remained of the letter in his pocket, the penciled words long disappeared, the edges as soft as cotton. It was the last he'd heard from Joseph, fifteen years ago, and he knew what it had said as well as he knew the Lord's Prayer. "Last night the moon was out full and it was so much colder than it's ever been at home," it began. My poor boy, the pastor would always think. What a terrible thing he'd gone to war. He'd been gentle his whole life — nursing a fox with a wounded paw or carrying spiders out of the house — and yet the pastor had been glad when he'd been called up, thought it would toughen him up. "When I get home I want to fish," he'd written. "That's what I dream about the most. And Mother's huckleberry pie."

The wind now howled like a pack of wolves, dolorous and fierce. The pastor turned his thoughts to his wife and how she would snap off both ends of green beans because she liked the symmetry. How after a day of rolling beeswax candles at the kitchen table, her hair would smell like honey. How when they were young, they would swim in the river, her dress billowing out around her like a spectral vision.

It looked like dusk, now, the sun obscured, the air cloudy and dry.

"Well, Martha, it's the biggest black blizzard I ever did see. They wouldn't know what to make of it back in Arkansas, now, would they?"

He was tired, his back ached, his finger joints were swollen from arthritis, his breath scratched his throat. He wanted to go home.

He wanted to be with his wife and son. He closed his eyes and felt the church shake, stones dinging the windows. He knew his faith was bowing under the weight of this test that would not let up.

There was a loud pop as one of the windows blew in, showering him in glass and dust. The wind whipped his hair, the glass cut his face, and yet he braced himself for what was to come, unwilling to hide.

By the time Samuel delivered his family home, the duster closing in, he couldn't stop thinking about Pastor Hardy and his faraway look that morning.

Annie tore strips from rags and dipped them in a paste of flour and water, sealing the window seams. Birdie brought in the cows, settling them in the barn. Fred, after losing the battle with his mother to bring the chickens inside, secured them in the henhouse. As Samuel drew tarpaulins over the boat and lumber and tools, he felt he had to go back to the church. Something was not right. He found Annie teetering on a chair as she hung a wet sheet over the kitchen window. He took the hammer from her and fixed the corner with a nail.

"I have to go back and check on him."

"Who?"

"The pastor."

"The storm's right outside the door."

"He doesn't have anyone else. I'll be back as soon as I can."

He turned then and rushed out the door.

"What do you think's going to happen to us?" Birdie asked. She and Fred sat together in her bed, huddled under the quilt, as the winds bit into the house and the darkness closed in.

Fred twirled his finger in the air.

"Not with the storm, silly. That's no secret. Everything gets dirty. Someone else goes crazy. You cough."

Fred coughed and smiled, his mask around his neck.

"I mean, are we going to just stay and stay and get older and sadder?"

Fred scrunched his forehead. Was everyone sad but him? He reached over for his notebook and pencil and scratched out, "What's wrong with here?" And then wrote again, "Cy?"

"Sometimes I wonder what he had for breakfast. I bet he doesn't have to eat wheat porridge anymore. Maybe he has a grapefruit. Did you know it's earlier in California?"

Fred shook his head.

"A couple hours or something. So when I wake up in the morning I think, Cy is still sleeping, and then I wish so much that I could be lying next to him."

There was scant light, so Fred hoped she couldn't see him blush.

"Someday you'll understand what it's like."

As the darkness grew, and with Samuel gone, Annie thought she'd join her children upstairs, but she stopped outside the door when she heard Birdie mention Cy's name. Since he'd left, Birdie spoke to her in short angry sentences, as if Cy's leaving were Annie's fault. She wished she could hold her and say she understood. She had more in common with Birdie than she could admit. But she knew how trying to talk to her would go. They were each spinning in the dark, like flies in a glass of water, flapping around for something to latch onto. Something cracked against the house, blown by the wind. Annie was furious at Samuel for going out in the storm. She felt her way through the hall to her bedroom and slid under the covers, pulling the sheet over her head.

"I'm afraid my whole life will be missing

him," Birdie said.

Fred found Birdie's hand and held it. "It'll be all right," he wanted to write to her, but it was too dim to read words on paper. Dust as fine as baby powder sifted through the window seams.

"No. It's not that. That's not it," Birdie said. "It's not just Cy."

He turned to her, the air thick.

"I'm pregnant," she said.

Snatches of images ricocheted in his head, piling up in a confused collage: pregnant, baby, animals, mating, Cy, nakedness, darkness, sweating, thrilling, strange, awful, the end. His sister was not his sister. She was something else, separate. Someone who could swell with a child in her belly. The secret felt hot in his head.

"There. I said it," she said. "I guess that makes it so."

"Take it back," Fred thought. "I don't want it to be so."

"It'll come in the spring," Birdie said. "If we haven't blown away by then." She turned to him. "You'll be an uncle. Can you believe it?"

Fred couldn't believe it. He kind of liked the sound of it, though. He could teach the baby things, like how the crows talk to each other with caws and warning cries and the

230

soft chittering of affection. But his thoughts were stalled by one cough and then another, and he spat dark goo into the piece of flannel he kept in his pocket.

"You okay?" Birdie asked.

He nodded. He was going to be an uncle. And an uncle needed to be strong.

CHAPTER 11

It wasn't Samuel who got to Pastor Hardy first. It was the man McGuiness, who blundered into the church half drunk, his boots crunching on broken glass, cursing God and the state of Oklahoma, which had treated him like shit since the day he was born. He'd been kicked out of Ruth's, tottering toward where he thought he'd left his truck, when he got caught, shoved around by the storm. The church had been the closest door, and now that he was inside, he scanned the place for anything of value. The collection plate was empty, but it was made of silver maybe. He stuffed it into the front pocket of his overalls. He wedged his face into the crook of his elbow to catch a breath.

"I'm here," the pastor said, in a wheezy shout. "Who's there?" Hardy turned in the pew, roused from his thoughts, and scrunched his face at the large figure coming toward him.

"Well. McGuiness. Looking to fleece me too?"

"Bet you got some whiskey at your place. Get up, will you?"

"I'm not going anywhere."

"Suit yourself."

Samuel pushed through the door with a towel over his face, disoriented by the swirling dirt.

"Pastor?"

"Go home to your family, Samuel," Hardy said.

But Samuel knew Hardy wasn't quite right, and could see now the cuts on his face.

"Help me get him over to the house," Samuel said to McGuiness.

"I know, you," McGuiness said. "You're Noah." He laughed and coughed. "You're goddamn Noah. Did you ride in on your ark?"

"Get his other arm!" Samuel shouted.

McGuiness complied, nudged by the hope of a drink, and they trundled the docile pastor out into the fury of the wind, feeling their way along the side of the church until the small clapboard house came hazily into view. The three men squeezed through the door, slamming it behind them.

Samuel helped the pastor over to a chair,

rinsed out a dirty glass, and filled it.

"Thank you," Hardy said.

"You weren't yourself today in church," Samuel said.

"What, no thanks for me?" McGuiness flung open cabinets, shoving aside plates and tins of salt and sugar. His gut knocked a jar of jam from the counter to the floor.

"It's in the one above the icebox," Hardy said.

Samuel recognized McGuiness, one of a handful of scavengers who roamed the county. He was as big as a bear, his hands broad and filthy. He smelled of beer and sweat.

"I won't ask you to leave, on account of the storm," Samuel said. "But I'll ask you to show some respect."

"Oh, okay, sure, Noah." He laughed and grabbed the whiskey by the neck and sat down at the table. "I haven't seen you in a while, Pastor. You've gotten old."

"Yes, well. It happens. The collection plate." The pastor held out his hand to McGuiness.

"In the spirit of this fine gathering." McGuiness pulled it from his overalls and set it on the table.

The wind whistled through cracks in the house. Samuel felt dislocated and uneasy.

He'd have to wait for the storm to pass before he could leave. He'd had experience with men like McGuiness before, but he was out of practice, and wished only to disperse the tinder of tension that might set him off. Back in Kansas, before Annie, he'd held his own twice with his fists, numbed by drink and youth. Once he'd awoken behind his shack on Gramlin's place to find his nose broken and his knuckle split, no memory of whom he'd fought or why. He'd lain there with the wet spring earth against his cheek and felt the sun on his back as it rose. He knew he ought to get up and hitch up the plow, but he felt small and petty and breakable. There was the earth and there was God. And he knew then that that was everything.

"Hey, Noah. Why don't you sit down and join the party. Bring over some glasses while you're at it."

The chair creaked under McGuiness's weight. He took a swig from the bottle, then absently rubbed his thumb along his half front tooth. Hardy slouched and his jowls hung. His face was dirt-smeared and defeated, a crusted cut above his eye. Samuel imagined he didn't look so well himself, thin as he was now and wind-whipped. He sighed and pulled two cloudy glasses and a jelly jar down from the shelf. The lamp cast a low yellow light on the table, the electricity surprisingly still on.

"You okay, Pastor?" he asked.

Hardy nodded with a grunt. "I lost myself for a moment in there, I'm afraid. I'm obliged to you." He sipped his drink. "How's the boat coming?"

"Got the ribs setting up. Fred's a good helper."

"I'm cheap labor," McGuiness said, a hint of challenge in his voice. "I don't know shit about boats, but you don't either, I suspect."

Samuel laughed. "I think I can make her float."

"That's what I said about that whore over in Beauville," McGuiness said.

The men drank. As he tipped his glass back again and again, McGuiness grew jovial, punching the others in the arms, telling tales of his exploits — "You ever wrestle a cougar? I didn't think so. Yeah, I did once. Breath smelled like dead fish. I won."

Hardy sank back, his Southern drawl softening his words, and Samuel felt the fire in his belly work loose his tongue.

"Let me ask you something," Samuel said. "Do you believe in God?"

"Oh, come on, Noah. Don't get all Bible-clutcher on me," McGuiness said.

"Do you?"

"I don't know. I mean, sure. But I have my doubts. Like the whole unfairness of life, for starters."

"I have had my own doubts," Samuel said.

"Faith in God is faith in the truth despite the doubt," Hardy said. "And truth is freedom. Jesus says it in John 8. I'll show you the passage."

"I'll take your word on it." McGuiness poured Hardy another drink.

"It's frightening," Samuel said quietly. Both men turned to him. "That kind of freedom."

"I'd never build a fool boat," McGuiness said into the silence that followed.

"You're a good man," Hardy said to Samuel, ignoring McGuiness.

"Am I? Maybe I'm as crazy as old man Dean."

"Elmer Dean thought the Germans were sending him messages through his teeth."

"Maybe they were," McGuiness said. "Maybe they told him to do a swan dive off the roof of the Fitzroy Hotel."

By now they were all good and drunk. McGuiness grabbed a tin of saltines from the counter and pulled down a plate of butter from the icebox. He used his finger to smear butter across a cracker, fitting another on top.

"Snack, anyone?"

The pastor held out his hand and McGuiness dropped the sandwich into his palm.

"My daddy loved saltines but we only had them when he was flush and we could actually go to the mercantile," McGuiness said. "One time my brother and me thought it would be funny to fill an old tin with cow pies and leave it in the kitchen so he would think it was his lucky day. We hid. He came through the door with two squirrels in his hand. His nose red and hair all crazy. We knew we were fucking dead." He laughed. "He whipped us, of course. Broke Jerry's arm. Never did set quite right. Made us eat the cow shit until we barfed."

Samuel and Pastor Hardy grimaced but McGuiness was chuckling.

"Christ, you are a pair of sad Sarahs. It's funny! To have to actually eat shit."

"My father used to make me pick out the switch I wanted to get beaten with," Hardy said. " 'Get your blade, boy, you're cutting it, too.' "

"Could you forgive him?" Samuel asked.

"He couldn't read or write and he was swindled out of his little piece of ground so he had to sharecrop alongside former slaves. He couldn't abide it. We ate corn porridge once for a month. He was a broken man. I forgave him before he passed on. But he comes back to me sometimes and I feel that anger all over again. I still want to smash his mouth with my fist."

"Shit," McGuiness said. "You-all are wrecking my drunk. So you taking two by two, Noah?"

"Maybe a cow. A hen or two."

"Who you letting on?"

"If you're worried," Hardy said, "you better get building your own."

"I ain't too worried."

They listened as the wind buffeted the house, the relentless sand roughing the windows. By now they were used to the whistle and moan, the droning world on the other side of the wall. Samuel closed his eyes and imagined the house being worn away. Annie and the kids seemed a faraway life, a world of darkness and dust between him and them. He was tired of seeing everything through squinted eyes, through a dirty mesh. He fell asleep, with a clunk of his head against the table.

Samuel was visited by the swirls of water, black like oil, the rain drops as fat as duck eggs. The voice a deep murmur in his head, so clear and strange, with the force of a thousand thundering buffalo. It filled him with awe, with humility. It filled him with terror. I am your servant, he said without speaking. I am here.

The men slept late into the morning, the sun sending knives of light through the dusty air in the house. The storm had moved on, leaving the usual mess in its wake. McGuiness, splayed out half under the table, was covered in fine gray powder. Samuel brushed off his shoulders, and wiped his face with his shirt. He could hear the pastor cough and gargle in the bathroom.

McGuiness hauled himself onto his side with a grunt.

Samuel rose and rinsed two glasses and filled them with water.

"You awake?"

"Go away," McGuiness croaked.

Samuel cleared a windowpane with his palm. The sky was an uncanny blue.

"I'll start coffee," Hardy said. He hobbled into the kitchen in his mended shorts and a T-shirt, the armpits stained yellow. Samuel was taken aback by the intimacy of seeing him this way. "God has given us a bright new day, hasn't he?"

240

The pastor's hand shook as he measured coffee grounds into a dented pot. He closed his bloodshot eyes. They were a battered bunch. Samuel's head felt hammered with each movement.

McGuiness heaved himself to his feet, ignoring Samuel's outstretched hand.

"Got sugar for the coffee, Pastor?"

"I wouldn't have pegged you for a sugar type," Hardy said.

"You don't think I'm sweet?"

"Not sweet, no. But you're not as tough as you seem, either."

"Says you."

"Says me. Sugar's in the canister there."

"What do you say, McGuiness? You should come to church sometime. Meet your neighbors," Samuel said. "We're not so bad."

"Darn if you ain't an earnest son of a bitch. Don't you ever drop the bullshit? I'm not looking for salvation." McGuiness laughed and shook his head. "I got to take a piss."

In the small, Spartan bathroom, he scratched his big belly and stretched his arms, his hands grazing the ceiling. Above the sink in the scratched mirror he looked grubby and bloated, his beard a grizzled mess. He knew what these men could never know: A man is who he is. That doesn't change. A thief is a thief. A bad man stays a bad man underneath. He'd been set at seventeen.

"You want to end up like me?" His father had raged at him for stealing from the collection plate at church. "How much you get? Give it here."

"No."

"No? You smartass pissant. This is my house."

His father was ramping up, his face coloring, his eyes roaming about looking for something to settle on, someone for him to rip into. Where was Jerry? Where was his mother? McGuiness couldn't remember. In his mind he saw only his father, a bully and a brute who smelled like animal guts. For some reason, the shovel was inside the house, leaning up against the door. It was as if he had planned it, so calm and quick were his movements as his father turned to light his pipe. A clean clang from behind with a shovel to his head. Steel against soft skull. McGuiness had never understood why his mother cried — how many times had his father punched her bloody? — that poor wretch with her mousy face and whispery voice, why she had slammed his chest with her two tiny fists.

He pulled his overalls back up. At the sink

he ran his wet hands through his hair. He spat. He wasn't drunk anymore, only parched and nauseated. On his way from the bathroom, he slipped into the pastor's bedroom. On the dresser was a small bowl full of coins, which he emptied into his pocket. On the bedside table, beside a Bible, was a small gold ring. He took that, too.

Dearest Annie,

I'm writing you in the midst of this latest abomination, the bulb flickering overhead, barely enough to see by. How will I get this letter to you without your husband seeing it? I haven't figured that out yet. But given the howling outside, I will have plenty of time to think of a delivery means as the night wears on and on. I am thinking of the time, not so long ago, that we waited out the dust in the car on First Street. Beautiful you were, even under a layer of dirt.

I hope that you are safe, though I wish you were with me here. I would read to you if the light held. I have a copy of *Pride and Prejudice* somewhere in the boxes of books I haven't unpacked since I arrived at this outpost as a younger man. Have I told you that I imagined myself some kind of cowboy when I left

Chicago? I still don't have any idea how to ride a horse. And truth be told, they make me sneeze.

I am a planet spinning out of orbit, Annie. I think of you and only you. Church today was devastating for me. You pulled away. What did it mean? I have gone over each gesture, each word, again and again. With so little time to talk, my imagination is fertile and predatory. Are you thinking of me too?

My brother has sent word that my father is sick. He is dying. I haven't told you about my father. He is gentle and hardworking — he owns a creamery — though when I was young I found him maddeningly small in his vision. Fulfill orders, eat at six, one beer with the newspaper, bed at nine. Ideas and ambition might as well have been pillow fluff. Maybe all sons feel this way about their fathers at some point, even favorite sons. Maybe it's part of growing up and finding one's own way. But I was mercenary. Not only did I choose to not work beside him as my brother did, and become a newspaperman instead, which he found a dishonest profession, I left, without a thought about what it might do to him. And worse, I've never gone back to visit,

244

after all these years. It is hard for me to admit this to you now.

I am going to Chicago. I don't know for how long. And here's the crazy notion that I can't wrest from the coyote's mouth. I want you to come with me, for a few days. Okay, there it is, finally, why I wanted to write to you. (In my old profession, that's what they call burying the lede.) I would like to walk around the city with you on my arm. I would like to show you Lake Michigan. I would like to take you to the Lincoln Park Zoo. Can you believe they have a gorilla from Africa? I would like to take you on your first streetcar. Think about it. You don't need to tell me it's not the right thing to do. But we live only once, as far as I know, and happiness should count for something, shouldn't it?

I know there are your children to think about. But a few days is what I'm asking.

It sounds like the roof is being yanked off by the wind. This storm seems different, darker and dirtier, if such a thing is possible. I'm sorry for the smudged paper.

I love you, Annie Bell. I wanted to say that to you at the church but I was a coward in the shadow of your troubled face. I love you. Come away with me.

— Jack

The mayor came down from his office, where he had spent the night of the storm, and walked out into a glorious day. He waved to Edward Banks who swept off the sidewalk in front of the post office. Jeanette, her hair pulled back in a scarf, wiped down the windows of Ruth's. There was a cool edge to the air, just a hint when the wind blew, which made him balloon with hope. The letter was folded in his shirt pocket. He had willed himself not to reread it for fear he would lose his nerve. He had yet to come up with a good excuse to drive out to deliver it, but he was undeterred. His heart was charging ahead, and he had no choice but to follow.

Jack sighed as he took in the state of the town, a layer of new dust, his own car tires half buried, a roll of barbed wire in the middle of the road. He had ten minutes before Jeanette would flip the sign to Open, so he kept walking. At the church he saw the blown-out window, but as he walked around to get a better look, there was Samuel's car, a small dune wedged against its rear. Samuel was here, and Annie was surely there.

He turned around and started to run.

CHAPTER 12

Annie lay awake in the dark morning, her limbs sunk into the bed. She was alone. She heard the door slam as Birdie went out to the barn for chores. Must you, Barbara Ann? she thought, before she remembered to be easier on her daughter. Remember, she told herself, what it was like.

When she'd taken her one and only trip to Kansas City, she had been Birdie's age. Her father had been invited to a Presbyterian council meeting, and her mother, in an uncharacteristic moment of vigor, had insisted they accompany him. Seventy miles in a hot and crowded train, but Annie didn't mind. A big city. Another state, even. She tried not to let on about her excitement to her parents, but she could not hide her upswing in mood.

"Nice to see you smiling," her father said. "Life is not too unbearable today, I gather. 'I can do all things through Him who strengthens me.' "

From her window, Annie watched the large industrial buildings begin to crowd the landscape as they neared Missouri.

"Maybe you can pick out a new dress for Annie while we're here," her father said to his wife. He pushed his round wire glasses up on his nose. "That one's a little short, don't you think?" As if she were not sitting right across from him.

"Yes, Reverend," her mother answered.

Reverend, Annie thought, like she was just another one of his fawning parishioners. What about a husband and a wife? What about love? It was no wonder her father had looked elsewhere.

"I read where each chandelier in the terminal weighs over thirty-five hundred pounds," he said.

"Isn't that interesting," her mother said. Her voice was feathery light, but her tone was flinty underneath.

"Let's not forget to look up when we arrive. Nothing like it back home."

When Annie stepped into the station's vast atrium, she felt as if the floor had dropped. She did look up, at all the dazzling crystals and starburst lights. She breathed it in until she was dizzy.

"I'm afraid I'm running short on time,"

her father said. "We'll meet back here. Five o'clock. Your watch is wound, Sarah?"

Her mother nodded. He patted her arm and left them.

Outside, the buildings rose fifteen stories in the sky and electric streetcars clanged. Annie felt herself expand. But her mother grew timid, stuck on the top step, stunned by everything moving around her.

"Can we ride on one?" Annie asked.

Her mother shook her head. "No, no. There's a café," she said, grasping Annie's hand.

Inside, women chatted and laughed, perched at tables in their brightly colored dresses, parcels at their feet. Annie ordered chocolate cake, which arrived on a gold-rimmed plate garnished with a strawberry rosette.

"Isn't this fun, Mother?" Annie picked up the strawberry, marveling at how it had been carved into a flower.

"It's quite loud in here," she said.

Annie let a bite of cake melt in her mouth, a small bite to make it last and last. But across from her, her mother frowned at the close chattering voices, the scurrying wait-ress, and sipped her tea. She seemed to be winding herself tighter and tighter, shrink-ing into her high-necked white dress. Her pale fingers twitched against her teacup.

"You remember the Thurgoods' son," her mother said. "He's just begun seminary."

Annie didn't answer. She did remember the Thurgoods' son from when they were kids — a nice quiet boy, his hair slicked into place — but she was unwilling to be drawn in by her mother, uninterested in her match-making. Her mother cared that he came from a moneyed family and that he would be a minister. She did not care about what would make her daughter happy. And then Annie began to feel the familiar confinement push in again, of her narrow Kansas life, of her mother thinking she knew best. The café at once felt stuffy, closing in, so small Annie thought she could touch wall to wall with her outstretched hands.

"William. A couple years older than you. He used to come to children's Bible study."

Annie still did not answer. She shook her foot and watched the activity of the city beyond the bright window and wanted to burst out through the door.

"You'd like him."

Annie snapped her gaze back to her mother. You don't know anything about what I'd like, she thought. But she would bide her time, figure out what was next. She'd smiled close-lipped and false, and had

251

said, "Let's go, Mother. There's a shop across the way."

It had been twenty years, but Annie could still feel that flinty defiance she had felt then. She sat up in bed and swung her feet around to the gritty floor. She feared Birdie had already locked her out the way she had done to her own mother. But at least Annie knew her daughter wanted to see the world, see something beyond the farm. Annie had felt that once, too. With Cy gone, Birdie still had a chance, if only she would take it.

Fred's door was closed. Annie turned the handle and stepped inside. It was like an eerie twilight, the windows covered. The whistling gurgle that met her sounded like an old steam tractor trying to turn over. It took her a moment to realize what it was.

"Fred," she said, shaking his shoulders, "oh, Fred." The dust rose in an airborne halo around him.

He sputtered awake and, after his body stilled from the coughs, he smiled.

"You sound terrible," she said. "You need cough syrup."

In the kitchen she mixed a drop of kerosene in a spoonful of sugar, the solvent vapors burning her nose. Fred hopped into a chair, his hair powdery, his lips drained of color.

"Take it all at once," she said, handing him the spoon.

He reared back with the smell of it and shook his head.

"That wheeze is bad. Go on."

Fred scrunched his face and choked it down, then gulped water to rid his mouth of the taste.

"I'll make pancakes," Annie said.

Fred's eyes watered. He hated this cure. His belly burned. He could feel his breathing ease, though, or he imagined it at least, the kerosene snaking into his lungs, clearing out the passageways.

"Get your mask on," his mother said.

He rolled his eyes and looped the limp mask around his ears. From the window, the rising sun showed a sky washed clean.

"Pop?" he wrote in the dust on the table.

"Stayed with Pastor Hardy. I expect he'll be home as soon as he can."

Fred was itching to get back to the boat. The hull was taking shape, barely contained by the barn. He loved working with his father, who was transformed in the smoky lantern light. He didn't say much, but he trusted Fred to do things right. To measure and steam and saw and set and sand. It would be the first boat Fred had ever been on. Sometimes when he was alone in the barn, he would overturn a milk crate and sit in the boat and imagine the rocking waves and surges lapping the sides. He would be the one gripping an oar to help steer them through the storm, his sister saying, "You can do it, Fred. Save us."

Us. He'd forgotten about the baby. He glanced at his mother, who of course didn't know. His mind jumped to his mother's apron, the one he'd found at the old house, but that and the mayor's visit, he could not make it all fit together right. He didn't like keeping secrets, and all of a sudden he had a whole handful of them. He rose to go find Birdie.

"Where are you going?" his mother asked.

He pointed out to the barn.

"Tell your sister it's breakfast time."

The morning was blessedly cool, as if the heat had finally worn itself out. Dawn had broken, but it was still dark in the barn. Greta's flank was warm against Birdie's cheek as she washed the cow's udder.

"It would be okay if you kicked me, honey, just this once," she whispered. "One swift one. Right here."

Greta lowed and stomped her foot, ready

for Birdie's fingers to give her some relief. Birdie waited, hoping the cow would get mad enough. But Greta just made a lot of noise. So she started on the milk, the stream clanging into the pail.

Did Cy ever wonder about what she was doing? That was the worst thought, that he never thought about her at all. She closed her eyes and concentrated and thought, "Cy. Can you hear me? There will be a baby."

She now had the smallest beginning of a belly, a slight rounded fullness down low. She knew the baby existed, of course, but it was an idea, like gravity. It had no connection to an actual thing that would tear its way out of her. It was not a he or she. It had no face, no heft. She imagined the screams, the groping fingers of a baby that was not hers. She knew she was not a mother.

Life was mostly about remembering or waiting, Birdie thought. Remembering when things were better, waiting for things to get better again. There was never a now, never a time when you said, "This is it." You thought there would be that time — when you turned sixteen, when Cy finally kissed you, when school got out — but then you ended up waiting for something else.

Now she dug her heels in against the passing of each day. She thought about the things that might make the baby go away. A knife slip. A punch. Getting pummeled by dust and debris. Women miscarried all the time. Why couldn't she? She prayed to God to take the baby away, but she knew it wouldn't work because that was not something you could ask for. What should she pray about, then? She prayed and prayed. God, do something.

Maybe she could move away and pretend she was a widow. Someone would marry a widow with a baby. There was no shame in that. "He was a good man. Died in a thresher accident," she heard herself say. No one would ever have to know. She would never come back to Mulehead. She would miss Fred. There would be that. She would be sorry to miss him grow up.

Birdie knew what she could not do. Turn out like Mary Louise VanCamp who'd given birth four months after marrying that Bible salesman. People in town called her Mary Louise VanTramp. There was something wrong with her son, but no one ever knew what. His eyes bulged out of his head and he ate dirt. Mary Louise had moved back in with her parents when the salesman disappeared. Pitiful. Shut away on a ranch out near Kenton.

Love is not something to be ashamed of, Birdie imagined herself saying. She would not hang her head.

"Who am I kidding, Greta?" She ran her hand along the cow's flank.

She slipped the full bucket from under the cow and brought it to her mouth, the cream foamy white on her lip, the milk warm and sweet.

She would miss that, too.

Birdie leaned her head into the open drive bay of the barn where her father and brother worked on the boat. A skeleton frame nosed up against the back wall, the front or back of the boat she couldn't be sure, ribs held in place with rough scaffolding. It was dim even in the growing daylight, and she tripped on a chunk of wood before righting herself. She picked it up. A two-foot sawed-off section. Maybe if she hit in just the right place. It was an awkward grip in one hand. Hit hard with everything, she told herself, do not chicken out. She took off her work shirt, crusty with the morning's milking, and touched low on her tummy with the board, knowing she would have to be precise. She closed her eyes for a moment as she took a breath, then pulled her arm back wide and swung, as if her own body were not the target.

It was a shock even as she knew the blow was coming. She threw up almost immediately, bile from an empty stomach, and she fell forward onto hands and knees. The rough end of the plank had scratched her and the impact had knocked her breath out. But within a couple minutes, the pain faded.

She sat back on her heels and waited for cramps or blood or some deep inside signal. She waited until all she felt was a familiar gnawing hunger. She whipped the piece of wood away where it landed in a far corner of the barn.

"Did he sound like this last night?" Annie asked. "And you didn't tell me? Was his mask on?"

Birdie took a big bite of pancake and put her fork down. She was amazed she could eat, yet here she was, again starving. Still pregnant.

"What?" she asked, mouth full.

"I just," Annie said. "We have to be vigilant."

Fred leaned his head back and balanced a pancake on his face.

"He seems okay to me," Birdie said. "Other than smelling like he might burst

258

into flames."

A trail of footprints tracked the kitchen, as if the floor were covered in first snow.

"You're not going outside anymore today," Annie said.

Fred stomped his foot, and scowled in protest.

"It's probably worse in here than out there," Birdie said. "Now that the sun's out, looks as clear as a bell."

Annie sighed. Her daughter was right.

"If I see you without your mask, young man, you'll be stuck next to me, cutting quilt squares and mending your father's pants for a week."

"I have a blouse that's missing some buttons," Birdie chimed in.

Fred narrowed his eyes at her from behind his mask. He pulled a pad of paper and a pencil from his pocket. "Hens," he wrote, holding it up for his mother to see.

"Go on," she said.

When he was gone, Annie felt newly uncomfortable alone with Birdie. She went to the sink and started on the dishes.

"Whatever happened to the VanTramps?" Birdie asked.

Annie dropped the frying pan into the sink. She exhaled slowly and turned to Birdie.

"Barbara Ann. The VanCamps. Don't be uncharitable."

Birdie scraped back her chair. She just wanted her mother to know without having to tell her. She wanted her mother to take on some of the burden, to make it better, the way she used to do when Birdie was little.

"The VanCamps. They were around and then they weren't."

"They headed to Texas. They had kin down that way."

"They ran away."

"They moved on. Sometimes it's the right thing to do," Annie said. She soaped a rag and went to work on the greasy pan.

Birdie stood.

"I'm the same as her," Birdie said.

"As who?"

"Mary Louise."

"What?" Annie wiped her hands on her apron and turned to fully face her daughter. "Why are you like her?" A quick glance at Birdie's middle.

Birdie stopped her hand before it reached her belly.

"Because —"

"Because Cy left?"

Birdie could shake her head or she could nod, reveal or conceal. She angled her body one way and then another, but her mother didn't read it as an answer.

"Cy didn't leave *you,* Birdie. He didn't have a choice. He had to go."

"I know," Birdie said. "But it doesn't make it easier."

"I know you can't see it now. But someday. You might see it as a blessing."

Birdie's shoulders drooped at the lost opportunity, at her mother's insistence that she knew best. She was now eager to be free of the stifling air between them.

"I would have thought Pop would be back by now."

"Probably helping out whoever needs helping."

Without comment, Birdie walked out and left her mother alone.

Annie untied her apron and sat at the table. She took a crescent of pancake left on Fred's plate and ate it with her fingers. It was a shame about Mary Louise, trying to sell the Bibles that man had left while looking after a child who was not quite right. What was a girl like that to do in this wasteland? she thought, as she stuffed more of the syrup-sticky pancake into her mouth.

Outside a car hiccupped and squeaked to a stop. Samuel. She rose and drank water directly from the tap to get the food down, then wiped her face on her apron. The relief she felt to have him home came as a surprise.

But it wasn't Samuel. Jack Lily. Her face lost its composure. An exhaled "Oh" escaped her lips.

"What are you doing here?" Her voice caught. She was angry at him for risking a visit, but desire curled through her veins like smoke.

"I know," he said. "Annie." His stillness eased her disquiet.

She could smell the soap on him, see the muscles of his jaw clench and release.

"What do I say about why you've come?" She looked behind her for Birdie.

"Just take this." He opened the screen door and handed her the letter. "Phones are out," he said more loudly. "Wanted to talk to Samuel about something."

Annie looked wildly about. "Okay. He's not here. Should be back any minute. Stayed with the pastor through the storm."

"Got a call from the *Cimarron*. They want to do a story." He sounded as if he was onstage, his voice meant for others to hear, his words rehearsed.

"A story?" she asked. The envelope was as light as a butterfly in her hand.

"They've heard about the boat."

"I'll tell him you stopped by."

He reached for her hand. "Say yes," he whispered.

Fred poked his head out of the coop and saw the mayor's green Model A. "Go away," he thought, not knowing why, just knowing. "Go away go away go away."

Annie swept out the house, starting upstairs to work the dirt down. She had not yet read the letter. Holding onto the broom took the shake from her hands. Outside another car door slammed. She stopped midstroke and listened for Samuel's familiar footfall on the porch.

When he looked up, he seemed startled to see Annie frozen midway down the staircase.

"Everything all right?" he asked. He scratched his head and looked down.

"Fine," she said.

He looked ghastly, his clothes unclean and rumpled, his hair sticking up above his ear. His eyes, though he wouldn't really look at her, were red and puffy.

"Pastor okay?"

"He'll manage. I thought it best to stay."

"Good of you."

The letter. She'd tucked it in her Bible and then hid it under her mending pile. She swept a dusty pile down a step. The letter.

"I found him sitting in the church. The window blown out."

"What was he doing?" She asked it, but it was an empty question. She knew well enough. She moved down the last two steps to the floor, clutching the broom and piling the dirt.

Samuel shrugged. "I didn't push him on it."

"There's coffee," she said.

"The children?"

"Fred's out with the chickens. Gave him some kerosene. He sounded real bad this morning." She wanted this to sting, but when she saw that it did, she felt sorry.

"I'll go see to him," he said, his face hangdog and contrite. "I'm sorry I wasn't here."

She moved the broom's bristles through the dust. The letter burned a hole through every other thought.

"Birdie went off somewhere to mope."

Samuel nodded, as if waiting to be dismissed.

"I'm glad you're back safe," she said.

He smiled at her, that open-to-the-world smile she'd fallen in love with.

"I best get some coffee," he said. He brushed by her, laying a hand quickly on her shoulder as he passed.

She listened as Samuel pulled a mug from the cupboard, scraped the coffeepot against the stove, poured a cup, and set the pot back with a clank. She waited, broom still, as he drank and, as she knew he would, looked out the window. Finally the back door creaked open and banged shut.

Annie leaned the broom against the wall and bounded up the steps to the bedroom. From the window, she watched Samuel make his way to the chicken coop. She dug out her Bible and pulled from it the envelope, flipping it over twice — looking for what? — before messily tearing at the flap.

Fred sat cross-legged on the wooden plank in the center of the hen house, wiping a rag over the once-white feathers of one of the leghorns. Since the first storm he had used his mother's flour paste and strips of rags to cover as many of the open seams of the coop as he could. He made sure the birds were in, with the door latched, for every storm.

The mask was stuffed into his pocket. His breathing was fast and ragged, as if he'd climbed all the way to the top of Black Mesa — the air blurred by bits of straw and dried dung and dust. He would do his best to stay clear of his mother today.

"Here, girl," he thought. He lifted the one

from his lap and replaced her with another. "Let Freddie clean you up."

"Son?"

Samuel pried open the door, the light making Fred squint.

"You spoil those birds so. Pretty soon they'll be wanting their water in a silver bowl."

He could see Fred's chest rise and fall quickly, the little concavity at the base of his throat sucked taut with each breath.

"Hard to get air in?"

Fred shrugged. Samuel ran his finger along the chicken's head.

"Are the eggs starting to taper?"

Fred pinched his fingers together to show a little. When the hens stopped laying, it usually meant cold weather was coming.

"I think we ought to get back to the boat soon, huh?"

Fred jumped up and wrapped his arms around his father's waist. Samuel was not quick enough to stanch the tears that gathered.

"Whoa there. Soon, I mean a little later. Got to clean up some around the place first. What do you say, after lunch?"

Fred nodded, his chin hitting his chest, his head too large for his beanpole body.

"You do a fine job with the hens. A fine job."

Fred smiled and pointed his thumb at himself.

Samuel remembered how Fred used to sit on Annie's lap, his head nestled under her chin as they sat after supper, her finger tracing his small translucent ear. It was his son's fragility Samuel feared, and he thought maybe it was his job to buck Fred up. Give him a gentle nudge. But now he could admit he felt jealousy, too. The closeness a mother was allowed. Once he had wondered aloud to Annie if Fred wasn't a little old to be sitting on her lap. He tried to keep his tone light. "I know he's your little one," he had said. He hadn't meant to, but he'd come off as accusatory somehow, or dismissive, and when she turned to him — she'd been peeling potatoes at the kitchen sink — he knew he'd been wrong to say anything. Her eyes were filled and she blinked furiously to contain them. Oh sure, he had apologized, taken it back. But she had surely lodged it away somewhere with the other times he had disappointed her. "He can sit on my lap as long as he wants." That was all she had said, and they'd never spoken of it again. The next time Fred climbed on her lap, she looked away. He had broken the spell, and Fred soon forwent the lap altogether, running off to play with his toy cars or get into Birdie's business. Samuel had, sadly, gotten what he'd wanted.

"Have you seen your sister?" Samuel asked.

Fred shook his head and twirled his finger in a circle next to his ear, a gesture he'd picked up from boys making fun of Jonas Woodrow.

"She's just a little temperamental these days," Samuel said. "She'll come around. See you for lunch. And don't think I don't notice your mask off."

Fred hung his head and pulled the mask from his pocket.

"Just make sure you have it on when you come in. No need to upset your mother."

Birdie walked just to go somewhere else. Ruth's, maybe. She had a dime in her sock for a sugar cookie or maybe some licorice from the store. She felt a flutter of hunger in her belly even after all those pancakes.

It was warm, but, at the tail end of summer, the edge was finally off, as if the bullying sun had lost a little of its will. The seeds were in the fields on both sides of the road for all the next-year-will-be-better folks, and now the hope would turn to snow — maybe it just needed to get cold again and the sky would open up — and the waiting was on again.

Halfway to town she saw Mary Stem on her bicycle riding toward her. Mary was her friend, she supposed, yet Birdie didn't really like her much at all. She was chirpy and tedious, not even that nice. But there was no detour, everywhere so starkly out in the open.

"My mother called out your way," Mary said by way of greeting. "But no one picked up the phone." She'd always had one eye on Cy, and Birdie knew she felt a certain victory in his departure.

"I must have been gone already. Can't say where everyone else was."

"What are you doing out here anyway?" Mary straddled her bike and adjusted the kerchief on her head.

"Walking."

"Walking where?"

Birdie shrugged. "To town, I guess. I don't know. Nowhere, really."

"That's weird, Birdie. Who doesn't know where they're walking to?"

Birdie saw Mary as she would be at forty. Same body, as straight up and down as a tree trunk, same nosy face. Hair shorter and starting to gray. The smug pinches of her mouth hardened into wrinkles.

"What did your mother want?"

"See if you wanted to come over. Daddy's filled a tub from the well. Thought we could cool off in it. I'm deathly bored from the heat."

"That would have been nice, sure," Birdie said, scanning the horizon, suddenly desperate for shade.

"Let's go then. I'm sweating and it's disgusting."

"Some other time, maybe. It's too far to go home and change."

"You can borrow a bathing suit from me. I have two. One's a little faded but still works okay. Has this little bow at the waist."

Birdie knew she couldn't squeeze into a bathing suit. Mary would home in on her tummy like a vulture to a carcass.

"I don't think so. Thanks, though."

"Oh please, please, please? I need your advice about my dress for the dance."

"School doesn't even start for another week."

"It's never too early. You better start thinking about it. With Cy gone and all. Set your sites on Luke Carlton. I'm working on John Bellows. That way, we can go together! Oh my gosh, what if we ended up marrying those two!"

I used to be like you, Birdie thought.

"I'm going to go home," she said. "I don't feel well all of a sudden."

"Oh, phooey on you," Mary said. "You're strange, Birdie."

Birdie turned without saying goodbye as Mary pedaled away.

Annie sat on the edge of the bed. Her face raged hot, her head dizzy. She imagined herself, or a smarter, more modern version of herself, walking with tall glittery buildings on either side of her, the blue shimmer of Lake Michigan in the distance. She didn't know what Chicago looked like, but she'd seen pictures of New York and had been, that one time, to Kansas City, so maybe it was a combination of the two. The wind would blow her skirt as she walked, her rounded strapped pumps hitting the sidewalk with decisive clacks as she crossed the street to a restaurant where she was to meet Jack Lily for lunch, the sounds of clinking teacups and low voices and forks against china as she pulled open the door.

Did she love him? She felt bubbly, the escape of it the headiest part of it all. She loved that he was different from anyone she'd known before, that he had chosen her. She loved his hands that had never worked a plow. How he made her body feel. The heat of it. But love? She couldn't quite reach it. Not yet. They'd barely talked, when it came down to it, so overcome by just being alone together. Love went beyond that, she knew.

From the window she could see Samuel leaving the coop and heading to the barn. How would it feel to leave him? There would be loss. There would be relief. She would miss him, the comfort of what she'd known her entire adult life. All that they shared. The children, of course. She could not run away.

She folded Jack's note into a square and then another and another. And yet, what would it be like to decide something for herself alone? A few days. And then she would come back. She looked down at her old flat shoes, unraveling at the heels. She could do it. She would go. Yes.

Her tired dresses hung in a sad bunch in the armoire. On the train she would wear the navy blue one she'd worn when they'd sat out the storm together. She pulled it from the hanger.

Birdie hadn't been to the Woodrow house since Cy left, and it now looked like it had been deserted for years, patches of shake gone from the roof, a dune almost entirely obscuring the front window, which was cracked and scratched. The front door had fallen over on its side. Anything of value, even the door handle, had been stripped.

She climbed through sand up to her knees at the threshold, and once through the door she called out, but was met with silence. She climbed the steps slowly. There, the window. There, the mattress, or what was left of it, chewed by some animal, now spilling its stuffing and springs. There, we were in love. Birdie crouched on the dirty floor without the slightest idea of what to do.

And then she felt it again, that same quivering in her belly from the morning. It came to her: quickening, the word like some medieval spell, whispered by women with knowing smiles. She'd heard her mother say it when she was pregnant with Fred. There was a baby in there and it just moved and I felt it, she thought, her hand against her firm tummy, still tender when she pressed her fingertips against it. It would be the girls who noticed first. Mary Louise VanTramp. Birdie Bell.

"I was thinking I'd go home for a visit." Annie stood at the sink and rewashed a bowl.

Samuel looked up, but she didn't turn around.

"See Mother and Father. It's been a long time. They're getting on."

"Oh." It was confusing to him, this sudden request. She never talked of Kansas. And it was an indulgence from a woman who asked for very little.

"Do you think I shouldn't go?"

"I'm just surprised is all."

"Just me. For a few days or so. Birdie can keep watch on the garden. As long as Fred is better. Seems as good a time as any. I know there's the money part. For the train."

"Of course you can go," Samuel said.

Annie felt a lightening all over her body, as if she might levitate off the floor. How easy it all now seemed.

"I'll make plenty of food before I go." Slow down, Annie, she told herself, breathe. "The children will be fine."

Fred figured Birdie had taken off for the Woodrow place. He had time before lunch to search her out, and then he would go to check on his bone pile, see what else he could add to it. Even though the bone meal grinder had gone away, someone would come back after the rains came and everyone needed fertilizer again. It occurred to him that the flood might wash the bones away, but by then he probably wouldn't care so much.

He trudged around to the back of the house and collected some pebbles, which he threw at the upstairs windows. Plink, plink, plink. Birdie appeared on the fifth throw.

Upstairs he found her darting about, madly pulling at the windowsill with both hands, her fingers bleeding as she grabbed at the edge of a warped wallboard.

"I want to smash something," she said. Fred stood with his hands in his armpits, unsure of her mood. "Oh, this'll work," she said, reaching for the broomstick lodged in the corner. "Go find something. It's going to be fun, you'll see."

Fred went into the other bedroom, where the windowsill was hanging from the sash. He kicked his foot against it until it splintered some.

"That sounded promising," Birdie called out.

He wrestled the wood free and held it in his hands like a baseball bat, tapping it against the window. It felt good and solid in his hands and he went back to his sister, whose face was pink and angry, and all at once he felt it too, that anger, at the dust and drought and his lungs and Cy Mack and God even, for how He let it all happen.

"One, two, three," she said.

She swung the broom handle into the window, first one crack and then another, and the third swing brought the glass down in a rain of shimmering triangles. "Go on," she said, panting. "Your turn."

Fred ran to the other room and put wood to glass with a power he didn't know he had. One shot and the window shattered into a spiderweb of cracks, which hung for a moment before collapsing to the floor in a heap.

"Nice one," Birdie said, leaning in the doorway. "You should do okay this year with the piñata." At the end of school festivities, Fred had famously yet to make contact with the papier-mâché animal — last year a pig — made by the older kids for the younger ones.

He smiled, speckled light on his face from the broken glass.

"It felt a little good at least," she said, and he nodded. "I wish we had some whiskey or cookies or something." She sat and he sat next to her.

It seemed impossible to him that she could be someone's mother. She was not one of those kids who seemed like a grown-up, like Betsy Meyer in his class at school, who quilted and studied her Bible. Birdie was just Birdie, running around the fields, churning the butter, always the first to jump from the mow no matter how much hay was below.

"Your breath still smells like kerosene," she said.

"Dragon," he wrote in the dust on the floor. He pulled a half-eaten lollipop wrapped in paper from his pocket and held it out to her.

"Root beer?"

He nodded and she took it, popped the sucker in her mouth. Fred reached over and took her hand in his, and, with only the faintest of resistance from his sister, held it in his lap without looking at her. They passed the lollipop back and forth between them.

He wrote "apron" on the floor.

"Apron?" Birdie asked.

"Mama's," he wrote. He pointed to the mattress. "Found it." There. What a relief it was to free the secret, to hand it over to Birdie. He thought he could even feel his lungs expand, just a little.

The storms had buried the bones, now a large gray mound like an elephant, cow femurs protruding like tusks. If he didn't uncover them, Fred wondered if they would be found years later like dinosaur bones, leaving the diggers to wonder why all these bones were in a heap in the first place. Maybe he should write a note and bury it as a clue. He ran his hand down the cow bones warmed by the sun and brushed back the sand, cool underneath, grabbing hold to pull the first one out. But the effort brought on the coughing and he fell to his knees, waiting until a little air got in. Maybe he could use the bones to build a fort instead, the larger ones as supports, the smaller ones in piles to shore up a doorway.

He sat to rest, and then he noticed it was getting dark, which meant he should head home. Then he remembered it wasn't even noon and he looked up to the green-gray sky, at the clouds of dirt churning across the plain.

The dust was back, the wind blasting him and swirling about, disorienting and vehement in its insistence. He was out near the old pond, but he couldn't see the cottonwood near its edge, couldn't see past his arm really, the air like webs, clogging his nose and mouth. The mask was still in his pocket. He got it on but it didn't help, so he yanked it off. He pulled his shirt off to cover his face, the grit stinging his chest like tiny pins.

He would do what the animals did and dig a burrow and wait it out. He wished he had a shovel. The sand slipped through his fingers and the bones were lodged deep. His eyes were going black around the edges, tunneling. There was no air getting in and he sucked hard and the black went away for a spell. He tried to yell, but if any sound came out, it was swallowed whole by the wind.

"Look at the crows," Fred thought. Where did they come from, and how could they fly around in the swirling dust? There were two and then more and then a hundred at least, all black wings and sleek heads, cawing their warning cries above, and he closed his eyes and flew with them far above Mulehead, his arms out, soaring and swooping, and it was as if he'd been flying all his life. There was Woodrow's place where Birdie was hiding out, a baby in her belly that would be a girl, he now somehow knew. Up here, Birdie! She had shoved the mattress up against the window to block the storm and she looked sadder than a motherless calf, all folded up on herself, but he knew she would be okay so he flew on and there was the farm, his father pushing the door of the barn closed to keep the boat from getting walloped. The boat! The boat with ribs like a sleek and mighty animal. Maybe it would flood and maybe it wouldn't but, Pop, it is beautiful, and Mama, what was she doing, he thought, wedged into the corner of her bedroom under a quilt. He wanted to go to her, to hug her because she was crying and there was nothing worse than seeing your mother cry. Some people carried the world and didn't let God take any of the burden and they trudged on and on, minute, hour, day, until it started again and their shoes were a little more worn but they still laced them up each morning. Mama, Pop, Birdie — he wished he could lift them up so they could see what he saw. He swallowed all their secrets and they were gone.

He missed them all so hard it felt like he might fall to the ground, but he was still a crow and he was being pulled along with the others. One led him to the barbed-wire nest and inside it was deep and cozy, so different than it looked from the outside. It would last these storms, last the winter for three new eggs in the spring, but he couldn't stay even though he wanted to. He felt the tug of the earth and heard the roar of the duster's wrath and he was heavy and he squinted his eyes open to see he was on the ground, back to the bones. His legs were getting buried and he couldn't move. He watched the dust build up around his knees. "I am here but I am not here," he thought. "I am somewhere in the middle."

He didn't remember what it felt like to be angry or sad or scared and they were just words, black letters on paper that didn't mean anything and the wind took them anyway and left him with something that was warm and still. His chest was pulsing as fast as a crow's and he stopped hearing the wind at all. There was no more air.

He would miss the chickens — "Goodbye, girls" — and oatmeal cookies and school that started next week and splashing in the Cimarron when it was a river and laughing and marbles and quiet snowy nights and even brushing his teeth and driving the tractor and spring and the clouds and his family, oh his family.

He would miss everything.

He must have fallen over, because when he looked up it was through a lattice of bones, and beyond was the bluest sky, and then the sky opened up, cracked in two, and disintegrated into a million wings. The wind had gone quiet, replaced by a barely audible murmur, and he took a breath as clear and big as the sun.

CHAPTER 13

After coming in from the barn, pushing a towel under the door — the windows were still covered from the last storm — Samuel fell into the sofa, his eyes stinging, his hangover a vise at his temples. Where was everyone? Upstairs, probably. "Annie?" he called out. But the wind took the sound away and his mind slid. He needed water, but couldn't lift his boulder head. The boat came to him as it would look finished, hulkish but cleanly built, bobbing on dark water. His family was safe, lit intermittently by lightning, their faces somber, searching.

His calling. He'd heard the words, hadn't he? Now he couldn't summon exactly what he'd heard. He shouldn't drink, that much was certain, the blood a gong in his head.

Annie squeezed the folded letter in her fist and let herself cry, muffled as it was by the wind outside. The storm was a kind of answer. Three days away. She could do that. Even if it were lie upon lie, a visit to her parents in Kansas as cover. A hotel room for Mr. and Mrs. Jack Lily. Champagne in the thinnest glass flute. A big white bed with a feather duvet and the electric city outside the window. She looked at the blue dress. It was too dark to find a decent button, let alone sew, so she shoved it back into the armoire.

She heard the door slam downstairs. Birdie was back. Samuel would have retrieved Fred. She'd left out potato salad and bologna sandwiches she'd covered with a towel, and there was leftover vanilla pudding in the icebox. The storm bit at the house, but it didn't seem to have the same venom as the one that preceded it. The sheets would hold over the windows well enough. Annie was pretty certain that what was left in the garden — broccoli, carrots, pumpkins, potatoes — was hardy enough to weather the wind.

She drifted again, this time to thoughts of a baby, a girl, with a dewy face and tendril fingers and plump limbs, in the crook of her left arm. Maybe with Jack Lily there could be another baby. Healthy. One who would never know a dust storm.

The dust hung in the air, filtering the light

like fog. She slipped the folded-up letter into the bottom of her shoe. When the storm passed, she would go to town and find Jack. Gusts of wind whined and shook the walls, yet she felt as alive as a hummingbird. She closed her eyes and imagined Jack's soft hands on her face. A collision of lips and bodies, a breathless tangle. She felt her face flush as a bead of sweat ran down her side. Love or not, he made her feel like she could be a different woman.

She pulled a small suitcase from under the bed.

It was Birdie who found him. She'd known somehow that Fred had never made it home, an instinctual hollow dread. When the winds had finally calmed she'd run, her feet sinking in sand, toward where the pond used to be, yelling for her brother.

He looked as if he had fallen asleep, reclined with his arms crossed over his chest — his bare chest, she saw as she got closer — and in a moment of irrational hope she tried to convince herself he could be napping, his head on his balled-up shirt. You had me so worried, Freddie, you little weasel. But it wasn't true. Her words were a false front, a wobbly cardboard façade, his legs almost fully submerged in dirt.

She clawed at his arms and slapped him across the face, that little-boy face as pale as bone. His head lolled back, his eyes not quite closed, the whites, their terrible blankness, even under a seam of dust. She willed another storm, the biggest anyone had ever seen, a blizzard of black and grit and death, which could go ahead and bury them together.

Jack watched the sky from the window, snatches of blue through the detritus the clouds left behind.

"Short, at least," he said. "If you can be thankful for something."

Styron brushed off a binder. "And we ate already. Don't forget about that. Good thing, too. I was dying for that hamburger. Hattie's on a new modern-lady thing in the kitchen. Some Moroccan dish last night with raisins in the rice. Went to bed famished."

Styron was comfortable now mentioning Hattie to his boss. His stories usually cast him in some hapless husband role. Last week he had asked her to marry him in an intimate moment at the close of the evening, hoping she would reconsider her ironclad undergarments. She hadn't, but here they were, engaged.

"She okay about moving out here?"

"She'll be glad to give up her job. Set up house for us here. I have my sights on that fine Victorian of old lady Hollister's. She can't live forever."

Jack shook his head and laughed. The house had been built with sawmill money. Three floors, ornate wooden detailing, painted blue, white, and pink, like a house Mrs. Hollister had once seen in San Francisco. The storms had taken off much of the color, but it was still impressive, and Jack couldn't help but feel a little embarrassed by his modest apartment. Styron had balls, money, and enthusiasm, which was more than he could say about himself.

"It's a nice house," Jack said.

"You staying up there until your father . . ."

His father was speaking to the dead, his brother had said on the phone. "He says, 'Elaine, I'll have cinnamon toast with my oatmeal,' as if she's in the other room," his brother said. "He talks to you, too."

Jack swept dust off the desk and into his other hand.

"Yes, I suppose that's right," he said.

His thoughts returned to Annie, where they'd spent most of the day. She had read the letter by now, of course, and the waiting

286

and wondering made his mind seesaw. What if he had gone too far? What if she said yes? He would leave for Chicago in two days. Oh, to have Annie come with him. Or to join him later, arriving at Union Station, her bright country beauty against the city's hard gray angles. Yes, his father was dying, but Annie would make it better. Her sun-freckled collarbones.

"How long's your guess?"

"A few weeks most likely. So don't clean out my desk just yet."

Styron laughed, his cheeks colored. "I hope you don't miss the flood. Or I guess I hope you do miss it. We'll all be swept away. Except for the Bells."

Jack's stomach clenched.

"Sun is out," Styron said.

And so it was.

Birdie dug Fred out of the dirt and got his shirt back on. She did not want to leave him for the hovering crows, did not want to leave him alone. She funneled all her effort into dragging him home. It was awkward, his body both floppy and heavy. It would have been easier to pull him by his feet but she couldn't bear the idea of his head bumping along the ground. She grabbed under his arms and had to rest after a few yards, her back screaming from hunching over, the baby in her belly kicking its tiny feet. Trade the life in here for this one, she willed. Please? His boy smell. His goddamn pile of bones. Stop crying, she told herself, swiping her eyes with her sleeve.

Sand filled her shoes. Fred's splayed legs left two grooves in their wake. Her parents didn't know yet. She envied them. Dear silent Fred with his stubborn cowlick and eager smile. Uncle Freddie. Life without him already felt small and cold.

As she rounded a hillock of sagebrush, the sky a cheerful, mocking blue, Birdie knew that there was nothing left for her here. She didn't know how or when, but she would go, even if it meant picking someone else's potatoes, even if it meant going it alone.

"The children, Samuel. Where are they?"

Samuel started awake, and squinted against the harsh light. "They know what to do by now when the dust comes."

Annie turned away and yanked the sheet from the window.

"Fred shouldn't have been out. Condition he's in." Her balled fists hit her thighs.

"He'll be fine, Ann."

There was someone out there, she saw now, shielding her eyes from the glare, a lurching figure coming over the crest. Birdie's yellow sweater.

"Here they come": her words out just as she realized that she only saw Birdie, who was dragging something, dragging someone, dragging. A quiet wail escaped just before the world shrank to the point of a pin.

Samuel went to the barn as the light sank. He breathed shallow gulps through his mouth and tried not to look at the boat's hull, the crate Fred had positioned as a seat, the notebook that read: "Ever row a boat?" "Will it rain for 40 days?" "What's this called?" "Why do I need to go to school?" "I can hold my breath for half a minute."

He pulled planks from the stack of boxcar wood, five-footers about, some painted red, others green, black, blue. He couldn't bring himself to measure Fred's shoulders, so he guessed two feet would accommodate him. With each pass of the plane, he thought a chant so as not to think — Water, soil, light, water, soil, light. A seed is both the beginning and the end. A seed, a seed, a seed.

He framed out the casket quickly, his hands at home now with wood and nails. It would be a patchwork coffin, but it would be sound. Fred's own little boat.

■ ■ ■ ■

"There's no point in asking why things happen. We don't get to know why." Pastor Hardy sounded angry, unconvinced. He blustered on, his Arkansas drawl like quicksand. "It is one of the terrible mysteries of faith. Even Jesus in his darkest hour asks his father, 'My God, my God, why hast thou forsaken me?' "

There was no wind, no clouds, no trees.

Annie didn't hear any of it, thankfully, or she might have run at him. She was made of tin, hollow and rusted, stuck on her feet, knees rigid. Samuel reached for her hand, but hers hung stiff at her side. The coffin he had made was colorful from the boxcar lumber, cruelly festive. Small. Her quilt, the one she'd made for Fred as a baby, padded the box, and the thought of all those stitches made as her belly had grown, finally, a full two years after the death of Eleanor, was what brought the sting to her eyes. She started to cant forward and would have keeled over onto her face had Samuel not locked her shoulders in the grip of his arm to hold her up.

She looked straight into the sun, her eyes a blur of hot light.

"We need not ask where our home is, because in the end we all come home to God."

Birdie cried into her hands. Everyone was there, damn near the whole town. Annie's people had not come — her father's rheumatism made travel impossible — and Samuel, his parents long dead, had lost track of any family that remained. They stood alone, the three of them, a small slouched huddle.

"God is never not there for us — hah — every minute, every hour, every day — hah — the light, the Lord — hah — the way, the Word — every minute, there to lift us — hah — God is our strength — hah — May the grace of our Lord Jesus Christ, and the love of God, and the fellowship of the Holy Ghost be with us all, evermore."

With a nod from the pastor, Samuel released Annie and stepped forward.

Annie could not stay to watch her son go into the ground. She would not listen to the pastor reduce him to ashes and dust. She turned around and walked, past her neighbors, past Ruth and Jeanette, past the Jensens and the Hollisters, past Styron and the chatty woman who would soon be his wife. Past Jack Lily, who raised his hand in greeting or sympathy or farewell.

She looked past him, stumbling on the

hard-bitten terrain, and kept walking.

Birdie told herself to remember how Fred would sit across the table eating his peas one by one with a fork, but it didn't work. It had been forty-nine hours. We have been left alone, she thought. All those times she had wanted to be left alone and now that was all she had and she would give anything for it not to be true.

The baby pushed her belly out some now, her dress tight, the black dress she hadn't worn since the Jensen girl died of fever a year back. The child had been laid out on her bed for a viewing, her skin eggshell white. Birdie had touched the girl's black curls when no one was looking, hoping they might feel different. They didn't.

She would go to school next week and try to forget everything. The dirt crumbled under the shovel, a dry splash against the coffin her father had made. Another shovelful and another. She would fill in the hole herself. Her father was on his knees grabbing the dirt with his hands. Get up, she thought. Get up.

Where was her mother going? No one went after her. Birdie watched her get smaller until she thought she would disappear.

Last night Birdie had heard sounds and had gone downstairs and there was her mother in her nightgown at the window. Birdie could see the outline of her body and it made her breath catch, like she hadn't thought of her as a woman before and here she was exposed. Her mother had secrets too, she now knew, like why had she gone to Woodrow's and taken off her apron? The mayor, the mayor. But there was nothing to make of it now, was there? Birdie wanted to say, "Mama, there will be a baby," but she didn't. Her mother's hand was flat against the glass, and then she turned around and her eyes darted shiny and Birdie said, "Mama," in case she couldn't see her, "are you all right?" She didn't say anything but turned back to the window and Birdie went up to bed where she listened to the muffled hiccups of her father crying into his pillow.

Ashes to ashes. Pastor Hardy could barely bring himself to say dust.

Birdie had the chickens now and she didn't care about them the way Fred had and they knew it. They scratched and rooted at her ankles when she filled the water. She wanted to kick them because he was dead.

Somewhere west the colors were bright. Green like she hadn't seen in forever.

Fred won't wait for the bus with me, she

thought, won't bounce along on those terrible wooden benches nailed into old Farlow's truck as he picked up every last farm kid. Fred won't be an uncle. Fred won't stumble and right himself and smile, always smile, even when kids teased him, even when he couldn't breathe.

Now they were less. The hole was filling with dirt. Someone had taken the shovel from her hands.

Jack lowered his hand. What he had meant by the gesture he wasn't sure, but now it seemed a wave goodbye. The window to Annie had been shut, he knew, and he would never know if there truly had been a way in. He could not offer comfort. He could not offer escape now.

'Tis better to have loved and lost, he thought, though he couldn't remember who had written it. Some poet who didn't know a thing. He watched her walk, her beat-up shoes against the scabrous ground, her arms wrapped around herself. He couldn't go after her, he knew that much.

Samuel insisted on lifting the coffin down by himself. The awkward weight and angle of the box made a corner drop hard into the hole. But leave it to Bell to have made a solid and handsome vessel for his son. Samuel climbed out and shoveled in dirt with his bare hands until Hardy helped him to his feet.

Jack knew it was all over. There was no reason to delay. He would leave for Chicago this afternoon. He would get in the car and drive away.

McGuiness could see the funeral from where he sat in the shade of a scrub juniper. The sad lot of stooped figures reminded him of toadstools. His jar of corn whiskey — Ruth had cut him off — was down to its fiery dregs. It was radiator distilled, probably full of lead, but McGuiness didn't bother burning it to find out. Since Joe had told him about the kid dying, McGuiness had drowned himself in hooch.

That serves you right, Bell, how do you like your great God now?

But he felt pity deep in his gut, like a quivering mound of gelatin. That poor son of a bitch with his conviction.

A prairie falcon circled above, eyeing a jackrabbit twice its size.

Fuck it all, he said. Everybody dies. Everyone's children die. Life goes on. He emptied the jar down his gullet, sediment and all, and came up wheezing. He coughed and spat. Now was the time to rob the old broad's place. Hurl the jar right through the window, make out with at least two fists of whiskey, if not the till.

But he'd gotten too drunk and had let himself feel bad for Bell and now he'd lost sight of the anger that usually pushed him to do such things. The falcon dove, and its beak speared the rabbit's neck just as its talons grabbed hold of skin and fur. The bird rose, unsteadily, its muscled wings working fiercely against the weight of its prey whose legs thrashed against the air.

And then there was Bell's wife — too skinny, but a looker nonetheless — no more than fifty yards off, walking toward him. He tried to scramble to his feet, but his boots skidded in the dry dirt and he fell hard, his back against the rough bark of the tree as he slid down. He was only up on his unsteady knees by the time she was upon him. She really was a waif of a thing — her black dress hung off her bony shoulders. McGuiness's swimming head kept him stuck there in his ridiculous prostration, afraid if he got up now it would frighten her.

"I'm sorry," he said, looking at the ground, his words thick and growly.

She looked at McGuiness for the first time, her faced scrunched, eyes vacant. She stopped walking.

"Can you drive me someplace?" she asked.

CHAPTER 14

McGuiness eyed his vehicle: the fender gone, the door rusted through and secured with rope. How long had it been since a woman had been in his truck? The seat was strewn with the evidence of his life: bits of copper pipe, an oily crowbar, wire cutters, an empty whiskey bottle, a filthy towel. How did he smell? Not good, he was sure.

"Let me just move some of this," he said, pushing it all onto the floor. "Okay. There you go." He thought he should help her so he stood with his hand out, but she didn't acknowledge it and climbed in, tucking her skirt under her as she sat.

Annie wanted to be away from that terrible digging. Away, away. From convention and expectations and everyone she knew. No one else's sorrow mattered. She focused on the crack in the windshield and then beyond to a vacant field where dust swirled in small billows, back to the broken glass, and then the distance, again and again. She would not allow herself to see her son's face.

McGuiness felt oafish and self-conscious, neither sober nor drunk enough, as he passed around to the driver's side. She bounced as he heaved himself behind the wheel, and he was hit with his own sweat-and-liquor stench. The funeral service had not yet concluded and here was Bell's wife beside him. He could think of nothing to say.

"Ma'am?"

She stared ahead, her gaze glassy and unfocused. He wiped his palms against his trousers and cleared his throat.

"Mrs. Bell? Did you have someplace in mind?"

She shook her head, so he started the engine with its chug and roar and pulled out slowly toward town.

"I'm sorry for your loss," he said, barely recognizing his tight, formal voice.

She turned away, unable to be polite, unable even to ask this brutish man's name. When Eleanor had died, Annie thought grief would snuff her out, thought it would close in like a sodden blanket, heavy over her face until she could no longer see or breathe. But her body didn't give in. She kept waking up. Her lungs took in air and let it out. Her heart went on with its callous rhythm. So here she was again with an ache and anger that pulled her skin taut. She knew better than to think death might relieve her. She would live on and on.

McGuiness drove past town, glancing at his passenger, checking to see if she might come to and ask him to stop.

"Time will pass," he said, trying again.

"I don't want to go home," she said.

Just drive, she thought. She didn't want to go anywhere. She didn't want to be seen. Where was there to go in a town where everyone knew you? She wanted to be swallowed by the open plains, the bitter glare of late sun, the inexhaustible sky.

"Oh, okay." He slowed the truck and spun around in a U, the rear tires dipping into the ditch until he gunned it back onto the road. He looked at her, waiting, but she still did not speak. He drove west because he liked it better.

They drove and drove, a brown expanse in every direction, the truck rumbling, the wind loud through the open windows.

McGuiness sniffed. "Fall's coming," he said. He'd forgotten for a minute about the boy and then remembered and shook his head. He needed more whiskey.

"You're not a farmer, are you?" she asked.

"I ain't a farmer, no."

And then Annie was quiet again for miles. Fields gave way to ranchland, and flatness to small rises. Dried-out thistles, stubborn wild sunflowers, and soapweed yuccas held ground along the road amidst the grasses not broken out by plows. She had never heard Fred say her name, but it didn't matter. It had always felt to her as if she knew his voice in her head. Mama, the moths are buzzing in the yuccas. Let's take a lantern and go out and see them tonight. Yes, my love, let's do that. She ground her knuckle against the corroded door of the truck, the sting quick and sharp.

They came to a small sign with an arrow pointing the way to Black Mesa, the highest point in Oklahoma.

"You ever been up there?" he asked, slowing to a stop. She didn't answer. "Want to see it?"

It was a nod, he thought, the slight bob of her head, so he turned north, hoping there was enough gasoline in the truck, the gauge long busted.

As they drove, small buttes began to interrupt the open plains, and groves of cottonwoods appeared, the most trees Annie had seen in years. Prairie dogs scooted into holes, a fat bullsnake lazed in the sun. The road looped and turned; down and then up again they climbed, surrounded by canyons carved deep into the sandstone. Annie had seen this place from afar, the high mesas in the distance, but there had never been reason to see it up close, and now it seemed the only place she could be, lost in this strange wilderness that went up and up. McGuiness jerked to a stop at the base of a steep slope, the truck's tires spinning gravel, until all was quiet except the scolding call of the chickadees in the juniper trees.

"Can't go no further," McGuiness said. "Except on foot. Must be five miles or so to the top."

Annie unknotted the rope holding the door closed and felt the marked coolness of the air, tufts of grass at her feet. She started walking.

"Mrs. Bell?"

McGuiness spilled out from behind the wheel, sober enough, and ran his hands through his greasy hair. Even he knew it was not a good idea to set out this late in the day — What about water? What about snakes? — but hell, here was a woman, a fine woman.

"Wait up," he said, as he hitched up his pants.

She didn't wait, walking fast, her mourning dress like a ghostly shroud ahead of him. He was soon winded, but he pushed on, keeping her in his sights. He wondered if his hands could fit all the way around that slender little waist.

It seemed the temperature fell with every step up, every step away from Mulehead. Annie felt she would never stop walking, no matter how many hours it took to reach the top. My child, my child, my child. All alone. And where was I? Her foot slipped on a crag, and her ankle twisted at an odd angle, but she didn't stop. A coldness had come into her. Her limbs, her head. Cold like the marble floor of her father's church. Her ankle hurt but she wanted it to hurt more. Nothing, she feared, would ever be enough to distract from her despair. She deserved everything.

"Hey," McGuiness said. "Sun's dipping. Don't want to get caught too high in the dark now."

"It's no matter to me," Annie said, surprised by the sound of her own voice, gravelly and low.

"Hard to tell how much longer to the top. With these steppes and ridges and all."

Her ankle was hot and wobbly. Annie paused to turn it this way and that, before taking in the man's dirty girth, the missing part of his tooth, his huge pawlike hands. A current ran through her, a quick and uneasy zip. She deserved whatever came next, too.

"Whew. You like a man to chase you, huh?"

She stared back blankly, her eyes puffy and gray. I should be afraid, she thought, as though she were watching herself from far away, but fear had lost its power. There was little left of her to take.

"Why don't we have a seat on that outcropping," he said.

Then his hand was on her back and he was guiding her off the path, into the scrub, and Annie knew things had taken a turn. She could run, she thought, or call for help, not that anyone would hear her, but she walked on. She would not scream, she knew. Do what you will with me, she thought. Make me disappear.

McGuiness wiped the dirt from a stone ledge, clearing a place for her to sit. Even he could be a gentleman, he thought.

Annie sat, her hands gripping her knees, every muscle as stiff and brittle as kindling. He scooched closer until their thighs touched, but she didn't move away. What awfulness happens next, she wondered. Disgust rose up in her at the man's smell, his dirty pants. He draped his arm over her shoulders and she had to brace herself for the weight of it.

He leaned into her. It felt so easy and right, as it had never felt for him, and he thought maybe this was what he needed all along to make a real go of it. A woman by his side.

"I'll take you for a steak later," he said.

She felt herself get smaller and smaller, a cold hard pebble. She wouldn't flee but neither would she make it easy for him. He rubbed her shoulder, but she sat still, watching the pale sky, the clouds going pink, wishing it were a week ago, a month, years.

She did not soften and McGuiness couldn't even feel her breathe. She was stone, and he felt like a dog sniffing after something and that familiar shame, that fury came creeping back into him at this woman who would not yield. We'll see, he thought. He twisted toward her, so he might squeeze both of his meaty hands around the delicate bones of her deserted face.

There was a clattering above them and two khaki-clad figures stepped down from a ledge. McGuiness dropped his hands, startled, and then he lumbered to his feet.

"Howdy, folks," one of them said. "Surprised to see anyone up this way." His glasses were dusted and he carried a small box under his arm. The other man held a burlap sack straining from the weight it held.

At the sound of voices, Annie felt a trickle of relief from some distant point outside herself for just a moment until Fred, oh Fred.

McGuiness spat into the dirt. "Who are you?"

"We're up there digging," one said.

"We're the dinosaur people," said the other.

"The fuck you talking about?" McGuiness said.

The man pushed his glasses up, looking from Annie to McGuiness and then back to Annie.

"Found a tibia," he said. "Looking for the rest of her. Forty feet long. From the Jurassic period."

"Bones," Annie said.

McGuiness relaxed his stance a little at the sound, at last, of her voice.

"Bones?" he asked.

"That's right. Dinosaur bones, fossils," the other man said.

"What kind of fool job is that?" McGuiness asked.

"You can see footprints," the man in the glasses said. "Not far from here. From an *Antrodemus.* Preserved in the creek bed about ten miles west."

Annie almost smiled. Fred would have loved this most of all.

"Best be careful this time of night," the other said. "The rattlers are out."

"Jesus," McGuiness said, eyeing the ground around his feet. "You all got any whiskey on you?"

"Are you okay, ma'am?" the man with the glasses asked quietly.

" 'Course she's okay," McGuiness said, spitting again.

Annie thought of Birdie and Samuel and how they would be needing supper, the tiniest speck of light somewhere that signaled she was still a wife and mother. It was happening again, all the little things to do, which would get her to another night and then another morning.

"The light's almost gone. Don't want to lose it entirely."

The other man shifted his heavy bag to his shoulder, eager to get going, but the man with the glasses stood waiting.

"We were just heading down," she said. "Done admiring the view."

McGuiness had lost his edge; his shoulders slumped in defeat. The moment was over. She rose and followed the men down the path. It was a choice, she knew, going back to the family that remained, back to who she had been.

McGuiness felt himself deflate, unable to rescue his mood. His stinking boots couldn't find good purchase on the descent, and he tripped, landing hard on his knee. She did not stop.

They drove silently back toward Mulehead in the indigo twilight; an orange glow still clung to the horizon. As they neared the end of the driveway Annie finally spoke.

"I'll get out here."

The house was quiet. The kitchen counter was crowded with food: casseroles, breads, pies, baked squash, canned pickles, strawberry preserves. Annie had forgotten about how the town mobilized for a death. The generosity automatic and unobtrusive. We do for you and you do for us, because out here we only have each other. She probably wouldn't have liked the anonymity of Chicago, anyway. Fred is gone, Fred is gone. She would not let herself remember him yet. Find room in the icebox, turn on the oven, churn some butter. It was easier to do than to feel.

She could hear pounding coming from the barn. Of course Samuel would be out there working on the boat, and it made her want to take a lead pipe and smash it to pulp. The goddamn boat. She splashed water on her face and pressed her eyes with a towel until the tears passed. A sliver of a thought — Jack Lily, Chicago, a seat on the train. It was light and air and forgetting. She knew he was already gone.

She went out the back door, stepping gingerly on her tender ankle, but couldn't bring herself to go to the barn. The air had a freshness that she'd been seeking for months. Summer was over. Birdie was going back to school and Fred was not.

"I hate you," Birdie said, kicking the coop door shut behind her.

"Did you eat?"

"Oh. I didn't see you there in the dark," Birdie said.

"I'm warming something up."

"Where'd you go?"

"I put a chicken-and-noodle dish in the oven."

"Mrs. Stem. Mary brought it in."

"I bet your father hasn't eaten anything today."

"Who's hungry, anyway?" Birdie shrugged and let her gangly arms fall.

Annie still had a child. She reached her arms out and cupped her daughter's face with her hand. That young and lovely face.

Her hair was unbrushed and sun-lightened, as it had been every summer since she was small.

"Why don't you go and lie down, Mama," she said.

But Annie couldn't lie down.

"I'll set out plates in a bit. You can help yourself."

Annie approached the barn and listened to the lull of sandpaper against wood. She stood just inside the door, her eyes adjusting to the low light, and there it was. The boat. It was a sight to behold, dwarfing the barn around it, solid and noble and true. Patchwork colors like the casket, but sanded clean with just a hint of hues in stripes along the body. Samuel was bent over the hull of the boat. He looked old to her, weathered and worn, smaller. He wore his sorrow in his hunched shoulders, the near fevered intensity with which he worked the wood.

"I haven't seen a boat since Kansas," she said.

Samuel stopped and stood up, but didn't turn around. He swiped at his eyes with his wrist.

"Nowhere to launch it since O'Malley's dried up."

There had been a night in their first year on the plains, the dugout dug, the stars in

310

July as bright as the lights of Kansas City, the heat like melted butter. They rode the wagon out to O'Malley's pond, a good five miles bumping over a rutted road, the horses clattering their bits, unsure of the night ride. She'd gone in the water in her dress, too shy to take off her clothes even though there was no one else for miles. The water was as warm as the air; she could barely tell the difference. Samuel had pulled off his shirt, but waited till she turned to take off the rest. He waded in and held her, her head against his shoulder, while she floated.

"I'll bring a plate out for you."

"Okay." He leaned against the boards scaffolding the boat, unable to fully look at her.

"You want bread with it?"

"I don't care about the food."

"I know."

"Fred used to sit on the crate there. Pretend to row."

"I'll leave you to your work," she said.

"Annie."

Her name in the barn dusk was the most plaintive of sounds.

"Are you still going to go?"

Annie felt like a marble falling, falling, falling into the blackness of a well.

"It might do you good. To see your folks."

Kansas. He was talking about Kansas.

"No. It was a dumb idea to begin with."

"You left today."

"I couldn't watch the dirt going in."

He nodded.

"How come we've never gone up to Black Mesa?" she asked.

"Black Mesa?"

"You can see a long way from up there is what I hear."

His eyes squinched, quizzical, but she held them with her own for the slimmest of moments. I am still here, she thought.

"We can go sometime if you like."

She nodded, the smell of sawdust too strong, and she felt the need for air.

"I'm going to go check on Birdie."

Without waiting for what Samuel might say, she walked out of the barn.

The baby moved. Birdie didn't think about whether it was a girl or a boy. She didn't care either way. It was her body, but it already felt like someone else's. She picked at the biscuit, pressing her finger on the crumbs to pick them up. The house was quiet save for the clock and the occasional settling beam. She thought of the funny papers yellowing on the floor of Fred's room.

Her legs were moving before she knew where she was going. She had to run. She burst through the kitchen and living room, banging out the front door, a stitch already in her side before she'd even reached the locust tree grove. Every direction was the same. Flat, colorless, known.

That left Woodrow's. Maybe she could do the job that she and Fred had started. Take down the whole damn thing, window by window, board by board.

She took the long way, by road, walking right in the middle, the shoes she'd worn to the funeral rubbing her heels bloody. It felt better to walk, to grind her feet against the pavement, to be headed somewhere, even somewhere as dismal as Woodrow's. The sky was a cauldron of purple and orange with the last remnant sunlight.

One of the headlights of the truck was burned out, the other a dim yellow, so it was right upon her before she noticed and skittered to the edge of the road. The truck slowed next to her as she walked, pumping her arms. She could feel it creeping along-side her and when she turned it was McGuiness, the scavenger whom she and Fred had encountered so long ago. He was here and Fred was gone. She could see the side of his mouth tug up even in the growing darkness, and she looked ahead and kept walking, rage in her mouth like metal.

"Want a ride?"

"Not from you."

He laughed. "Well, ain't you a spitfire."

He did not scare her. She felt as impermeable as a river stone.

"I won't bite."

There was some dank crevice of her mind that wanted to say yes, to ride the current all the way to the bottom. She felt the baby kick. The moon was waning, sickle-shaped with piercing ends.

"I know it was your brother," he said.

She would not look at him.

"Sorry. All's I'm saying," he said.

She turned and walked straight into a stubbled field.

"Suit yourself," he called after her, before rattling away toward town.

It was so dark at Woodrow's, she had to feel her way along the walls, the wallpaper ribboned and curled up under her palm, planks rough underneath, up the stairs to the bedroom. Glass sparkled on the floor beneath the windows. Sweaty from the walk, Birdie peeled off her mourning dress, glad to be free of it, and lay down in her underwear. Her abdomen swelled in a small taut pot where she rested her hands.

She was plain tired and closed her eyes.

Maybe her mother had needed a hiding place, too, and that's all it was. She'd taken off her apron — a break from rendering lard, canning tomatoes, washing trousers — to just sit for a minute by herself. She knew her mother's life was hard, never gave her credit for it, and now Birdie felt a black nugget like coal, sharp-edged in her throat, with the thought of that life closing in on her, too. She had been a silly girl to think she knew better.

The wind was calm tonight and brushed in through the broken-out windows. Are you up there, Freddie? she thought. And for a moment the loneliness ebbed and her thoughts drifted and she was floating in blue salty water, bobbing and buoyant, and it didn't matter that she couldn't swim because it was like she was suspended by a giant invisible hand.

Annie brought a lantern, not trusting the slim moon. When Birdie had not returned by nightfall, she set out to look for her, bleary with sleeplessness and grief, crazed by the thought of her one remaining child out there, at the mercy of every evil thing. She walked, her ankle throbbing, toward

Woodrow's, the thought of which brought a gust of sorrow for what she had done there, but she pressed on through the chaparral that grabbed at her legs, the surprising cry of a coyote — she thought they had all vanished — a sad moan in the distance. Fred had died all by himself. That little boy she would have kept little forever. Please let him not have felt scared. But with whom was she pleading? Annie's toe caught an old root and the lantern bobbled, sending its halo of light in a dance across the dune along the fence. She would wake up every day and think, He is gone, and feel that gutted feeling anew. Can the strawberries, He is gone. Hang the sheets, He is gone. Lie down for sleep, He is gone.

The old house leaned like a beached ship, the front door half buried. How fast it had become a relic, a ruin. Here she had been with Jack Lily, and now she felt as dull as clay. Inside she held the lantern high.

"Birdie?"

She listened for noises, but heard only the insects, the cricket song anemic and spotty. When she had come here with Jack, she had never looked around, and the forlorn kitchen was now barely recognizable. Thick webs traversed the sink; one broken teacup upside down on the counter. She wondered if the Woodrows dreamed of coming back here one day, and what would be left if they did.

Annie walked to the staircase and climbed slowly, the steps sagging underfoot.

"Birdie?" Her voice sounded foreign and strained in the darkness.

And there in the silvery light was her daughter, her head on her bunched-up dress, stretched out like a resting nymph, and Annie's first terrible thought was, She's dead too, until she saw her chest rise and fall. Annie sank to her knees and blinked against the image of this body in front of her, more womanly than she had realized, her daughter's hair spilling over the side of the mattress where she herself had been loved by Jack Lily, and where, Annie knew, Birdie had lain with Cy Mack. Oh Birdie, she thought, and before she could reach out her hand, she saw the belly, unmistakable in its firm, smooth insistence. Annie knew on this day that had gone on forever, a day that had sliced her thin, that her daughter was carrying the most profound of secrets.

There would be a baby.

CHAPTER 15

What happened to fall? Samuel wondered. A few weeks at the most. Some tillers came up from the planting, but they went dormant too early. At least the growth gave the cows something to eat, better than the dregs they were going on before. The snow came in gray gusts, too little to prime the soil. Thin light, early dark, penitent cold.

He knew they were all waiting for the big snow that would help the crop that was in. No one said it out loud, yet everyone thought it, prayed for it, believed it.

Samuel sat apart from the other men at Ruth's, siphoning a beer. His eyes were downcast, his hands heavy on the wooden bar. Since Fred, he found solace here sometimes where the others, with enough life trouble of their own, left him be. It calmed him to hear them talk, their broken-in voices. He listened to two men sitting one stool away, farmers he'd seen before but wouldn't say he knew.

"I hear they got an X-ray machine over at the shoe store in Beauville."

"X-ray machine?"

"So they can see where your toes are at in your shoes."

"Why in hell they want to do that?"

"To get a perfect fit."

"Must be the strangest thing to see all those bones of your feet."

"Ruthie? Got any peanuts or something? My stomach's talking."

Samuel watched little Ruth walk toward them, her white bun high on her head, her cherry-candy lipstick bleeding into the seams around her mouth.

"Kidding me? You-all would never leave," she said. "You been courting that beer all night as it is."

Samuel was glad for the distraction from the grim business of winter. At home, the three of them trudged forward, hunkered down by the season, each doing and doing — boat, school, house, larder, church — without looking up,

"How old are them dinosaur bones, any-way?" one of the men said.

"Thousands of years old. Millions? I don't know."

"Before Adam and Eve?"

"It's confusing, isn't it?"

The men lowered their voices, but Samuel could still hear them, Ruth's mostly emptied out by now.

"Speaking of the Old Testament, you hear about the boat?"

"Heard about it."

"I almost wish the damn flood would come. Sorry lot he drew," one of the men said.

Jeanette, who had sauntered in from the café, stood in front of them and blew smoke in their direction. "Will you two just shut up?" she said.

"It's all right," Samuel said.

"I meant no disrespect," one of the farmers said.

Samuel nodded, not caring what people thought. Jeanette fiddled with the radio dial until she hit on a crackly big band number.

"So the mayor never came back."

"Can't really blame him."

Samuel was sorry about that. He had liked Jack Lily, appreciated his seriousness, his equanimity.

Jeanette stubbed out her cigarette in the old snuff tin on the counter and filled Samuel's beer.

"We're stuck with that college kid," one of the farmers said.

"Think you could do better? Throw your old hat in the ring then," she said.

"You know me, doll face. I'm not good for much."

She laughed.

"I do believe that's the first time I've ever heard you tell the truth," she said, shaking her backside as she walked away.

"I hear Dwight's got himself on the dole."

"A fiddle don't pay the bills."

"We're all a bunch of fools trying to farm the desert."

"Can't argue with you there," Samuel said. The men nodded in solemn agreement.

He watched the calendar, always eager to x out another short and brutal day. He watched the weather, hoping for snow deep and white but settling for gray pellets that felt like buckshot on his skin. We watch each other, Samuel thought, so tired of these careworn faces.

"We got eggs," one of the farmers said.

"No shit?"

"The girls are laying."

"Well, hell. Here I thought spring would never come."

Ruth rang her cowbell for last call.

"Don't make me go, Ruthie."

"I'll be open tomorrow." Her tongue

rooted around her teeth until she worked something out. "You can dream about me in the meantime."

Samuel drank what was left in his glass, lifting it again to get the very last of it. He had made it through another day.

Samuel and Annie didn't talk about what they had lost. Annie packed Fred's shirts and pants and socks with holes in them and half-used notepads and rusty toy cars and comic strips and bitten pencils and egg tabulation charts and a postcard Samuel had sent him from Oklahoma City — the only mail he'd ever gotten — and the pillowcase that still smelled faintly of little-boy hair, in a small tin trunk she took out to the old dugout.

And then Samuel raised his eyes one day and they had done it, it was March, and they had made it through the freeze. He could feel the earth, himself, soften, ever so slightly. He could go longer without gloves on, work longer without lights on. Spring is God's promise, Pastor Hardy said.

The chicks had begun to peck at their shells from the inside, breaking through. Spring came barreling in like a circus train, with colors, sounds, and smells they had all almost forgotten were possible. The grass-hoppers were gone. The still-damp ground held, and the warming days brought the wheat out, tillers reaching up to the sun.

Samuel had finished the boat.

Styron was giddy. The ground was still exposed for miles and the snowmelt had not been enough, but the communal sense in Mulehead was that, with spring, things were looking up. But more important, Jack Lily had written to say that he was staying in Chicago indefinitely, tying up his father's affairs, managing the creamery with his brother. Styron would be acting mayor until the next election. He shoved the piles of papers on the mayor's desk ceremoniously to the side with a sweep of his arm. Hattie had given him a glass owl paperweight, which he moved to the desk, along with his "big idea" binder and his coffee thermos. He left the ledgers and budgets and tax codes and federal guidelines for assistance where they were.

It was only weeks until his wedding, and he thought of Hattie now with great affection. Her adoration. Her warm hands and ready laugh. He didn't worry about love. He would christen the old Hollister house the Mayoral Mansion. He and Hattie would spend their wedding night there, amid the smell of borax and new paint.

"Styron."

He bolted up as if caught in the act itself.

"Sorry to come unannounced." It was Samuel Bell. How small he looked, Styron thought, with his sunken cheeks and hanging trousers.

"The mayor's door is always open," Styron said, arms wide.

Bell cocked his head a little and pursed his lips.

"Jack's not coming back. Got the word this morning."

"Congratulations, then. You've been doing a fine job of it already, I suspect."

"Appreciate that." Styron remembered then how Gladys Abernathy had cornered him after church a few weeks back.

"It's a disgrace, this business with the Bell girl," she'd said. "Flaunting it like that. In school. In front of the other children. It's obscene is what it is."

"What would you have me do, ma'am?"

"Make her take her studies at home."

Have you forgotten about the boy they lost, he'd wanted to ask her.

Styron felt for the Bells, so he had been dragging his feet on the matter. There had been an anonymous letter, too, last week, signed "Concerned mothers." People down on their luck were always looking for something to chew on to make them feel worthy.

"I was in town, thought I'd stop by," Samuel said.

Bell wasn't going to ask about going on assistance, now, was he? Styron thought.

"What's on your mind?" Styron asked.

"The boat's done."

Styron clapped.

"Well, goddamn. Excuse my language."

Styron imagined the ark in the center of the town square. You decided what you had that no other town had; then you marketed it until the cows came home. You told people it was a place to visit, you made it so.

"I could use some help. To get it out of the barn."

"Great, great. Let's haul her out!" Styron was nearly at the door. "Can I get a ride with you?"

"I've got Ford and Jensen and his boys coming Saturday round noon. Lunch, of course."

"Oh, sure. Saturday. Saturday would be fine."

"Bring Hattie if you'd like. Annie could use the company."

■ ■ ■ ■

At school no one derided Birdie, but no one talked to her either. Mary Stem counted discovering Birdie's pregnancy as one of her greatest achievements. Birdie had made it a good way into winter before the whispering had begun. Mary noticed that Birdie could no longer button her coat. Before the truth had come out, Luke Carlton had asked her to the dance. She'd sewn two side panels of floral fabric into the dress her mother had made her for her sixteenth birthday. A week later, he'd disinvited her with a smudged note he'd handed to her on the bus.

Birdie's chair was now so far back from her desk she had to lean over to get pencil to paper. It was a good thing she had to make an effort to reach, or she was sure to fall asleep. She took her shame and rolled it around in her mind until it came out as defiance — she didn't care much about school, but she never considered that she should stop coming, and, after Fred, her parents didn't seem to notice much of what she did. Her father had his boat, which he had taken to sleeping in, working until exhaustion, then dragging himself under a load of blankets in its center. Her mother cleaned and cleaned, determined to rid the house of every last speck of grit and dust. When she wasn't cleaning, she read books — her only outings were to church and to the library in Herman — boring old ones like Birdie had to read for English class. With spring, she had her garden. Her mother looked at Birdie strangely but she never got angry. Disappointed, of course, but distant. There had been no great scene and there wouldn't be.

She thought about the apron sometimes. Why was it there, Mama? Her mother wasn't forgetful, didn't lose things. Birdie turned over her suspicions in her mind: she and the mayor together behind the church, him driving all the way to the house, talking through the screen, Fred had told her. There was what you saw and there was the hidden life underneath, and you don't know it when you're a child and then you do and growing up doesn't seem so great anymore. And then she remembered the day she and Cy had come upon Jack Lily at Woodrow's. Where Fred had found her mother's apron. The mattress. Putting the two of them together there made her feel suspended, the ground out of reach. She tried to push the idea away. If it was true — and how could it possibly be true? — it was better to let it be, she told herself. Jack Lily was gone. Her mother was not.

It was increasingly difficult to milk the cow, but she went out morning and night to tend to Greta without complaint. She never saw her parents talk. When Birdie spoke, it sounded too loud in the silent house. Her words hung in the air until she wasn't sure if anyone had heard her at all. An elbow poked out, or a foot or a fist, as the baby turned over, the whoosh a feeling she had not gotten used to.

Birdie was glad for school, if only to get out of the house. The classroom smelled of chalk and old wood and musty textbooks, but it was comforting. I will remember this room with fondness, she thought, when I'm a thousand miles away from here. She did not have a plan. She dreamed of jumping a train heading west. She dreamed of oranges.

Annie didn't mind cooking for the men. It was good that Jack Lily didn't come back, she told herself, but it was hard to shelve possibility, the hazy what-if. She had finally unpacked the suitcase she'd hidden under the bed. She diced winter carrots and cut the eyes from potatoes, and now, everything with him seemed so long ago. When the

world had Fred in it. When she was different.

Samuel called her Annie again all the time
now, a new gentleness in his voice. They
were careful with each other, hesitant,
unsure. They refused to disagree. Whatever
you'd like. It's okay with me. You're right.
You don't? Okay, I don't either.

"Annie? Styron's not here yet, but we're
going to get started."

"Okay," she said, pulling a remnant feather
from a chicken.

"Wish us luck."

She smiled. "You'll do just fine."

It was the kind of day that made them all
forget about how bad it had been. Just warm
enough in the sun, the air thick with the
smells of earth and dung and hay. Ford, a
squat man with a thick neck, farmed to the
south, and wiry Jensen, who had come to
Mulehead at the same time as Samuel,
farmed toward Beaver with his grown sons.
There had been a time when the three had
joined together for threshing before they
each got their own tractor-pulled machine.
They had all come to the Plains looking for
a future, and Samuel knew they were as tied
to the land as he was. No number of dust
storms and weak yields would chase them
off. They didn't talk about what the boat

was for. But they answered the call because they were neighbors, because they had history.

"You sure we're getting this thing out?" Jensen asked.

"We're going to try," Samuel said.

"I guess we got God on our side," Ford said, eliciting a chuckle from Jensen's two sons.

"Maybe he'll give us a little push," Samuel said, smiling.

Styron arrived with Hattie done up in a purple dress with a matching hat. An enameled peacock brooch sat high on her chest. The men stopped and watched as they got out of the car.

"Mayor of Mulehead," Ford said under his breath.

"And his queen," Jensen's son added.

"He's here to help," Samuel said.

Styron jogged over, his cheeks ruddy.

"Gentlemen," he said.

The others nodded.

"Thanks for coming," Samuel said.

He pulled open the doors of the barn, and the sun shot through to the boat, illuminating the hulking midsection, whose supports pushed right against the barn walls.

"You son of a gun," Jensen said. "You really did it."

Styron looked like a boy who'd hooked his first fish. "Outstanding," he said.

The men squeezed into what little space remained, the bow and stern each nearly touching a wall. A hutch across the beam for shelter, a deep hull for storage, covered over to keep it from filling with rain. The boat was massive, not graceful, perhaps, but radiant still, varnished a dark umber, nearly glowing in the midday sun.

One of the Jensen boys ran his hand along the flank.

"You did this all by yourself?" he asked.

"Fred helped me a bunch," Samuel said, dropping his chin.

"A fine vessel you've made here," Jensen said. "I don't pretend to understand. But I know good work when I see it."

Samuel touched the man's shoulder in acknowledgment.

"What do you say, boys?"

With claps and hoots they shook off the reverential tone that had befallen them.

Samuel had already dismantled part of the mow so they could take the boat straight out.

"Get wheels under it on both ends. Use the truck if we need to," he said. "It's heavy. We're going to have to move it inch by inch."

"Sure, sure," Styron said, unsure of where to direct his energy. "You built a goddamn ark, man!"

"I mean, is it too much to ask to have the house ready for our wedding reception? They said the curtains would be ready last week. I ordered this gorgeous rose damask print they had to ship from Philadelphia. Can you imagine? All the way from a big city in the East?"

Annie let Hattie chatter on. She patted the biscuit dough onto her floured board. Hattie had brought a green bean casserole and was now slowly, arduously, peeling apples for a pie. Her pace will change, Annie thought, when she has children.

"I'm sure they will be lovely," Annie said.

She thought of Fred and how he used to run and skid into his seat at the table, his smile revealing the chipped corner of his front tooth, from when he was six and it wasn't even in all the way and he slipped climbing into the bathtub.

Birdie came in from the chickens, her big belly stretching her dress — one that had been her mother's — tight.

"Oh," Hattie said.

Birdie stood with her hands on her back, chin thrust straight out, refusing to demur.

"Hello, Miss Daniels," she said. "Looks like a boat is getting born out there."

Hattie, at a rare loss for words, merely nodded, a smile lagging.

"Birdie, help with the table," Annie said.

It took hours of lifting and maneuvering to get the boat atop the two old tractor axles Samuel had rigged. He tried to chain the front axle to the truck, but the boat kept slipping, so they pushed and adjusted, pushed and pulled, little by little, bringing the boat out into the sharp light of the day.

"Where you want it?" Ford huffed, leaning against the stern. "I think we can get it rolling now that it's out."

"Over there beyond the barn will be fine," Samuel said.

Annie, Hattie, and Birdie set out supper in the locust grove. The wind was light, the air dry and warm. The men washed up and joined them.

"Maybe the dust is all finished with," Hattie said. "It feels like a fresh start, doesn't it? Today is as bright as Christmas. Wouldn't that be wonderful, if it went back to how it was and we could forget all about that terrible dirty time?"

"It would, Miss Daniels," Samuel said.

Annie didn't sit to eat, moving back and

forth from the house with pitchers and platters. Birdie stayed in the kitchen, happy to wash dishes away from the chitchat.

"He did it," Birdie said.

Annie wiped her hands on her apron and leaned for a moment against the icebox.

"He did it," she said.

"Do you ever hope the flood actually does come? Even a little bit?"

It would prove Samuel not crazy. It might save the land. It would change the way she thought about God.

"I wouldn't wish for destruction like that," she finally said.

"It would change everything," Birdie said. "It's always the same around here. Everything just goes on like always."

"Well, not quite like always," Annie said, nodding to the baby, with the slightest flash of a smile.

Two nights later, the sky lit up with jagged flashes, thunderheads bunched and boomed, nearing from the north. Samuel rubbed his chin and watched from the porch. This certainly was rain, and the wheat was already a little ahead of where it had been last year. Lord, Lord. The boat, with its flat bottom, sat sound where they had set it down, visible when the lightning streaked the darkness. Bring the rain, he thought. Let it come.

Annie and Birdie, unable to sleep through the growing rumbling, soon joined him, and the three of them heard the rain start, thwonking against the wood of the boat. And then, as if a giant bucket had been tipped, the rain fell in torrents. Samuel stuck his hand out and it felt like nails against his skin. Water pooled on the still-droughted ground, running down the eroded grooves. It sounded like a freight train, the downpour deafening. And it kept coming, hard and fast, covering the dirt first in puddles and then in streams. Thunder cracked and Birdie scampered back toward the door, but Annie held fast beside him, the wind whipping her nightgown.

For a moment, Samuel felt himself rise up, lifted by awe and belief. Could this be more than rain? He felt a warmth pulse in the center of himself. My God, you are here, he thought. I have built a boat and you are here. He closed his eyes and felt waves crashing in his head. You were right, Freddie, you were right.

"This is more than rain," he said finally, his voice loud and strange.

Annie had forgotten what a real rainstorm was like, how it boomed to life with its

335

cymbals and snare drums. Like those tantrums Birdie used to throw as a toddler, fists to the floor. Her face was wet. But she would not move away from it. Grief had made fear a powerless object she could hold in her hand. One child had not been enough for God, He had to take two, she thought. We know everyone we love is going to die, but we don't know it, can't possibly believe it, she thought, or long ago I would have gone and started digging until I had a hole big enough to lie down in.

In a flash of lightning, Annie glimpsed the water rushing below the porch, like those summer storms when she was a girl and the saplings would bend all the way to the ground, the runoff from the roof a waterfall against the front steps. Her mother would worry the edge of her apron, fretting over her peonies.

Fred oh Fred my little Fred, Annie thought. Her anger was still there, red and shapeless, but it had settled some into a bone-deep sadness. There were moments now too that dug out a little space. Like the ruby blooms of Texas paintbrush that had begun to appear. Or Samuel's gentle hand on her back when she was at the sink. Or even the boat. It was a thing of beauty. Even she could see that.

Birdie went into the house to get dressed. The girl was ready to burst. But Annie forgot it sometimes, her mind distracted. Haul the water and turn the soil and plant and weed and coax and tend, keep going another day. There would be a baby and wasn't that a wonderful thing? She knew she should tell Birdie that. She should tell her that all the other mess didn't matter.

Annie stood next to Samuel on the porch. He would never know her cruelty of heart. Samuel, Samuel. His kindness and his faith. Here she was. She took his hand.

I will come back to you, she thought, if you come back to me.

CHAPTER 16

Birdie returned to the porch with a cardigan, its buttons straining over her bulging nightdress. She clutched a small suitcase she'd found days before in the dugout, one her mother had brought out from Kansas, its clasps rusted, the leather ripped along the seam. She held her shoes in her other hand.

"Are you going somewhere?" Annie asked. She still did not believe a flood was coming.

"I figure it's now or never for the boat." Birdie had packed a few things, underwear and socks and the dress her mother had made her, which wouldn't fit now but would fit then, after, when she was herself again. She didn't really believe a flood would wipe out the land, either, but she felt excited by the gathering water. Here was something different. And just maybe her father had been right.

Now that the moment was upon him,

Samuel didn't quite know what to do. He'd imagined them dashing aboard for safety. The water was rising, but it was a slow ascent, only up to the first porch step.

"It's just a rainstorm," Annie said, but she had to yell over the din.

Birdie held her palm out into the pummeling rain.

"It looks like a flood to me," she said to her mother. Jack Lily is not here anymore, Mama, she thought then, and we are. "Better to be together, isn't it?"

Annie didn't answer, but she knew Birdie was right. These were the two people she had left.

They looked at Samuel, his shirt soaked through. It was his moment and he looked unsure, his eyes darting from the rain to Annie to the darkness where the boat waited for them. His feet felt shackled to the splintered boards of the porch. Above them a gutter yawned and snapped free of the house.

"We can stay dry under the roof there." He pointed, even though he couldn't see the boat. "I built a bench under it."

He had not thought about how to get the milk cow onto the boat. Should they get some of the chickens? Fred would have insisted.

"I'm going inside," Annie said.

"Annie," he said.

"I'm getting on," Birdie said, and walked down the steps and into the water and stinging rain.

"Barbara Ann!" Annie tried to reach her hand but Birdie was off, stepping carefully, water over her ankles, wading toward the boat with her suitcase.

"Go get some clothes," Samuel said.

"I'm going to bed," Annie said. It was the one last fight she had in her, but it didn't take.

"No, you're not," he said. "Come with me."

She was crying now, relinquishing her position, relinquishing everything. She went into the house and grabbed a dress and some shoes from the wardrobe that had been hers as a girl, the one that had made it out in the wagon all those years ago. She didn't bother with her small box of keepsakes — she couldn't really believe the world was being washed away — but she did take the picture Fred had drawn of the barbed-wire crows' nest. They would not get to start over, but there was a relief, she admitted, in the rain, in something she didn't understand. She let the tears come to a hiccupy end. Who knew what would happen now, but she might as well wait it out with what remained of her family.

The water was up to her knees when she stepped in, surprisingly cold, and it pulled at her with an insistence that teased her balance. Her feet slipped in the mud below. Rain pelted her head and ran into her eyes. Samuel held her arm and led her to the boat where Birdie waited, hair matted to her head, her hands resting atop her belly, a borrowed tabletop. Looking at Birdie, it struck Annie that something wasn't right, hadn't been right for a while. The girl seemed divorced from her condition, neither anxious nor hopeful, as if her body were not her own. She squeezed next to her daughter on the rough-hewn bench, and the smell of wet wood and pitch made her nose itch. The rain went on and on, but there they were, Annie thought, safe. She took Birdie's hand, rigid at first and then limp.

Samuel could not stand straight in the boat's shelter without knocking his head, but neither could he sit, his restless feet dancing forward and back. His hands jittered at his sides. He stuck his head out the doorway and brought it back in, water running off his chin.

"I've water and some food below," he said. "But it's too late for a ramp to get Greta up. Water's too deep."

The water curled around the boat, swirling in eddies, and splashing up the sides.

Part of Annie wanted the water to rise and rise. If Samuel was right, she would have to believe, would have to find peace. She couldn't tell how high the water was, but it seemed threatening, gaining strength. Something banged into the hull, but whatever it was disappeared in the rushing water. And then she felt it. A lurch.

"Pop?"

Samuel scrambled out to the bow and stood in the rain, his eyes outward to the darkness.

The boat moved again, and then the front began to slide a little back and forth with the current.

"You did it, Pop!" Birdie shouted, laughing. "You were right."

Annie stood in the doorway looking toward the house, her body hard and still, as if she were carved from some pale stone.

The boat slid forward an inch and then stopped, slipped again, dragging against the ground.

Samuel felt himself expand, filled with a joyous kind of light. The boat lifted, starting to float. The land would be wiped clean, they would be wiped clean. They would be saved. "Praise," Samuel said. "Praise be."

The boat inched its way atop the water, yawing and pitching in the storm. The water swallowed the ground and the bases of the locust trees, flooded the dugout up to its roof. They couldn't make out the house through the darkness; it was as if it had already floated away. Samuel had a pole he'd fashioned that he tried to use to steer, but the boat was too heavy in the current and it listed one way and then another. They were moving, really moving, and Samuel grabbed the gunwale just before slipping off himself.

"Samuel," Annie said, a new force and clarity in her voice. She held her hand out to him.

He scrambled back to where she and Birdie sat soaked, despite the roof, and wedged himself between them.

Now that they were on the boat, he feared the destruction that was to come. The house he had built would be brought down. Mulehead would be gone. There was room on the boat for others. But he knew they were miles from anyone. There would be death and ruin. It was too much to think about.

He had felt such lightness only moments before, but now he was falling hard, dread dragging him down. I have done what you asked, he thought. But what about everybody else? How is that right?

The stern got stuck and the boat pivoted a quarter way around before spinning back. Annie, drenched and oddly calm, waited for Samuel to tell her what was next, or just waited for where this vessel would take them. She could see no further than the rain. The night was black. She braced herself against the frame of the hutch as the boat jerked back some, then forward.

There they sat, Samuel, Annie, and Birdie hand in hand in hand on the small bench, when the boat crashed headlong into the barn, taking out part of the wall and narrowly missing the milk cow whose distressed cries could barely be heard over the rain against the roof.

The ark was grounded, half in the barn and half out, its brief journey at an end.

The rain began to ease soon after, as if on command. The Bells righted themselves, but they did not speak. They sat for a long while on the boat as the storm dripped to a halt. They watched the water slowly recede.

"Everyone all right?" Samuel finally asked.

"Sure, Pop," Birdie said. He smiled a naked smile such as she hadn't seen since before Fred died. He stood and peered up, the last drops falling in a languid rhythm.

And then he laughed.

"I didn't want a flood," he said, "when it came down to it."

He could hear the runoff sluice below, a shallow pond around them. He pulled off a hanging slat from the barn wall and tossed it onto the deck.

"I'll put a kettle on," Annie said.

Samuel felt calmness like a fire-warmed blanket over his shoulders. He had been tested and he had been spared. He believed that. He felt neither pride nor regret, delight nor despair. He just was. A man, a farmer. It was the most solid he had felt in months. There was flickering sadness there, too, for the feeling of purpose that was gone. He was just like everybody else. Returned. He thought of Fred and his small arms sawing in the lamplight and how together they had built this beautiful, worthy thing.

Samuel didn't know that there would be years of dust storms yet, years before the conservationists and tree planters came, before terracing and crop rotation transformed the fields, before grasses held the soil down again, before the end of the drought, before farmers tapped the Ogallala

Aquifer, that endless-seeming source of water, before waterwheel irrigation turned the Plains into a grid of giant green circles, before the Ogallala began to run dry, a resource only thousands of years of rainwater could replace. But in the still of the aftermath of the almost-flood, he felt something restored in him. He had his small family. He had his old farm. It had rained. He had hope.

He didn't yet know that Styron would have the boat towed to town, to the center of an old parcel of land that had once held the feed store. Crows would make a nest in the hutch. People would come to see it from neighboring towns, and, when Styron finally got his sign up on the highway, the curious would trickle in to see the Ark of the Plains. Samuel wouldn't mind. He'd let go of the boat as soon as the rain had stopped.

"I'm going to bed," Birdie said, yawning. "What time is it? It must be almost morning." She climbed off the boat on her own before Samuel had a chance to help her.

The birds had begun, twittering and chirping, the air heavy with the smells of mud and wet spring green. Annie thought of the wildflowers that would burst up in the coming weeks. She would burn the old letter from Jack Lily. She would not begrudge Samuel his faith. Maybe God posted signs visible only to those with eyes to see. She wasn't one of them, but she could accept that maybe her husband was.

"Let me help you down, Annie," Samuel said.

She took his hand. There is grace here, she thought.

A day passed and the water was sucked into the earth. The dugout had filled, leaving it a dank and mucky pit. Inside, the trunk of Fred's things had floated, most of its contents spared. Annie saved a lot of what she had canned, though some of the pickle jars had cracked. The last of the wheat sacks were sodden and would soon mold. Samuel would fill in the old rooms and raze the roof. It was time to dig a proper cellar.

At the kitchen table, Birdie closed her history book. She laid her head on her arm on the table. Annie stood near the sink peeling and cutting carrots for roasting. They could hear Samuel repairing the barn wall, pounding in slats of lumber he had at the ready.

"I thought you had a test this week."

"Tomorrow."

"You haven't done much studying." Annie glanced at her and went back to the carrots.

"I'm sleepy," Birdie said. "What does it really matter?" She would have to leave school when she had the baby anyway.

"It matters to do well. To learn. It's easy to be common, Barbara Ann."

The comment nettled her. She stared at the red loops of her mother's apron strings, which hung uneven and limp. After Fred, Birdie had tried to bury what she suspected about her mother. But she suddenly felt so tired, of secrets, of the whole past year, she wanted to fling open the door and be done with it. She said it before she could change her mind.

"Your apron."

Annie stopped chopping.

"Fred found it, he told me. At Woodrow's."

Annie shrank into herself, pulled in close around a cold polished center. She had thought the affair had been hers to put away. But that was too tidy an ending, she knew, to how she had strayed. Of course Birdie had caught on. How reckless Annie had been.

"He did find it there," Annie said. She kept her voice up, holding on to the slim chance the moment would pass without incident. "Didn't even know I'd lost it."

She started again with the knife, but

nicked her finger. She held it in the faucet stream before bringing it to her lips. She closed her eyes and waited.

"I can't make sense of it," Birdie said, quietly.

Whatever Birdie knew, it was enough. The truth, with its steely resolve, had a way of making itself known.

"Neither can I," Annie said.

So it was true, Birdie thought. Her steadfast mother. Birdie had hoped against reason that she had been mistaken. But she wasn't really surprised. Even Fred had known something. Oh Freddie, how she missed him.

"The mayor," Birdie said.

Annie stood still and silent.

"You and the mayor," she said. "Mama." But the words fell sad and soft. Birdie could not make her anger rise.

"I stayed," Annie said, barely above a whisper. "I would have never left you and Fred. I'm your mother above everything." She squeezed her bleeding finger in a towel and held it to her chest. There was a pause in the hammering outside, and then it began again.

Birdie started to cry, couldn't help it. She wanted to go back years. It was dizzying how you could just send your life in a different direction. One choice and then another.

"I'm sorry," Annie said. "I'm sorry." Her chin quivered. "I don't forgive it."

"Does he know?"

Annie shook her head. "I love your father. Will always." She dropped the blood-dotted towel in the sink.

Birdie thought of Fred's small coffin and knew that more punishment was not hers to mete out. So much sadness let loose. She felt so old. Older than sixteen, older than the moon. Birdie couldn't help but feel a kernel of wonder. Her mother, who never seemed to yearn for anything. All that I don't know, she thought.

Annie walked closer and placed her hands, firm and warm, on Birdie's head.

The pain started in the early morning a couple weeks later, like a low ache Birdie couldn't quite locate. She didn't think much of it until it felt like monthly cramps, and it took her a moment longer to realize she didn't get monthly cramps anymore and oh, Lord in heaven it was April. Flashes of tightness came through the morning as she milked Greta and fed the chickens, rising through her until they died back down. It should not have been a surprise that this day would come but she was shocked, overwhelmed by how her body had taken over.

Annie came in, dirt across her forehead and rare color in her cheeks, to find her daughter doubled over, the bones of her knuckles straining against skin, clutching the table ledge.

She pressed on Birdie's lower back until the spasm passed.

"I don't know what to do, Mama," Birdie said. "I don't want a baby." She cried then, her hands in fists against her forehead.

"We will be fine, Barbara Ann. Let's walk."

The wind was up, but the ground was sticky with new mud. They passed the mangled barn Samuel had begun to repair, the boat still sticking out.

"Think people will ever stop talking about us?" Birdie asked.

"People are always going to talk," Annie said. "If it's about us or not is neither here nor there."

Birdie winced as the grip of labor rose to its height, and she squeezed her mother's strong hand until it passed.

"No one will ever see me the same."

"You won't be the same, after today."

"I know it."

"It's not a bad thing. Even if it's not what

you want."

"Like lima beans."

She is so young, Annie thought. But she had been, too, and she had managed. Mothers managed.

"There is good about it, too, Birdie," Annie said. "A child is always a blessing."

Annie knew enough to be a midwife. Most country women did. She laid out towels and tore sheets into squares, boiled a knife and a clothespin for the cord, warmed water for the cleanup, spread old newspapers on the floor near the edge of the bed. She sudsed her arms in lye soap to her elbows. Samuel stood by as his wife, transformed by agency, bustled about.

"Get a big bowl," she told him.

"For the baby?"

She shot him a withering look. "The placenta, Samuel."

Samuel had birthed animals his whole life, but had not been allowed at his wife's births, shooed away by the attending midwife, and he found himself stuck in cement, unable to react or move as he wanted. In those leaden days after Fred's death, when Annie had told him about Birdie, he had felt the revelation from a distance and marveled how, at another time, the news would have stirred thoughts of his daughter's sin. Now he could do little more than mourn the loss of her freedom, his daughter who had always been perched on the edge, ready to take off. But there was buoyancy, too, giddiness even, in welcoming the arrival of the newest Bell.

"Soap up," Annie said. "I'll need your help."

Downstairs at the sink, Samuel pressed his palms together and prayed for help, until Annie called for him and he snapped to it, lathering the harsh soap up to his armpits.

He raced back up to their bedroom.

"Baby's coming," Annie said. She smiled then, a quick small smile that opened her face, and Samuel saw goodness there.

"Grab her leg," Annie said.

Birdie clung to the iron headboard, and Samuel placed his hand on his daughter's wobbling leg.

"Hard. Grab her thigh and push it back. Come on now."

He did as he was told, holding his weight against Birdie's leg as a little dark head crowned.

Birdie grunted and yelled and Annie told her to push and Samuel, bewildered, waited for his next instruction.

"Hold both legs. Hold them steady," Annie said. She crouched under him and ran her finger around the baby's head to ease it out and Birdie let out a sound that was both scream and primal moan.

"Birdie. Barbara Ann Bell, you listen to me," Annie said. "You are doing just fine. Now push."

In that moment of fire and pain and fear, when the baby's head inched its way out and Birdie felt herself rip open, she knew. I will go, she said to herself, I will go. It was decided. Go, go, go, she said to herself as the baby slid out into her mother's hands. I will go.

It was a new configuration of family. Give us this day our daily bread, Samuel thought. The baby girl turned from bluish to pink as Annie rubbed her with a towel. She cut and clamped the cord, as the baby let out her first cries. She wrapped her with an expert one, two, three swaddle of a blanket and placed her on Birdie's chest.

"You hold it, Mama," Birdie said, handing her back. She scooted down into the mess of birth on the bed, turned over, and fell asleep.

CHAPTER 17

Birdie closes the door quietly behind her and walks away, one step and then another and another. It's dark but the birds are already busy. Her old dress, which she hasn't been able to wear since the fall, doesn't fit right — her body still soft and bulging — but she is back to herself, or what passes for herself now. The sun is close. She can almost feel the coming of the light. She does not look back at the house. The risk is too great. She is leaving everything. It's been a week since the baby; as she walks, her belly feels empty, loose, and she keeps touching it to remind herself of where her body ends.

A skirt, a shirt, a sweater. Extra socks and underthings. A smooth stone Fred gave her that he thought looked like butterscotch. A napkin full of biscuits. A jar of water. Twenty-two dollars from her father's dresser. She knows he would have given it to her if she had asked, not that it makes her feel better about taking it.

She walks. The crack of light on the horizon announces the morning. The inevitability of the sun comforts her. Do not think about what you are leaving, she tells herself, or you will get nowhere. There will be time for that later. There will always be more time for that.

Birdie walks west, and then she will walk south, in the direction of Amarillo, where she will pick up Route 66. She will walk and walk. She hopes to hitch with a family, since plenty of people are moving that way. She knows to stay clear of men alone, though she also knows, in the reaches of her mind, that there will be sacrifices along the way, compromises she will make to get where she wants to go. She thinks back to the day of the first dust, when she didn't yet know a damn thing. What if she had not gotten pregnant? What if Cy had taken her with him? The what-ifs can go on forever if you let them, she heard her mother say once, and Birdie knows she was right about that. "What if" will get you nowhere, and she has many miles to go.

There is light now, the ground still damp with dew. Birdie turns around and can just make out the sign for Black Mesa to the north. The dinosaur people are still up there. They found footprints, and now they have found bones. She thinks about bones, porous and strong, smoothed by sand and bleached by the sun, buried, waiting to be found. Maybe it's like that for her, she thinks. She will bury her childhood in all this Oklahoma dust and it will wait for her to come back someday to dig it up. Even now, when all she wants to do is leave, she knows that she might spend the rest of her life looking back, wondering about those bones. It will take a lifetime to organize her memories of Oklahoma into a coherent shape, a story she can tell herself without falling apart.

The early sun warms her back, and in front of her, the High Plains sky extends to eternity. It is quiet enough that she can hear the sound of her shoes against the pavement, a soft, insistent tap, tap, tap. The breeze is gentle and intermittent. She breathes in the sharp and earthy smell of sand sage and lemon sumac mixed with rich clay loam. It is beautiful out, the kind of day that coaxes roots from seeds, and Birdie cannot say whether she is happy or sad. She will miss the land, the sky, and the space between. This place will always be her place, despite its capacity for cruelty, despite what has been lost. The yearning will go on and on.

But for the unknown she harbors hope as fragile as a tiller shoot. Seventeen will surely be better than sixteen, she thinks. Mama and Pop have a baby now. She will be their girl. And that is all Birdie will allow.

There's a car somewhere, getting closer. She can hear the rattle and puff of a worn-out engine. She has walked west and now it's time to turn south. She is tired and would welcome a ride. For a moment, she fears it will be her father come to fetch her, but then the sound of the car isn't quite his and she breathes deep and lets it go. She isn't scared. She feels powerfully alone.

She arranges her face in a smile, and turns and waves.

Annie awakens to the baby's cries. She listens, hoping Birdie might be able to soothe the child, but the baby cries on in frantic bleats. The dawn is violet. Annie goes to her daughter's room. She can see immediately that Birdie's bed is made up and empty. She goes first to the cradle and lifts the flailing baby, resting her cheek against that tiny softness until she quiets.

Birdie has left a short note on her pillow, her loopy scrawl filling the paper from edge

358

to edge.

Dear Mama and Pop,
I am going. I'm not going after Cy or
anything like that. But I'm going west
just the same. I know all the reasons why
I shouldn't. It's just what I have to do. I
will be okay so don't worry about me.

Love,
Birdie

Annie flips the paper looking for more,
then reads it again. Gone west. Gone. Her
breath — held for how long — eases out
and she feels herself smaller, older. She does
not think, Go after her — she knows already
there will be no hope if Birdie doesn't want
to be found — but neither does she think,
Let her go. Her daughter alone in the world.
She heaves air back into her lungs.

The new sun cuts sharply through the
window. The baby gurgles and yawns. Annie
can't remember how Birdie looked as an
infant and she feels a panic rise about
forgetting. How do you remember everything? What will be lost? She catalogues the
details: the uneven spray of freckles across
her nose, the slight pigeon-toed stance, the
way she works a walnut from its shell, so
intent, so serious about getting all the meat

out. Her face on the Ferris wheel in Oklahoma City, open and expectant as they swooped up and up.

The baby dozes; her lips purse and then settle into sleep. Annie pulls a quilt from the cradle and wraps her, the same way she swaddled all of her children. She sits still and breathes quiet shallow breaths.

Annie knows she should run to wake Samuel, but she wants to be alone a little longer. She already misses Birdie with a fierce ache. She will not let herself think of all the possibilities, the dangers, or they will overcome her. She closes her eyes and imagines Birdie on a train, the fields slipping by until she is free.

The baby squirms away from the eyedropper of sugar water and milk, screws up her little wrinkled face in confusion and dismay and cries until Annie holds her to her breast and she latches on, soothed until she falls asleep.

Annie moves the rocking chair outside into the shade of one of the locust trees and rocks Rose. She and Samuel named her the day Birdie left. In recent days, Samuel has taken to walking Rose around and talking to her about how the leaf sheaths are emerging from the tillers of the wheat and how the robins have returned and laid their blue eggs and how when Birdie and Fred were small they used to hide up in the haymow in games of hide-and-seek. Annie fashions a sling out of flour sacks and wears Rose while she weeds and waters her garden or hangs out the wash or shells the peas. They are like first-time parents again. They never put the baby down, always checking, touching, cooing.

Wrapped in the baby quilt she made for Birdie, Rose has pink cheeks and her mouth is puckered and Annie holds her soft fragile head and feels an ease in her chest as something finally gives. That infant face has laid claim on her. The dust will come again, she knows. But on this day, the land spread out before her, she allows herself to return to what she once loved about it — the mad colors of the wildflowers, the sporadic green of the dormant wheat coming to life in the fields. She does not feel whole, no, but she has a baby in her arms, and that feels as close to right as she has ever hoped to feel again. Beneath the damage she can still find moments of wonder, hints of joy. Would she even say she is optimistic? It isn't the shiny optimism that lifts Samuel, but it's a hard-won kind, born from the depths. A choice.

It is enough.

She cannot accept yet that Birdie is truly gone, her first girl, her strong impulsive one, her survivor, her daughter who, in the end, knew how to want more. Part of her thinks, Go, Birdie, go. Go on and find something else, go on and take what you can get. But the other part of her watches the road at the edge of the farm, will watch it always, hoping she will see her walking home.

ACKNOWLEDGMENTS

Thank you to:

Sarah Bowlin, my talented and generous editor, who made this book so much better.

Elisabeth Weed, my agent, friend, and advocate from the beginning.

All the folks at Henry Holt. Every writer should have a team this good.

My first readers: Alex Darrow, Susannah Meadows, Jessica Darrow, and Michelle Wildgen, whose kindness and guidance nudged me forward from a first draft.

Christina Paige. Boise City, baby!

Jennifer Sey, Mark Sundeen, April Saks, Carolyn Frazier, Andrew Wilcox, Lance McDaniel, Amy Sweigert, Carol Lawson, Lynn Kilpatrick, Darin Strauss, Lewis Buzbee, Sabine Laerum, Emma Fusco-Straub, Curtis Sittenfeld, Emily Bell, Michael Donohue, Dune Lawrence, David Khoury, Maartje Oldenburg, Melissa Kantor, Ben Gantcher, Rebekah Coleman, Meredith and Jennifer

Bell, Aaron Sanders, and Denise Wood Hahn.

The Twin Cities contingent: Pamela Klinger-Horn, Beth Slater Winnick, Nina Roberson, Frank Bures, Bridgit Jordan, Jeff Chen, and Karen Ho.

My friends from the University of Utah Creative Writing Program.

Bob Barry and the Wednesday crew at the LIU pottery studio.

The Meadows and Darrow families, always.

Alex, Indigo, and Olive. You are the best.

ABOUT THE AUTHOR

Rae Meadows is the author of *Calling Out,* which received the 2006 Utah Book Award for fiction; *No One Tells Everything,* a *Poets & Writers* Notable Novel; and most recently the widely praised novel *Mercy Train.* She lives with her family in Brooklyn, New York.